USA TODAY bestselling author **Emily E K Murdoch** is read in multiple languages around the world. Enjoy her sweet romances writing as Emily Murdoch, and steamy romances as Emily E K Murdoch. Emily's had a varied career to date, from examining medieval manuscripts to designing museum exhibitions, working as a researcher for the BBC to working for the National Trust. Her books' settings range from England 1050 to Texas 1848, and she can't wait for you to fall in love with her heroes and heroines!

Also by Emily E K Murdoch

The Wallflower Academy miniseries

Least Likely to Win a Duke
More Than a Match for the Earl
The Duchess Charade
The Prince's Wallflower Wife

Discover more at millsandboon.co.uk.

THE DUKE'S MEDDLESOME MATCHMAKER

Emily E K Murdoch

MILLS & BOON

First published in Great Britain 2026
by Mills & Boon, an imprint of HarperCollins*Publishers* Ltd,
1 London Bridge Street, London, SE1 9GF

www.harpercollins.co.uk

HarperCollins*Publishers*, Macken House, 39/40 Mayor Street Upper, Dublin 1, D01 C9W8, Ireland

ISBN: 978-0-263-41866-8

01/26

For Amelia.

And to PB, PB, BB, and BB.

Chapter One

December 31, 1811

Miss Aphrodite Oliver settled deep into the luxurious seat of Rules, the best restaurant in London, and beamed across the room at the gentleman making his way back to the table.

It had all been perfectly planned. Of course it had. She had planned it.

A proposal at New Year, after all, was a wonderful idea. When Aphrodite—or Ditty, to her sisters—had first heard of the idea, she was rather astonished she had not thought of it herself. Preening ever so slightly, and who could blame her, she smoothed down her long skirts and held her fan just above her nose, her hazel-green eyes wide above it. It would not do to be recognised…

'Another glass of champagne, Miss Oliver?'

Ditty looked up and beamed at the serving-man. 'Isn't it wonderful?'

The man hesitated, evidently unsure what on earth she could possibly mean. 'It…it is?'

She nodded at Mr Matthews, who was still weaving his way through the many tables. 'He. Mr Matthews. He'll be proposing marriage tonight.'

The serving-man's eyebrows raised. 'He—he will?'

'Naturally,' Ditty said smoothly. 'It was a delicately made introduction, has been several months of courting, a most respectable time. This is, after all, one of the best restaurants in London—and it took a great deal to convince the chef to prepare my preferred menu, I can tell you. The finest champagne—yes, I will have a glass, thank you. And the speech! Oh, the story I could tell you about the speech...'

Her voice trailed away.

She had worked hard on that speech. Being one of the most respected proposal planners in the *ton*—far more difficult than a matchmaker—one had to make sure each proposal speech was quite different. It was one of the things that made her the best.

'He is going to sit, then speak of his affection. The speech is all prepared,' said Ditty proudly, sweeping back a curl of her chestnut mane which had escaped its pins. 'Then just as one would think no more romance could be packed into an evening, he will slowly lower himself onto one knee, take her hand in his, and present it with a promise of his devotion and a request that he be made the happiest man in the world.'

She sighed happily. It was the perfect plan. Thank goodness she had put so much work into it—those late nights in her cramped rooms shared with her sisters, Thalia and Calliope, were all worth it.

Strings. The violinist she had organised for just this moment started to gently play a melody from Handel's *Rodelinda*—a favourite opera.

The serving-man cleared his throat. 'And…and you do not mind? Knowing so much about the proposal before it occurs, I mean. Is it not unusual for a woman to know precisely all the details? No offence meant, miss.'

Ditty blinked. *What was he talking about?* 'I beg your pardon?'

She fixed her stare onto the man standing beside her table who suddenly looked as though red-hot coals had been applied to his feet.

'I just—I only meant—'

But Ditty could not listen to him now.

Breath hitching in her throat with all the excitement, she watched a beaming Mr Matthews walk toward her. Their gazes met. *He is so happy*, she could not help but think. So happy. And so was she.

And then he strode past her table and sat at another. 'I am sorry for taking so long, my dear, I wanted to ensure our order was exactly understood.'

Miss Evans, soon to be Mrs Matthews, smiled. 'Not at all, my love.'

Ditty nodded and made a small tick in the notebook before her. Everything had been going to plan—his walk to the kitchen had taken approximately ninety seconds longer than they had scheduled for, but the violinist had managed to cover the gap. She would have to remember to tip him an extra half crown—not something one would have been able to do in Almsbury.

Her stomach lurched and she forced aside the emotion she could ill afford at such a crucial juncture. She did not miss living in Almsbury. She was perfectly happy in London.

Ditty looked up and saw to her surprise that the serving-man was still standing there, his mouth now open.

'He...he's not proposing to you?'

Ditty frowned, bemused. 'Why on earth would he?'

Only too late did she realise the misunderstanding. Stifling a laugh, she tried to see it from the man's perspective.

She had been speaking as though Mr Matthews and herself—*of course.* 'I'm a proposal planner.'

'A proposal planner—'

'Hush!' Ditty glanced around the restaurant, then glared severely at the serving-man when her gaze fell back on him. 'Do you want to put me out of business?'

Not that it would be hard, she could not help but think. After her father's death, matchmaking had been considered a respectable way for her to support her two sisters and their rather unconventional mother: a wonderful way to bring together what ought to be romantic, and imbue it with the practicality and organisation she had become famous for—even during her time in finishing school.

Most people were...well, so slapdash with their courting.

But not Miss Aphrodite Oliver. Her proposals were perfect. The trouble was, fewer and fewer people were investing in a matchmaker these days, let alone a proposal planner. Love matches, heaven forbid, were starting to become the fashion. Mamas hoped for introductions, rather than made plans for matchmakers.

It was ridiculous. It was starting to make finding clients difficult.

A small movement just ahead of her made Ditty focus. 'Go away!' she hissed to the serving-man, flapping her hands.

It was about to happen. The moment she had spent the last three weeks planning, considering, obsessing over and finalising within an inch of her life.

Ditty glanced at her notebook.

7:11 pm: Mr Matthews begins making romantic speech. Key points: gratitude for her support as he finished studying medicine, his recent introduction to her sister and family, finally finding the perfect home for them to live in.

She nodded approvingly. Achievements any couple should be proud of. She had insisted Mr Matthews include them.

The table she had chosen was expertly positioned— just close enough to listen in on each word her client uttered, but just far enough away that she could not be under suspicion.

'Miss Evans, you know that I have been courting you for five months now—' Mr Matthews began.

Ditty had to work hard not to nod along. Yes, precisely as they planned. She had forced the gentleman to practice in a looking-glass for the last four days, so he should be well rehearsed by now.

'—and your support while finishing my medical studies, I cannot thank you enough—'

It would have been a better idea perhaps, Ditty mused, doodling on her notebook, if Thomas had been able to attend. He would have made a perfect excuse to sit here. Sitting with the gentleman who was courting her would have given her the perfect excuse to continually look up…and over his shoulder and beyond him to her client.

But Thomas was busy tonight, apparently.

'On New Year's Eve?' she had asked earlier today on their customary Thursday morning walk.

He hadn't really seemed to be listening. 'Happy New Year's Eve to you!'

Ditty had closed the door in his face none too gently, and put it from her mind. She had a client proposal that evening, after all.

And Mr Matthews was doing a rather superb job of it. She examined him with an expert eye—she had been organising matches for…what was it, four years now?

Ditty worked hard to keep her eyes open as Mr Matthews continued. She'd been up late all last night, putting the finishing touches to this proposal. *It had to be perfect.*

'—and with the property I have now found, everything just seems to be falling into place…'

Two proposals a month, every month, for four years— though the festive period had naturally slowed that down. No wonder she was tired—but then, London hardly lent itself to slowing down since losing her father five years ago, because she had two sisters and a mother to support.

Ditty ticked off another element of Mr Matthews's speech in her notebook. This had to be perfect: she had no further matchmaking clients, something deeply concerning. True, it was near the end of the Season, but she had not expected such a decline. She would have to hope new clients would emerge in the New Year, as they always—

Her shoulders stiffened. Though her thoughts had wandered in another direction, her ears had still been listening all the while to Mr Matthews's speech. The speech had been going so well, and now was going so wrong.

Ditty glanced up, trying desperately to catch the eye of the idiot. *What does he think he is doing? He has now completely deviated from my script!*

'—and I adore you, everything about you,' Mr Matthews was saying, eyes bright. 'Every day spent with you is one I want to continue forever. You complete me in a way…'

Ditty rolled her eyes. *Romance!* What, did the man think one could just pluck romance from the air, like ordering a cravat from a haberdasher!

Romance was what she orchestrated, but it took weeks of planning, more coin than most people knew what to do with and her own special approach! One couldn't just spout romance at the drop of a hat!

Oh, this was going to be a disaster. From the angle

she was sitting at, Ditty could not see into the eyes of Miss Evans but she could well imagine.

With a heavy sigh, Ditty prepared herself to rise from her seat. Well, this could not be blamed on her, at the very least. She had prepared for all eventualities, as she always did, and—

'Yes! Yes, I will marry you!'

Ditty blinked. What? Miss Evans wasn't scheduled to finish hearing, much less accept Mr Matthews's proposal for another six minutes. She didn't need to look at her notebook for that detail; she had memorised the schedule. Naturally. As any good proposal planner would.

The fool! The festoons of rose petals to be showered on them would now be entirely mistimed!

But there was nothing she could do now. Ditty watched, half despairing, half fascinated, as Mr Matthews rose from his knees and kissed his new fiancée reverentially.

The chink of champagne glasses, sipping of the bubbly liquid and muttered joyous nothings that were not, clearly, for her ears.

Glancing up, she caught the eye of the violinist and told him with the nod of her head, silently and from at least ten yards, precisely what to do.

The violinist began playing the overture from Mozart's *Magic Flute*. That told the proprietor of Rules restaurant that it was time to bring out the mock wedding cake with copious candles, dazzling and glorious, lighting up the whole restaurant. The bright lights indicated to the florist she had hired, through much difficulty, to start scattering rose petals over the heads of the happy couple.

'Oh, Mr Matthews!'

'Anything for you, my dear.'

Ditty smiled as she relaxed back into her seat.

Well, the timings were completely off, she would never have sanctioned that sort of nonsensical speech—*every day spent with you is one I want to continue forever, indeed*—and she would be forced now to pay double to everyone else involved for the change in plan.

But it was a success. Of course it was. It was one of her proposals.

The tiredness she had managed to keep at bay suddenly rushed through her. A dull ache in the back of her neck, a throbbing in her shoulders, a heaviness to her head. The pins in her coiffure were far too numerous and her stays far too tight.

Perhaps she would take a week off before seeking out her next client, Ditty mused as Miss Evans burst into happy tears. She'd earned it.

Twenty minutes later—*as per the agreed schedule*, she could not help but think to herself—she rendezvoused with the happiest man in the world just outside the door to the kitchens.

'It went perfectly!' Mr Matthews said excitedly, a light in his eyes Ditty well recognised. It was the look of a happy client.

She nodded. 'All of my matches are perfect. Though you did go off-script, Mr Matthews.'

He blinked as though he had never heard of a script

in his life, and they hadn't spent the last few days going over and over it. 'What?'

'The script we agreed,' Ditty said patiently, resisting the urge to simply return home and collapse onto the chaise. 'The one that detailed your appreciation of Miss Evans's support through your medical degree—'

She could not continue for Mr Matthews was laughing too heartily. 'Appreciation? Miss Oliver, I am in love!'

I can see that, Ditty wanted to say. *But what about the plan?*

'I could not hold in such emotions during such a time—I had to speak from the heart!'

'The heart,' Ditty repeated, trying not to smile.

They were all the same, these romantics. They all believed they had a better understanding of romance than she did—she, who made a living from it!

But there was no point in arguing with them. It was why Thomas was such an excellent match for herself. They both had no interest in the pointless Valentine-style performances that filled so many courtships these days.

They knew where they stood.

But of course, now so did Mr Matthews. Ditty smiled. 'I am happy for you, Mr Matthews. I will be leaving now, but enjoy your evening, and your New Year.'

'And you, Miss Oliver,' Mr Matthews replied, beaming. 'And may you find true love!'

It was all Ditty could do not to roll her eyes as she departed from Rules into the freezing cold London air.

True love.

Ditty had never had much cause to believe in such a

thing. Her parents had loved each other and what had that gained her mother? Nothing but heartbreak. She had barely considered a gentleman until six months ago, when she had come across Thomas.

'Excuse me,' she said, pushing past a happily clamouring crowd taking up much of the pavement.

One of the men leered. 'Happy New Year, ain't it?'

'Not quite,' Ditty said with a wry smile as she left the chattering group behind.

It would not be New Year until she dined with Thomas. Her sisters could never understand what she saw in him, and she trotted out the same speech she always gave.

He was solvent. He was unmarried. And he understood her passion for planning.

What else could a lady want?

Ditty pushed back a curl of golden brown hair as a familiar face stopped by her side.

'Miss Oliver!'

'Hullo there, Pat,' she said brightly, stuffing her hands into the pockets of her heavy winter pelisse. The postman's chirp put a smile on her face. 'You're out late.'

'Post never sleeps, miss!' the man said happily. 'I thought you would be at home, but here you are—and here you are.'

Pat handed her a letter, relatively thick and sealed with a symbol she recognised.

Ditty smiled. It was perhaps one of the most foolishly romantic things she had ever done, she mused as she pulled off a glove to open the letter. Selecting a bespoke seal for Thomas so she would always recognise his letters was not something she had ever done before, though it had a certain charm about it. But it had not been designed for romantic purposes, she had been quite clear about that. A proposal planner received a great many letters, and knowing his in a moment was a practical solution.

Besides, he lived right on the other side of London. Miles away, hours of walking if there was not a hackney cab to be found. And they were both so busy—sometimes they could go weeks at a time without even seeing each other.

'G'night, miss!'

'Yes, good night, Pat,' Ditty said vaguely as she looked down at the letter, sidestepping a couple nuzzling together in a doorway. She didn't even need to look up. Kissing couples were merely the backdrop of her world.

The seal easily broke and Ditty pulled out two pieces of paper. Oh. Thomas hadn't written to her, after all. Oh, there was a short note…but the other paper within the envelope appeared to be from a solicitor.

A solicitor?

Miss Oliver,
Please find your cessation of relationship notice
enclosed.
Yours respectfully,
Thomas Wright

Ditty blinked. It was a little formal, to tell the truth, even for Thomas. Her thumb was cold in the freezing

December air as she opened up the other piece of paper, entitled 'For Aphrodite Oliver, 31 December, 1811.'

And stared.

No. Surely she could not be reading—

'Careful now!'

Ditty gasped as she almost strode straight into someone—but they were beaming.

'Ditty, you'd lose your head if it wasn't screwed on!' Thalia said with a snort. 'Got lost?'

Ditty's features relaxed into a smile as she grinned at her brash, outspoken and frequently irritating younger sister. 'Lost?'

Thalia pointed up at the building they were standing outside. 'You've walked straight past our door. Something exciting in that letter—is Mama returning soon from her visit with Aunt Louise in Brighton? A new client, maybe?'

There was such hope in her voice, Ditty almost winced. Her sisters had been so understanding with her the last few days as she started to fret about this proposal concluding and leaving her with no income to speak of.

But her sister could not be more wrong.

'Not really,' she said awkwardly, suddenly conscious they were standing outside in a bustling street. 'Come on, I'll tell you upstairs.'

And so about ten minutes later, Thalia was curled up in an armchair while Calliope poured them all hot chocolates. Calliope had a pencil shoved in her hair bun— an occupational hazard of being an artist—and Thalia slowly worked on adding pâté de guimauve, or what she called 'marsh mallows,' arranging them carefully in their mugs. Her passion for poetry and beauty meant she was always looking for perfect balance.

And while they did that, Ditty told them.

'A…a cessation of relationship notice?' Thalia said, eyes wide, legs tucked under her. 'No.'

'Yes,' said Ditty ruefully.

'No!' Calliope thrust the hot chocolate into her hands with wide eyes.

'Yes.' Ditty nodded.

It was hard to believe, even saying it aloud. She and Thomas had never spoken much about the future—at least, not after they had mutually agreed to court.

What had been the point? Ditty had elaborated on her five-year plan, indicated precisely when she would need Thomas to propose if he was serious about courting her, and gave him a copy of her weekly schedule. He had sent her a notarised copy of his own five-year plan by the early-morning post the very next day.

They understood each other. Better than anyone. Better than all these romantics.

At least, she had thought they did.

'I have never heard of such a thing!' Thalia said expansively, slopping hot chocolate over her hand with her wild gesture. 'Oops.'

While she licked her hand, Calliope looked firmly at Ditty. 'And you had no idea this was coming at all? He didn't say anything to you about this?'

Ditty hesitated, and took a sip of the delicious steaming hot chocolate to give her time to think.

Not that she needed it. She and Thomas hadn't spoken for…why, it must be a week now. Perhaps more than a week. No, it was definitely a week: he had called on Christmas Day, according to their landlady, who lived in the rooms below them, and she had missed it because she and her sisters had been out for a bracing walk—but she had read his hastily scrawled note and returned a note in kind. He had probably read it.

That counted, didn't it?

And she should be sad. She should be, yet sadness would not come. There was a strange sort of ache, an emptiness. Was that what one was supposed to feel when one's courting gentleman ended things by letter?

'Ditty?' Calliope's eyes were looking more concerned with every passing moment.

Ditty leancd forward, snuggling into the large, misshapen chaise that took up most of the small drawing room of their lodgings. 'Honestly, you mustn't worry.'

'Mustn't worry—mustn't I?' Thalia stared as though Ditty had grown a second head. 'You don't have any clients, which means no income, Mama is on her jaunt to Brighton but the money will run out soon and your gentleman friend just abandoned you!'

Ditty winced.

'Well, fine, not abandoned per se,' said Thalia swiftly. 'But still, he is no longer courting you, is he?'

'I suppose not,' Ditty said, looking at the letter in her hand.

The paper from the solicitor was short and to the point. That was one of the things she had always liked about him. Thomas never blathered on about nonsense, he always got straight to the purpose of his conversation.

Addressing: Miss Aphrodite Oliver
From: Mr Thomas Wright
Notice: You are formally given notice of Mr Wright's decision to terminate the courtship between you.

He understands this may come as a surprise, but he has given much thought to the matter, and after consideration has concluded there is nothing more to be gained from the connection.

Your letters, the two books and note of your weekly schedule will be sent to you forthwith. You may dispose of his items in any manner of your choice.

The excursion to the theatre organised for January 18 has been cancelled, as has your dinner arrangement for February 14.

Please do not contact Mr Wright to discuss this matter, as it is now closed.

'Read it out again,' Thalia said firmly, tucking her long skirts over her. 'I need to hear this for myself—properly, now I'm concentrating.'

Ditty smiled as she saw Calliope roll her eyes. 'You never listen!'

'I'm listening now!' said Thalia defensively. 'Besides, who can be expected to take in such a thing the first time!'

It was starting to sink in, even Ditty had to admit. The cessation of relationship notice was, though she could only admit it in the privacy of her mind, the perfect example of their courting.

'Ready? So it says, "You are formally given notice…"'

Ditty was not interrupted once as she read out the letter to her sisters. It was rather odd to do so, in truth. Having it there in black and white felt strange; speaking it aloud made it real in a new way.

Thalia sighed heavily as Ditty reached the end. 'Well, there's nothing of his here, he's not much of a gentleman for visiting, is he?'

Ditty shook her head. No. For some reason, he had never visited their rooms.

'And does he have many of your letters? Anything like that?' That was Calliope's question. Her hair had been unpinned now, as they were in the privacy of their own rooms, and she looked worried.

Now she came to think of it, Ditty wasn't sure she had sent much correspondence to Thomas. His rooms were far away and she had visited but twice, her letters usually perfunctory and designed to organise another walk or visit to the opera.

And that should bother her, should it not? That there was almost nothing left, now that he had summarily departed her life, to prove that they had once been…what, to each other? Had Ditty ever defined it? Was that why this strange ache was already fading?

She shrugged. 'A few letters, perhaps. I have probably loaned him a few books…'

Calliope snorted. 'You and your books!'

'I like my books,' Ditty said defensively. 'They're a portal into another world!'

A more ordered world. Sometimes, when life got too much and Ditty didn't feel able to share with her sisters precisely all the thoughts swimming through her mind, she removed all her books from their shelves in her bedchamber, cleaned each cover, ensured no bookmarks had been left in them or dog-ears created by her sisters and then reorganised them.

Alphabetical by author.

Alphabetical by book title.

Chronological by composition.

Chronological by printing date.

Colour of spine...

There was nothing that could make Ditty feel more grounded, more herself, than seeing all those beautiful books elegantly arranged in a fresh way.

She looked up to glimpse Calliope giving Thalia a furious, 'Our sister is heartbroken and we shouldn't be criticising her!' look.

Ditty sipped her hot chocolate. 'Perhaps it's for the best.'

Calliope frowned. 'You think so?'

'I don't feel that upset about it at all, to tell the truth. More shocked. Surprised, not sad,' Ditty confessed, finishing her hot chocolate. 'Mmm. That's good. Is there more?'

Calliope rose immediately and took her mug. 'So you really don't mind the man you've spent months courting has ended things by a letter from his solicitor? With a—what did he call it?'

'A cessation of relationship notice,' Ditty supplied.

Calliope snorted. 'Why are men so…so…'

'Exactly,' said Thalia firmly. 'You know that gentleman my friend at the studio insisted I meet without giving me any details about him?'

Ditty said nothing. She could have told her middle sister, the first person who had helped her get on her feet when she had followed her to London, that meeting gentlemen in such a manner was rarely a good idea.

'You said you didn't have any requirements for a husband,' Calliope was pointing out fairly.

'He had a glass eye!'

Ditty smiled as she accepted the second mug of hot chocolate. Calliope was snorting with mirth now, her hair all tangled with ribbons and paint stains on her bodice. That was what you got, she thought wryly, with artists.

Thalia, on the other hand, was pursuing poetry. Just as artistic, but far more patient. One had to be, when you had to wait for the words to come to you.

Her stomach twisted. And the only reason her sisters could pursue these passions as ladies of leisure was because she had decided to work. She was the only one in the family standing between them and destitution, a heavy fall from grace considering their comfortable life when Papa…

Ditty cleared her throat. She would not think about it. She would not think about the nightmares of her mother being cast out onto the street. Not think about how she was the only one who thought practically. The only one who worked.

Discreetly, of course. And respectably. A proposal planner was a very respectable profession.

It ceased to be a profession when she couldn't find any more clients…

'Look, I have the best idea,' said Calliope suddenly, interrupting Thalia's monologue on why having a glass eye was not a character flaw, but it had caused a great deal of confusion when she thought he was flirting with another woman in Hyde Park.

'I mean, I almost shouted at him right in the—'

Ditty raised an eyebrow. 'Calliope's good ideas usually end up—'

'Disasters, is that the term we agreed?' Thalia quipped.

'I think *catastrophe* was the one we chose,' Ditty said over Calliope's protests.

'Ditty!'

'Well, they so often are,' said Thalia firmly, settling next to Ditty on the chaise. 'Remember that time when you said your bedchamber would feel bigger if you painted it black?'

'And it does, doesn't it?' Calliope objected.

Ditty started to giggle. 'Only because that big chunk fell out of the ceiling!'

'Well, how was I to know steaming off the wallpaper like that would cause damp—'

'And that time you assured us if we bought an additional kettle, it would take half the time to boil water for tea?' Thalia added.

Calliope pointed to the fireplace where their two kettles sat. 'We use it every day!'

'Of course we do,' giggled Ditty. 'As a receptacle for biscuits!'

The three of them fell about laughing and all the tension Ditty had not realised had collected in her stomach started to fade away.

So, she wasn't going to be entering the New Year being courted. What did that matter? She had a profession that was not entirely failing, more books than most people would know what to do with, a mother who thankfully did not completely interfere in their lives and two sisters who would support her no matter what occurred.

What could possibly distract her from that?

Chapter Two

January 23: 20 days until the proposal

'You really mustn't go wandering off like that,' Henry Paisley, freshly minted Duke of Glanyrafon, and long-suffering only doctor of Brexley, said sternly.

The woman looked up with wide eyes. 'Why?'

'Now, you know why,' he said, trying to keep his voice severe, even as he pushed his dark brown curls from his eyes.

That was the trouble. Unless he really piled on the guilt, they never did anything he said—and they always promised they would, and then always crept off somewhere!

'You know I'm giving you these rules because I want to keep you safe,' Henry said, finding himself tempted to wag a finger and resisting the urge. 'Everything I do is to keep you safe—all of you—and these restrictions are because I can't trust you.'

She opened her mouth in mock horror. 'You don't trust me?'

Henry sighed heavily as he straightened to his full, rather towering, height. 'No, Mavis. I do not. Now go back to the library and take your medicine.'

Mrs Mavis Curll, who was at least seven and eighty but refused to tell Henry her precise age, waggled an eyebrow. 'I'll only go if you accompany me. I always feel better with a handsome gentleman on my arm.'

It was impossible to stay angry at any of the residents of the Lodge for Gentlemen and Ladies of a Certain Age. Henry had tried to remain stern, fiercely so, for several months—ever since he had opened the place.

But there was something just so endearing about the ladies and gentlemen in his care. Their knowledge, their experience, their wisdom—it all combined to make them the most marvellous escape artists, and they did so with such smiles of innocence…

'I put up with this in the spring and summer,' Henry said warningly, taking Mavis's arm and walking her into the building and down the corridor toward the library. 'But in the winter—'

'I know, I know, I could have a fall,' Mavis said, waving a hand cheerfully as she grinned at a few residents coming the other way. 'But you'll always catch me, won't you?'

Henry could not help but smile. Yes, if he could, he would. If he had enough hands, arms, legs, brains, he would follow each of his residents around with cotton wool, desperately trying to keep them safe. But he was just one man, and they'd had to let another nurse go only last week. The ledgers just didn't account for such things.

And he wasn't going to charge his residents more—not when they had so little.

His stomach twisted in a painful knot but he tried to ignore it as they entered the library. 'I will do my best to catch you, Mavis, but it would be a lot easier for me if you just stayed—Avril Vickery, what do you think you're doing?'

Slipping Mavis's hand from his arm, Henry rushed toward the elderly woman who was struggling with her skirts and had apparently been attempting to climb out of a window.

'I just wanted a breath of fresh air,' Avril said innocently, guilt all over her face. 'Is that a crime, now?'

'Well—'

'I'll have less of your cheek, young Henry,' Avril said with a mischievous wink. 'You may be a duke now, but that doesn't impress me!'

There was so much to think of, so much to do, so much to organise.

So much to worry about.

Trying to push the sinking sensation away from his mind, he affixed a smile. 'I quite understand.'

The place needed at least three more nurses, and someone to organise things for them all to do, he thought wretchedly. And here he was, the owner of the place, wrangling with the elderly, trying to prevent them from escaping and slipping on the ice. When he should be at his desk, working out how to afford coal for the fires until March...

'Henry!'

He started and grinned weakly at Avril, who was glaring. 'I do beg your pardon, Avril, I was thinking—'

'But still, you have been far more preoccupied than normal,' she pouted. 'Even for you, Your Grace.'

Your Grace. They must be worried about him.

Not that Henry ever demanded the honorific. It seemed the sort of thing a fool would do, after a gentleman unexpectedly came into a title after slogging at medicine for a decade.

His mother had never even mentioned it. The granddaughter of a duke! Never given a hint of it—not that the knowledge could have prepared him for the letter which had arrived less than a year ago. Two uncles and his cousin dead in a shipwreck. No more male heirs… except himself and his brother. And as the elder…

The recently inherited Duke of Glanyrafon tried to smile as best he could, keeping deep within him the doubts that had been plaguing him the last few months.

Inheriting a duchy had for a short time—mere days— been simply wonderful. The freedom it would give him—the power, not just to change his own life, but to better the entirety of Brexley, of those beyond. He could patronise artists and musicians, travel the world…

All the joy of such an inheritance had been swept away when the bills had started pouring in. Now the damned title was a millstone around his neck, one he ignored as best he could.

Henry's heart twisted. Whenever he wondered whether he was doing the right thing by staying in Brexley, the small town nestled in the hills where he had been born and raised, he just had to spend more than five minutes in the company of his residents. They were always able to see the world straight.

'Medicine, Mavis,' he said sternly. 'Then let me listen to that heart.'

The older woman pouted, but swallowed a gulp of the tonic and sat quietly as Henry placed his ear over her heart. He closed his eyes, losing himself in the mechanical nature of his training.

Thur-thump. Thur-thump. Thur-thump.

His own pulse quietened. 'Much better. Keep taking your tonic regularly—'

'But this does not explain the preoccupation our young gentleman has,' Avril was saying crossly, as though her inspection of him had been interrupted. 'And I think I know what it is!'

There was such a triumphant air in her voice and knowing look in her eye that Henry froze.

Surely...surely she could not know?

He had done his best, the last few months, to keep the impending pressures away from the residents. The last thing they should have to worry about, he had told himself firmly, was whether or not they could afford dessert on Sundays.

They'd already had to cut it from dinners during the week, and no one had complained. Henry had been wracked with guilt when he'd made the decision the summer last year, but no one had mentioned a thing.

But could Avril have worked it out?

No money! It was ridiculous—a dukedom had fallen

into his lap, but the estate had been mortgaged to the hilt and had debts pouring from everywhere. There was no money. Just a ridiculous title.

'You think you know what it is?' Mavis said, leaning forward in her chair.

Gossip, Henry thought ruefully. *We'll never be in short supply of that.*

'Our young Henry,' said Avril victoriously, 'has a lady friend!'

There was a moment of ringing silence, and then several things happened at the same time.

Mavis gave an exclamation of glee and clapped her hands together.

Avril beamed up at the Duke, absolutely certain in her statement.

And Henry laughed aloud.

A lady friend? He couldn't recall the last time he had even thought about…well. Not since Georgiana. But that had been—what, two years ago now? Three years this spring. His stomach curled tightly, as it always did whenever he thought of the woman who he had thought would be his wife.

But he had far more important things to worry about. Like how they were going to replace the pipes when they eventually cracked, as was certain to, in the next six months. Then what would they do for water?

'A lady friend?' Henry said aloud with a forced chuckle. 'The ideas you come up with, Avril!'

Avril's face immediately fell. 'You mean to say there isn't one?'

He shook his head. 'Not in the slightest.'

Mavis scowled. 'And there you were, getting me all excited, Henry, telling us about your wedding.'

'It wasn't me who said anything of the sort!' he protested, finally giving in to temptation and pointing a finger at Avril. 'She was the one who—'

'And why isn't there a lady friend, eh?' Avril cut across him, evidently uninterested in his blustering. 'A handsome chap like you—'

'Well-educated.' Mavis nodded in agreement.

'From an excellent family—'

'A duke now, by all accounts—'

'So?' Avril demanded. 'Why are you not finding a nice lady friend?'

Henry swallowed. It was the conversation his mother attempted to have with him every week, and he was not about to have it again. 'Because,' he said aloud with a genial grin, 'how could I possibly fit another woman into my roster—it's already packed with you two, and half the residents here!'

Their chuckles were good-natured and Henry felt his shoulders relax.

Because it was true in a way. Being the doctor and owner of a place like the Lodge was not just a full-time occupation—it was a lifestyle. Henry could still remember the moment he had stepped into the mouldering main house, with its collapsed ceilings and damp-stained walls, only for the housekeeper to apologetically say that the Lodge was the only place on the estate even close to still standing. Henry had hardly been able to breathe;

he had already given instruction to open up the Lodge for the elderly and infirm in Brexley, his first step—of many, he had hoped—to serve the community that he loved so much. Now he was a resident with them.

Inheriting a duchy was all very well, but when it came with a crumbling manor and an even more crumbling Lodge house, Henry had planned to continue his medical practice in the town to provide for it.

That was, until Prinny—the Prince Regent!—had sent a rather pointed note, delicately explaining that dukes did not take wages.

He was hardly one to throw the elderly onto the street. Henry's father, the previous vicar at St Elsbeth's, would never have approved. So the Lodge continued, and Henry tried to make his deceased father proud, and ignored the mortgages on the estate and the debts piling in.

'Distracted again, poor boy,' Avril said lightly. 'Be off with you, Your Grace.'

And so he did—only within fifteen minutes he was already groaning.

It probably wasn't fair of him to groan, but he couldn't help it. After finally deciding to return to the grounds-keeper's cottage—the repair of which had taken all his immediate funds last year—Henry had thought he would gain himself some peace and quiet as he ran through the place's ledges. That moment had ended the instant his horse slowed to a trot and entered his stables, the dog cart behind it squeaking terribly—he really should get the contraption examined—and he saw it.

His brother's fancy new chaise and four.

What was Charles doing here?

Henry had to shove a brace back into position on his dog cart twice before it held, and when he dismounted, something did not sound good. He really needed to get the man at the Brexley Staging Post to take a look at it. Trouble was, he didn't have the coin to really get it fixed.

Henry rubbed his jaw as he closed the stable door with a creak, and turned to look at his home.

'There you are!' Charles grinned as he stepped out of Henry's cottage and waved. 'I've been waiting an hour! Do you know how much that time's worth?'

Henry chuckled as he strode up the short path. 'You charging your own brother now?'

He clapped the younger man on the back and grinned as they strode into his pokey hall.

'You know I'd always give you preferential rates,' Charles winked. 'But when you're a lawyer—'

'You dullard,' teased Henry, shrugging off his greatcoat and hanging it on the stand before beckoning his brother into the dingy kitchen. 'I assume you are here for a drink. Tea?'

'Always,' groaned Charles.

As the kettle was placed on a newly lit fire, Henry distracted himself from the unexpected visit by bustling about the place, choosing two cups and taking the milk from the pitcher by the back door, the wintery weather keeping it cool.

It wasn't that he didn't like playing host to his brother. Charles was pleasant, as brothers went. He was wealthy, a man of his own making—and he had never crowed about it, always taken care of their mother, and was courting a young lady who'd received their mother's seal of approval, a difficult task.

But still. Henry's bones ached from the fourteen hours he'd just spent at the Lodge. If it wasn't one thing, it was another. Fixing the broken cistern in one of the out-houses. Checking up on their four seriously ill patients, reviewing the medication for all sixty residents, arbitrating the arguments between Avril and Mavis.

All he wanted was a long bath, a strong pot of tea and one of those horrid dry pies that one of the sellers from the market always dropped by of an evening.

Charles grinned. 'Aren't you pleased to see me?'

Henry snorted as he poured the tea. 'You only come to call when you want something, little brother.'

'Now, that is not true!' protested Charles. 'At least, not entirely.'

They had the same scruffy dark hair, the same lop-sided grins and the same inability to tell a falsehood. It was part and parcel of being the vicar's children, he had always thought.

'So what do you want?' Henry pressed, slipping onto a chair by the table.

Charles grinned. 'I wanted to tell you something. Something important.'

Despite himself, Henry leaned forward. 'Something important?'

Charles nodded, and only then did Henry notice the nervous excitement radiating off him. He was bouncing on the balls of his feet. It was the sort of thing their mother did when she had a secret she was bursting to tell.

She never managed to keep hold of it.

'Well?' Henry pressed, knowing his brother wouldn't be able to hold it in for long. 'If it's something to do with work, you know you cannot tell me—'

'It's Miss Yorke,' Charles blurted out. 'We're getting married.'

Henry stared. *Getting married?*

He had known Charles was courting Miss Yorke. They had done so for almost three months. She had even moved with her father to Brexley, which their mother had seen as the ultimate sign of interest.

Truth be told, sometimes Henry almost forgot she and Charles weren't married.

'You—what?'

'We're getting married,' said his brother happily. 'I'm getting me a wife!'

Just in time, Henry remembered that what he was being told was something he should be excited about. He rose from his seat and stepped around the counter. 'Why, Charlie, that's—that's great!'

He pulled his younger brother into an embrace and found much to his consternation that tears were prickling in the corners of his eyes.

This isn't about you, Henry told himself firmly. This was about his brother—about Charles and Miss Yorke. Their happiness. *Not about your loneliness.*

'That's…that's great, such great news,' Henry said aloud as he pulled away from his brother.

Charles evidently saw the brightness of his eyes, but thankfully mistook the emotion. 'I know, if only Father was here. But Mother is delighted, absolutely ecstatic. I think if Miss Yorke isn't too careful, she'll be moving in with us.'

Henry snorted and brushed at his eyes as he returned to his chair and coffee. 'Now, that I would pay good money to see. So, tell me all about it,' he tried to say as graciously as possible. 'How did you propose?'

And that was when Henry knew something had gone wrong. At least, not wrong. Different. Far different to what he had expected.

'Oh, I haven't proposed yet,' Charles said easily.

Henry blinked. 'You—*what*?'

His brother sipped his tea. 'Oh, this is the stuff. You know I've been trying to cut down on tea, I read in a newspaper that it may not be the cure-all some think it is. You as my doctor should know all about that, but I can't help but—'

'Charles,' said Henry firmly, hating to interrupt his brother but needing to work out precisely what had happened. 'What do you mean, you haven't proposed yet?'

'Of course I haven't proposed yet,' Charles said slowly. 'What, you think I can just concoct something like that on my own? No, I've hired a proposal planner.'

Henry burst out laughing, but his laughter swiftly faded away as his brother looked at him steadily, with no hint of mirth in his eyes. 'You…you cannot be serious?'

'Why not?' Charles shrugged. 'Just because I have found a match, doesn't mean that I don't recognise the importance of getting this proposal right. You wouldn't have a baby without a doctor or midwife, would you? You wouldn't buy a house without a solicitor. Why would I not bring in the professionals for this?'

Henry's jaw fell open.

Well...it sounded so logical when his brother said it like that.

But what on earth was he thinking? Couldn't he just summon up the right words for Miss Yorke and ask her to marry him? Was a proposal planner really necessary?

'A proposal planner. To plan your proposal,' he repeated, testing the waters.

Charles nodded.

Henry simply could not get his head around it. The idea someone who barely knew you could create such a special, important moment...

It did not bear thinking about.

A very small cruel voice at the back of his mind wondered whether having a proposal planner would have made any difference with—

No, Henry told himself sternly. *No, he could not think that way.*

His brother was frowning. 'You're not excited.'

'No, no, I am,' Henry said hastily. 'At least, I will be. Once you've proposed, and Miss Yorke has said yes.'

'Oh, she will.'

'I don't doubt it,' said Henry with a dry laugh. 'But still...a proposal planner.'

'You're judging me,' said Charles accusingly.

Henry bit his lip before replying, but the hesitation was more than enough. 'I—'

'You are!' Charles sighed, putting down the teacup on the table. 'I should have known not to tell you—I should have known you would think this foolish!'

'It's not foolish, exactly, I can see why you—it's just, well,' Henry said lamely. 'You cannot manufacture romance, you know? You can't buy it off the shelf, or plan for it. It's not like that.'

'And what would you know about it?'

The words were spoken in anger and Henry knew that. It wasn't his brother's fault that his heart had been broken, that he had thought he had love…and then watched it walk away. That the knife had been twisted all the deeper when just two months later, Georgiana had returned, all smiles and joy, when the newspapers had written about his sudden assent to grandeur and title.

He had loved her. Loved the idea of her—he had wanted to marry her.

And she had not wanted to marry Dr. Paisley.

She had been rather eager to marry the Duke of Glanyrafon.

Henry's jaw tightened. Would he ever be free of the memories of her? Of the regret, not that he had loved her, but that he had been so wrong about her?

The remorse swiftly rushing across his brother's face was genuine. 'Henry, I'm sorry, I—'

'No, it's fine,' he said as easily as he could manage.

Charles looked stricken. 'I didn't mean—'

'I know,' said Henry calmly. 'I know.'

The two brothers stood in tense silence while Henry tried to think of a way to extricate them both from this situation. 'So, when's the big day? The first one, I mean, the proposal?'

His brother smiled awkwardly. 'I thought February 12. Just before St Valentine's Day, you know.'

'So…what, twenty days away?'

Charles nodded, and for some reason, looked awkward again. 'Yes…which reminds me.'

Henry fixed his brother with a piercing stare. *He knew it*. 'What do you want?'

His brother raised his hands in mock surrender. 'It's just a small favour!'

Henry groaned. 'I knew it—I knew you wanted something, you only ever come over when you want something!'

The cheeky grin across Charles's cheeks, however, was one he knew well. Had he ever been able to resist helping his brother out? Did he ever want to?

'I have a big case tomorrow, one I can't leave the office for, and the proposal planner arrives on the midday stagecoach.'

Henry sighed. 'And you want me to meet them.'

He'd say yes. He knew that. He'd never been able to say no to his brother.

Charles grinned. 'Thanks, Henry.'

Chapter Three

January 24: 19 days until the proposal

Ditty stamped her feet in the freezing cold air and wondered why to goodness she had thought this was a good idea.

Because, she told herself as the few other passengers on the stagecoach passed her as they left the staging post, *this is the only client you have right now.* Even if he was a small-town lawyer in the middle of nowhere.

London was her home now—small towns, they were filled with naught but sadness and grief. At least, that had been her experience.

But the offer of a job had been better than nothing, especially with Mama running up debts in Brighton with no thought to practicality, and Thalia and Calliope unable to hold on to a shilling for more than a week. Guilt seared her at the very thought, but it was not so much uncharitable as realistic.

Mama…she had never truly recovered from Papa's death. It had been Ditty who had stepped up and sold off the house and most of their things to cover their unexpected debts. Ditty who had spoken to the tax collector and tried to explain that her father had always paid his taxes. Ditty who shielded her sisters and her mother from the constant need for just another shilling…

As soon as Ditty could earn money it was spent, and no matter how much she tried to save there was always an emergency, always a debt to pay.

Perhaps it was better that their mother was staying with Aunt Louise in Brighton. Safer that way. Cheaper.

Ditty's stomach twisted with the familiar panic of it. She had to earn money, she had to keep them afloat. If she were careful, her sisters would never need know the load that her shoulders bore.

She looked up and down the road. No hackney cabs.

She turned back to the staging post. No…staff?

Ditty sighed heavily, her breath blossoming out before her in the cold. Where on earth was she?

Well, at least that was a question she could easily answer. Right opposite her on the side of the road—the only road, it appeared, that went into the town—was a huge, beautifully crafted sign.

Brexley. Home of romance!

Ditty snorted. Right.

But even her cynicism about the destination for her next client couldn't completely dull the anxiety twisting in her stomach.

Her worries were natural, she tried to tell herself. It was her first job outside of London—who knew if there was even a restaurant in this town! And finding a superb violinist? That was surely going to be tricky…especially if she couldn't find her way to her lodgings.

Casting her gaze up and down the road, she bit her lip. He was supposed to meet her here, wasn't he?

'You all right there, miss?'

Ditty spun around. A beaming older man, dressed in a country jacket, breeches, working boots and a knitted scarf that almost trailed onto the ground, was before her.

'Mr Cantelli,' he said, tipping his hat. 'Not good for a young lady like yourself to be out here on your own.'

Ditty pulled her pelisse closer around her and pulled her trunk nearer her ankle.

In London, words like that would be the opening of something sinister…but he did not look sinister. In fact, he looked quite the opposite. A cheerful local.

She swallowed. Not something she was accustomed to. Goodness, it had been years since she had last left London, now she came to think about it.

When had she grown so cynical?

'Thank you for your concern, sir,' Ditty said with a brief smile. 'But I'm meeting a gentleman here. Paisley.'

Mr Cantelli's eyebrows shot up. 'Goodness. Old Paisley, eh?'

Ditty nodded uncertainly. This might have been a mistake. For all she knew, Mr Paisley wanted to keep the entire thing secret, and she had a growing suspicion news of her arrival on the stagecoach, which arrived daily at Brexley, would be around the town before she arrived at her lodging at the local inn.

Goodness knows what an inn here would be like…

'Well, much as I don't like to leave you here alone, old Paisley is one to be trusted,' said Mr Cantelli grandly. 'Good afternoon, miss.'

'Good afternoon, sir.'

Ditty watched as he walked away along the road, his stout boots far more suitable than the elegant shoes she had decided on in the early hours of that morning. If she'd known there would be so much snow on the ground…

Where was this man?

Pulling off a glove and wishing immediately she hadn't, Ditty opened up her reticule to check the letter this Mr Paisley had sent her.

But before she could open it, her eye was dragged to the newspaper clipping beside it. Despite all her better instincts, despite knowing it would only make her sad, she opened it and read it for the millionth time.

PROPOSAL PLANNER RUINS ROMANCE

In this exclusive interview with Lord Edward Kilkerney, second son of the Earl of Kilkerney, we can reveal there are predatory individuals right here in London looking to prey upon those in love.

Believe it or not, there are actually 'proposal planners.'

These are people who will charge you a king's ransom to do precisely what you would have done anyway: propose marriage to the lady a gentleman is already courting.

Lord Edward has exclusively revealed to the newspaper that, after contracting Miss Aphrodite Oliver (a name which is surely carefully calculated to lure in the gullible) as a proposal planner, he was in the end forbidden from proposing at all by the sharp woman.

'I wasn't able to talk about my feelings,' Lord Edward told our reporter. 'Miss Oliver said it was quite impossible!'

Despite coming from an excellent family, Lord Edward was informed by Miss Oliver that he was in fact forbidden from making advances toward the young lady who shall, for her sake, remain nameless. As though Miss Oliver knows anything about matrimony, being a spinster as she is herself!

It should shock us all that romance is being commercialised in this senseless fashion, and we at the newspaper can only hope Miss Oliver, and others like her, leave their professions and do some honest work instead—or better still, marry and let their husband care for them.

Ditty's heartbeat was heavy in her chest as she reached the end of the article.

It had been her own fault. She had asked her sisters to put aside any newspaper articles that mentioned her. She had done it at first to make sure she heard all the lovely responses she was certain to receive—and she did receive a few. But after refusing to assist Lord Kilkerney's son in forcing—*persuading*, the peer had said—the man's latest paramour to accept his proposal, the newspapers had grown a little cold…and now this…

Ditty stuffed the newspaper page into her reticule in the hope she could forget about it as soon as she was no longer looking at it. Doing so dislodged two notes that her sisters had clearly hidden in her reticule for her to find.

Don't read any articles from the newspapers! I'll tell you why when you get home. I mean it, ignore! Good luck with Brexley. You will be marvellous. Much love—Thalia

It's absolute nonsense, you never would have forced that idiot to say or not say anything—ignore it! Keep your head up. Did you write to Mama? Does she have sufficient funds to remain in Brighton? Calliope

Ditty smiled, despite herself. She had good sisters, but they were too late. She had read and agonised over the article long before she had seen their notes.

Well, all it means is that I have to astound here, she thought sternly as she opened the letter from her new client. She would impress him, help him impress his future fiancée, and then she could at least return to London with her head held high.

It was times like this she wanted her books.

Ditty cast her gaze down the letter from her new client, scanning for the important line. There it was.

You will be met at the staging post and taken to your lodgings at the local inn.

The sound of horse's hooves made her place the letter in her reticule and look up. There it was—a carriage.

Not quite a carriage. A very old dog cart, by the look of it. Ditty's nose crinkled as she examined the rust around the wheel arch and the rotting wood.

Not the sort of conveyance one would expect a wealthy lawyer in any town to own, but then, this was the countryside. Perhaps she should not get her hopes up too high.

And so it was that she tried to address the driver with a beaming smile as he pulled the horse's reins to a halt.

'Mr Paisley.'

The man glared. 'I suppose you could call me that. And you are Miss Oliver.'

Ditty nodded. Well, she could see why the man was about to become engaged. Those eyes—piercing and bold, enticing from the moment their gazes caught. Any woman would be transfixed. His clothing was suitably fashionable but well-worn. Very well-worn, in some places. Dark, unruly hair, a chiselled jaw that would surely only be more handsome once he smiled.

He did not smile. 'Well, let's get this over with.'

Ditty's smile faded. *Over with?* The man wasn't going to do her the courtesy of helping her get her trunk into the back of the dog cart—or assist her up to her seat?

'This isn't London, I'm not a coachman,' the man said with a grumpy sigh, as though he could read every single thought in her mind. 'Aren't you getting cold?'

She certainly was, but the weather was nothing to the frosty temper in his air.

Ditty's mouth fell open before she was able to force it shut. Why on earth did the man hire her if he had no intent in being the least polite? Wasn't that what small English towns were famous for—their sense of community and their charming inhabitants?

'Do you want to leave anytime soon?'

Ditty glared, allowing just a fraction of her irritation to surface, but then she calmed herself and smiled tightly. 'Yes. Give me a moment.'

The back of the dog cart did not lower as she had expected. She was forced to heave her trunk over the wooden slats, though she was not quite strong enough to get it over, and she knocked a piece of the rotten wood clean off.

Ditty stared at it in horror. Not five minutes in the man's presence, the man who could make or break her reputation as a proposal planner, and she had damaged his property!

'Ah,' she said helplessly. 'I seem to have—'

'Oh, don't fret about it, the thing is falling apart,' said Mr Paisley with a shrug.

Ditty heaved her trunk a little farther onto the dog cart with great difficulty, panting slightly as she finished. When she struggled to clamber up into the passenger seat, her new client held out a hand but did not look at her.

In turn, she did not look at him—but she could feel

him. His hip pressed against hers, the tingling it created, something she should absolutely not be feeling.

'Ready?'

Ditty placed her reticule on her lap and could almost feel the folded newspaper article within it. It would be the end of her reputation as a proposal planner if she did not manage to make this man smile. And his future betrothed, of course.

'Ready,' said Ditty with a deep breath. 'To Brexley.'

Henry concentrated on the road rather than on the pretty woman beside him in the dog cart.

Not pretty. He didn't have time to get distracted by that sort of thing. Romance was for those who wished for their hearts to be broken…and he had already experienced enough of it to last a lifetime. Besides, he had a duchy to restore to its former glory.

That he would, Henry had no doubt. There was a surety in his character which had been there since he had been a child, one which had greatly irritated his brother, and it told him that there would be a solution. He would find it, and before the town—before his brother—ever found out just what a burden inheriting a duchy really was.

It was thanks to Charles he was here at all, Henry thought dryly, and not up at the Lodge. Nancy needed that bandage looking at, and if he did not settle the debate about whether the whist-table could be left out in the card room, he would soon have a riot on his hands.

But here he was, picking up a proposal planner.

Proposal planner.

Henry snorted, but shot another quick look at the woman beside him.

In truth, she wasn't what he had expected.

What had he expected? Some sort of fancy Londoner, he supposed. A maidenly aunt in an impressive gown and parasol trimmed with lace, and shoes that had no business being anywhere save for an opera house, with no idea what she was doing in a small town.

But this woman was wearing a bulky pelisse and had managed to heave a rather heavy trunk up without too much difficulty. He'd felt embarrassed about that, but his tongue had tied and his mind had filled with a haze as he looked at her. There was a knowing glint of intelligence in her large eyes, and her mouth—

Henry's gaze snapped back to the road as he drove them toward King's Street. *Don't even think about it*, he told himself sternly. She was here to manufacture romance for that fool of a brother of his, and that was all.

'What is your name again?' he said quietly.

So far as he could make out, he would have said she looked piqued at the question. 'Ditty.'

Henry glanced at her with a wry grin. 'I'm sorry, you're named after a short tune?'

A flush tinged her cheeks, highlighting her prettiness in a way Henry tried not to notice. 'It's Aphrodite, actually, but I prefer Ditty. Aphrodite Oliver.'

Henry snorted. *Of course it was.* Aphrodite? What sort of parent gave an innocent child such a name?

No wonder she had ended up a proposal planner. A

name like that would make anyone start considering romance a business, not just a feeling.

'I see.'

Silence fell again between them and for some reason, Henry felt a prickling of discomfort rushing up his spine.

Why did he feel the need to fill the silence? He was a doctor, for goodness' sake, had been long before he had become a duke; he was the master of lingering silences which his patients and residents filled with what was really on their mind. It was a knack.

So to his own utter surprise, he said gruffly, 'And you think you'll be able to do it, then? Get Miss Yorke to say yes?'

Ditty folded her hands in her lap. 'I have a 100 percent success rate, Mr Paisley, but it is not entirely down to me. I am trusting the courting has been going sufficiently well enough to receive a proposal before I start making my plans.'

Henry nodded. Well, that at least made sense. He would have warned Charles off her immediately if she'd swanned in making all sorts of vague promises.

They didn't need a charlatan in Brexley. The town could be too trusting as it was.

Mr Paisley. It had been a long time since he'd heard that. The Duke of Glanyrafon was his formal title now, no matter how much he hated it.

'And you make your living doing this because…'

Why did his mouth just have to talk?

'Because I am better organised than most people, and because my father died and left myself and my sisters and our mother penniless, and because as I am not the one whose judgement is clouded, I am able to make better decisions,' said Miss Oliver firmly.

Henry almost laughed. 'I'm sorry, whose judgement is clouded?'

He drove onto King's Street as he spoke, the long, winding street that formed the spine, the very heart of Brexley. His stomach swooped as he looked at the bustling little town; the Cantelli restaurant, the church on the corner with Vicar Melview carefully pruning his roses, the butchers, the library, the bakery on the left.

Precisely as he had known it, all his life.

'Well, yes,' said the proposal planner beside him, as though what she was saying was perfectly obvious. 'People in love cannot be trusted, can they? It's a chemical imbalance. No, they need someone who can think clearly, who can plan, organise, schedule—but be creative.'

There was such passion and eagerness in her voice, Henry found himself—much against his will—nodding along.

Then he stopped and cleared his throat.

It was so easy, then? To be blinded to reality, to lose oneself utterly in a feeling that could not be trusted—

But no. What he had felt for Georgiana…that had been real.

It had not been reciprocated, in the end…but it had been real. That was when he had promised himself never to allow such weakness, such vulnerability in his heart again.

Still. Henry glanced at her as he took a right, toward the only inn in town.

She wasn't what he had expected. No prim and proper madam, no scheming swindler out for his brother's money.

Just…a woman. With a thick pelisse, and a scarf wrapped around her neck. Hands in slim leather gloves. A beauty that needed no adornment, a beauty his body responded to, even if he did not wish it to.

'We're almost there—the Rose and Crown. Mrs Fletcher took it over when her husband died and her rooms are good.'

She nodded, and Henry found himself prickled that she had not responded. Well, he knew how he could make her respond, didn't he? Not that he would be so uncouth as to say—

'I can't say I care for your profession,' he said eventually in a nonchalant voice. 'Matchmakers and proposal planners the pair of them, it all seems most ridiculous to me. Manufacture romance—I don't believe in it. But there we go.'

For some reason, Miss Oliver was looking absolutely astonished. 'I beg your pardon?'

'I just think it's a tad ridiculous,' Henry said wretchedly. Here he was, opening his big mouth… 'But that's neither here nor there, it's not up to me to—'

'But it most certainly is— How dare you bring me here under false pretences!'

Henry frowned as he pulled up outside the Rose and Crown. *False pretences?* He'd brought her straight to where Charles had said, had he not? Taken time out of his busy day to do it, too. The least she could do was thank him!

'Though I will admit, I am relieved to see there is another businesswoman here who understands the brief.'

Henry blinked. What on earth was she talking about? 'What?'

'The inn,' Miss Oliver said, pointing at where they were approaching. 'Brexley themed, I assume? I saw the sign. "The home of romance"?'

He glanced at it. It was only when an outsider pointed it out that he really noticed it, but she was right. Mrs Fletcher had rather gone overboard. The windowsills were painted pink. There were little painted hearts, and since when had the weathervane been a little Cupid?

Henry winced. All for the idiotic St Valentine's Day Festival. The most ridiculous idea to make their town thrive in all the world.

Well, he didn't have to put up with this for much longer.

'You are welcome,' he growled, pulling the dog cart to a stop and glaring.

To his utter astonishment, the proposal planner was glaring back. 'You have the audacity to bring me all the way out here, in January, too, when I may not be able to get a stagecoach back home for days!'

Henry's eyes widened. 'No, you can't go back,' he blurted out.

That would be the last thing he needed—to upset his

brother's proposal planner before she even stepped into the inn!

He should have kept his mouth shut. What had he gained but to see ire etched all over the woman's face?

Still. He wouldn't be a man if he did not notice just how pretty she looked as she grew angrier.

'I most certainly can go back if I want to.' Miss Oliver was almost bristling, she seemed so angry. 'When you hired me—'

'Hired you?' Henry stared. 'Me?'

What on earth was she talking about? Him, hire her? He'd started walking down that road before and it had ended in nothing but pain. There was no chance he—

Oh. Oh, now he understood.

But the proposal planner obviously hadn't. 'Yes, when you hired me! I have to say, Mr. Paisley, I wish I had requested some references of you, rather than merely supplying my own. I have never been so insulted—'

'Ah,' said Henry knowingly.

Miss Oliver scowled, evidently miffed she had been unable to continue her speech. 'What?'

He smiled half-heartedly. So swiftly had he wished to transport the proposal planner that he had not even bothered to introduce himself. All this misunderstanding would have been avoided if he'd just enacted the good manners his parents had given him.

'I think I've discovered the confusion,' he said slowly.

The proposal planner was still glaring. Henry had to admit himself impressed.

Well, she was here all alone, wasn't she? She'd turned

up in a town she'd never been to before, to meet a gentleman she'd never met before, and got into a dog cart with someone who hadn't even made his full name known.

Despite himself, he was impressed. She was bold. Brave.

Alluring.

'Confusion?' she said, narrowing her eyes. 'There is no confusion—I'm here to help you propose, and—'

'No, you're not,' Henry interrupted. 'You're—'

'I most certainly—'

'Will you just let me speak, woman! You're here for my brother. I'm *a* Paisley brother, yes, but not the one who hired you!'

Miss Oliver stared for a moment, blinking at this new information.

Henry's stomach twisted. This was all so avoidable, and now she was going to meet Charles with a poor opinion of him.

Not that it mattered. Why did he care what the proposal planner thought of him?

'Your…your brother.' Miss Oliver spoke slowly, as though trying out this information and seeing what she thought of it.

Henry's mouth curved upward as he saw, out of the corner of his eye, Mrs Fletcher come out to welcome her new guest.

'Look, my name is Henry Paisley. You're here for Charlie—Charles,' he corrected hastily. *There would be time enough to explain that he was also the Duke of*

Glanyrafon—another time. 'My younger brother. My better mannered, lawyer brother.'

Was it his imagination, or had bitterness crept in there?

'He's the one who wants to get married, he's the one who hired you and he is the one who asked me to meet you at the staging post,' Henry said, speaking faster now as Mrs Fletcher approached. 'Look, I am sorry I offended you, it's just a misunder— Oh, good afternoon, Mrs Fletcher.'

Mrs Fletcher beamed. 'Ah, you've brought my new lodger.'

Henry smiled faintly. That was the trouble with staying in the small town you grew up in. Everyone knew you from a child. All your foibles, all your mistakes... and had supported you through them. Helped you grow.

He wouldn't want to be anywhere else other than Brexley.

'Here she is,' he said aloud. 'Aphrodite, the goddess of love. I'll carry her trunk in for you in a moment, Mrs Fletcher—just got to clear up something first.'

Henry watched Mrs Fletcher's gaze dart between him and the proposal planner, and tried to keep his groan inward.

Of course. Of course the old lady would start to construct some sort of idea he—

'Oh, young Henry, you take as long as you need,' chirped the innkeeper with a smile. 'I'll be right inside, you know where to find me.'

She almost clucked with delight as she returned to

her door, Henry saw with a wry smile. Well, there was nothing much else for the women of Brexley to do than marry off the younger generation, he supposed.

'You are not my client,' said the proposal planner slowly.

Henry turned back to Miss Oliver. 'Absolutely not,' he said firmly.

She examined him for a moment, and heat grew in his chest at the attention. Not because it was her, naturally. He would have felt discomforted if it had been anyone.

'Well,' said Miss Oliver finally. 'Well. That changes things.'

'So you'll stay?' Henry said eagerly. He wouldn't be the one to ruin things for Charles. After all, it had been the one thing their father had asked of him, on his death-bed, Henry's years of medical training still not enough to keep the man he loved alive.

Look after your brother, whatever you do.

The proposal planner stepped down from the dog cart—which he had to assume was a good sign.

'My brother is a good man,' Henry snapped, trying to ignore the heat roaring through his body as she stepped closer. 'I want him to be happy.'

'Even if you think I am some sort of charlatan,' Miss Oliver said, halting before him and gazing up at him through long eyelashes.

Henry swallowed. Charlatan? Yes, that was one word for her. It wouldn't be particularly accurate. *Beauty.* That was more accurate. *Temptress*, for it was tempting to lean down and taste—

He stiffly stepped back, half wondering how he'd managed to get himself into such a situation. *Honestly, man. Pull yourself together!*

Miss Oliver was examining him closely. 'It appears most difficult to please you, Mr. Paisley.'

God in His heaven... 'All I am asking is that you fulfil your agreement with my brother,' was all he could manage. 'He is the only family I have left.'

Something flickered in Miss Oliver's gaze. 'I'll stay,' she said shortly, walking around for her trunk.

Henry almost tripped over his own feet to get out and retrieve it for her. It was the least he could do.

'Good,' he said, handing her the heavy thing. *What did she have in there?* 'I'm glad you're staying.'

'I'm not staying for you!' Miss Oliver bristled. 'I—I am already fatigued by avoiding your displeasure.'

They stood there for a heartbeat, glaring at each other, until Miss Oliver snorted, turned around and stamped over to the inn.

Henry watched her go. *Well!* That would be the last time he'd ever be tempted by Miss Oliver!

Chapter Four

January 25: 18 days until the proposal

Ditty smiled encouragingly. 'Ready? The first place we want to start is with a history of your courtship. Then likes, dislikes, passions. Then we'll move on to a review of the town and where might be best to locate the proposal.'

A spark of excitement rushed up her spine.

This was, perhaps, the most exciting part of the whole process. The very beginning, when all options were open and she could let her imagination run riot.

Proposal while galloping across London in a game of tag? Why not?

Proposal in a boat in the middle of a lake? Of course!

Proposal after clambering to the top of St Paul's Cathedral, looking out over London? She'd organised that, and the other two, and plenty more besides.

But with a new client, there was always the chance their story would give her an idea she had never considered before, and that was what made Ditty so excited about working with Mr Paisley.

Charles Paisley, she corrected silently as she waited for her client to speak. Certainly not the Mr Paisley she had first encountered.

Will you just let me speak, woman! You're here for my brother. I'm a Paisley brother, yes, but not the one who hired you!

Ditty shook her head to push the irritating man's words from her mind. What did he have against proposal planners, or romance, anyway? Why would a man like that be so determined to make her life difficult just as she arrived in a new town?

She had long ago abandoned the hope for romantic love—seeing her mother fall apart after her father's death had been terrible indeed. To love, it was clear to Ditty, meant to grieve, and she would not, could not do that again. She would not allow anyone else into her heart if it meant it being torn apart when she lost them.

Mr Paisley—he had told her to call him Charles, but Ditty had a hard time with that, it was most indecorous—was frowning. 'Likes. Dislikes?'

Ditty nodded as she leaned back in the comfy sofa in the man's drawing room. Soft wintery sunlight drifted through the wide windows overlooking a garden that was spacious and, in the summer, undoubtedly beautiful.

Her client was seated opposite her in an armchair across a console table. He looked perturbed.

She waited another minute, and then smiled. 'It can

be difficult to get started,' she said softly. 'Let's start with a history of the two of you.'

Charles looked up with panic in his eyes. 'Why does this feel like giving a deposition?'

Ditty chuckled, and that seemed to immediately put the man at ease.

He sat back more easily, crossed one leg over the other and shrugged. 'Sorry, Ditty,' he said, evidently far more at home using her nickname than she was using his first name. 'It's just—I am sure you can understand. Being a lawyer, this feels more like an interrogation than— Henry!'

Ditty froze. The door had just opened behind her but she had rather assumed it would be…well, she wasn't sure who she thought it would be. A maid perhaps, supplying additional cakes. A footman bringing a message. A clerk from the law firm. Miss Yorke was, according to Charles, visiting a cousin for a time while she tied up the sale of her and her father's home. She wasn't due back until the day before the planned proposal.

But it wasn't her.

Henry Paisley, the irritating man whose displeasure she had managed to avoid for almost a whole four and twenty hours, stepped into the room and halted as he awkwardly met her gaze. 'Ah.'

Ditty held up her chin, trying to show him she was absolutely unworried by his presence.

She wasn't. But then, she could not deny her heart had skipped a beat as she caught the gaze of the older Paisley brother. There was something about him, even though she could not stop thinking about how annoying he had been. There was something she couldn't quite put her finger on.

It brought out a passion—no, an anger in her that no man, not even Thomas, ever had.

Perhaps that was what was most disconcerting.

'Henry! Come in, sit and meet—oh, but of course, you two would have met yesterday,' Charles said with a beaming smile. 'Come, sit.'

Well, it spoke well of Mr Paisley, Ditty had to admit, that his brother was so evidently delighted to see him. That was something.

But it was their disagreement yesterday on the drive from the staging post to the inn that surely explained why Mr Paisley looked so uncomfortable. 'My apologies, Charles, I didn't realise you were with… I can come back another time.'

'Don't be daft, man, sit! I'd be glad to have your input, it turns out I hired a proposal planner for good reason,' said Charles with a laugh.

Ditty watched the two men with interest. Now this was fascinating. The moment Mr Paisley stepped in, Charles had perked up and changed into a confident man, eager to demonstrate how confident he was. Fascinating.

The dynamics of brothers, she had always assumed, was rather complicated. But this was something more.

Mr Paisley bit his lip. Ditty found her attention drawn to the curve of his jaw. 'I really can't stay long.'

'Sit, man, how many times do I have to say it?' his

brother said genially. 'I'm about to give Ditty a full and true account of Miss Yorke and my courting history. You can add to it, tell me where I went wrong!'

And there it was, Ditty thought. Just a hint of painful truth in that sentence. What had happened between these two brothers—or was this just what happened when a younger brother had the impressive law firm, the house and the lady of his dreams?

She wasn't even aware what Mr Paisley did for employment, or whether he was a gentleman of leisure—as the eldest, he would have inherited whatever family wealth there was, surely—but whatever it was, it couldn't be that prestigious. Not driving a dog cart like his around the place.

'Fine. I've got five minutes,' said Mr Paisley quietly.

There were a myriad of seats available in the large drawing room, but Ditty found her breath caught in her throat as he moved toward the sofa upon which she was sitting. Surely he wouldn't—

He wouldn't. Mr Paisley walked straight past her, not giving her a second glance, and sat in a chair across from his brother.

Ditty managed to slowly let out the breath she had been holding.

She was being ridiculous. She was here to work, not become distracted by irritating gentlemen who did not appreciate her skills.

'How did you meet?' she said aloud, turning her gaze to Charles.

He grinned. 'Oh, you should have been there, Ditty.

I was in Marchester—the nearest city, I happen to have a number of clients there...'

Ditty nodded as the man spoke, jotting things in her notebook.

It was a standard situation. Introduction by mutual friends, courting whenever he went back to the city, and then—

'She moved here?' Ditty found herself interrupting.

Charles nodded. 'With her father. He sold his law practice, he was planning to retire anyway, and—'

'But—here?'

She immediately wished she had not done so, even though the temptation had been too great to resist.

Moving to this tiny town *once* Charles had proposed—now that, she could understand. But Ditty had never encountered someone moving out of a city to a town like *this* before a proposal had been accepted. It was unheard of!

'You might find,' came Mr Paisley's voice quietly, 'there are a few charms here in our town you can't find in a city.'

Ditty shot him a look. As if he could know—had she not lived in both and found only grief in a small town? At least in the city it was easier to forget, easier to be distracted from life's hardships. 'I was asking your brother,' she said sweetly, turning back to Charles. 'So, she and her father moved here.'

There was a twinkle in his eye as he continued. 'That she did. When I realised she had given up so much for me, and was the best sort of woman I could ever meet, I knew I had to marry her.'

Ditty nodded. That made sense. The calculation had been made, and he was a lawyer, he was used to weighing up cases. She would struggle to find a better offer, and so he wanted to ensure that no other gentleman noticed the same thing.

'Wonderful, that is most helpful, thank you,' she said, jotting down another few notes. 'Likes and dislikes.'

'Mine?'

'Yours, hers, the two of you together,' said Ditty, looking up and smiling. 'Don't worry, there won't be a test. It's just to get an understanding of the two of you, see if I can spot an opportunity to maximise the romance.'

A snort came from her left.

Ditty glared over at Mr Paisley. 'I'm sorry, did you have something to say?'

'Me? No, not at all,' said the most irritating man on the planet, raising up his hands. 'Just…interesting.'

Interesting? Interesting? What did that mean?

Ditty knew she should ignore him—knew she would only get more irritable if she engaged with his nonsense.

But really, what did he think he was doing? This wasn't his proposal, it was his brother's, and she was going to do an excellent job. So why did he keep interrupting?

'Interests,' she said firmly, turning back to Charles.

His gaze flickered between the two of them for a moment, before his shoulders once again relaxed. 'Right. Interests. Well, we both like good food…'

There wasn't anything particularly unusual in the list he gave her. Ditty wrote them all down diligently, regardless. There was every possibility something might come to her later, when she could leave this frosty atmosphere the elder Paisley had brought with him and return to her room at the inn.

She almost smiled just to think of it. Now, there was a woman who understood how to manufacture romance. Every single inch of the room she had been shown to was covered in love hearts. Every surface, the wallpaper—even the gas lamp had a pink heart-shaped cover.

'Well, I've got some good places to start here,' Ditty said aloud. Charles beamed. 'Now, Mr Paisley—'

'I told you, call me Charles.'

Ditty forced a smile. 'Well. Charles. You contacted me because you wanted to ensure the perfect proposal—'

Another laugh.

She turned to glower at Mr Paisley. 'Do you not have somewhere to be in that falling-apart dog cart of yours?'

'Yes,' said Mr Paisley steadily, holding her gaze. 'Somewhere I could be doing far more good than you are, I'll be bound.'

Ditty's mouth fell open. *Well! How could he say such a thing? It was outrageous!*

'Now, Henry,' his brother began.

But she was not about to let that slide, and she did not need a man, even if a client, to defend her. 'Then why don't you go there?'

Heat was flaring in her very bones, but Ditty was not going to allow herself to be overwhelmed.

'Because I want to make sure my brother isn't being robbed,' Henry said calmly. 'You never know, someone coming from London, making all sorts of promises—'

'I make no promises, no guarantees, save that of a perfect proposal!' Ditty could hear the pain in her own voice and hated he was able to disquiet her so easily. 'It's up to my client, your brother, what happens next, and I don't know why you would need to—to check up on me!'

'Just doing my brotherly duty.'

'So what precisely is the problem?' Ditty asked Mr Paisley sharply, heart hammering in what could only be anger. 'All I have done is come to your precious town and tried to do my job.'

Henry stared at the woman who appeared determined to take offence.

His problem? His problem?

Wasn't it obvious? Didn't the whole world think it odd that anyone, let alone his brother, would pay another to ask perhaps the most important question of his life? The longer he had sat listening to Miss Oliver *do her job* the more infuriated he got.

'You honestly don't know?'

The words had slipped from his lips before Henry could stop them, but he could already see his brother was not happy about it.

'Henry, go back to the Lodge,' Charles snapped, all geniality gone. 'You're not helping here—'

'No, let him stay and explain himself,' said Miss Oliver sharply, slamming her notebook shut in her lap. 'I want him to justify what precisely is going on here.'

Henry swallowed. He had not intended this to become so confrontational. He supposed he should be grateful they could have this out in the privacy of his brother's house, rather than outside Mrs Fletcher's inn.

But he couldn't just keep his opinion to himself—he never had. He wasn't about to start now just to make this proposal planner feel better.

'It's simple,' Henry said, prickles of discomfort radiating across his chest. 'You cannot manufacture romance, *Miss Aphrodite Oliver*, no matter what you're called.'

There. He'd said it.

Part of him was pleased with himself. He wasn't going to allow himself to be pushed about by an outsider, especially one who was likely charging his brother tens, perhaps even a hundred pounds to be told to wear a nice cravat, say nice things and follow the ridiculous new fashion of offering a ring. There had been Paisleys serving as vicars of the church here for four generations—five generations were buried in the church graveyard. His grandfather, Henry knew, had helped build the road that led into the street, his great-grandfather had assisted in digging the well. Paisleys had built this town, and he wasn't going to allow just anyone to come here and disrupt the way of life.

But for some reason, Ditty did not look disquieted. In fact, her face remained motionless.

The silence elongated, increasing the tension in the room. Henry swallowed. Why didn't she say something?

When she eventually did, his shoulders sagged with relief.

'I'm sorry, I'm waiting for the rest of your speech.'

Henry stared. *His speech?*

'I think I should be getting back to the office anyway,' came Charles's voice from a long way off. 'It's busy as I said the other day. Henry, why don't you come with me and—'

'Speech?' repeated Henry, ignoring his brother. 'You think I need to justify myself further?'

'I think manufacturing romance is not a crime,' said Miss Oliver sweetly.

Henry tried not to notice the dimple that appeared in her left cheek as she smiled. It was most disconcerting to feel a rush of attraction to someone who was so entirely and utterly at odds with him.

'I didn't say it was a crime,' he said aloud, trying to inject more forcefulness into his voice. 'But there are plenty of things that aren't crimes that I don't agree with, and charging people for the simple practicality of proposing—'

'Oh, there is nothing simple about my proposals,' Miss Oliver cut across him with a glance at his brother.

Henry bristled. Of course there wasn't. She had to prove her worth, didn't she? Justify why she was going to charge her brother a small fortune for the pleasure of—

'Really?' As he had expected, Charles's ears had pricked up. 'Nothing simple?'

'Oh, no, there are many wonderful details I can add to your proposal, weave in from the very beginning,'

Ditty said, turning away from Henry and beaming at his brother.

'It's not about…' Henry began.

'For example, for one gentleman whose lady had a history of dog breeding, I was able to gather over four hundred of her favourite breed into Hyde Park as he proposed,' effused Miss Oliver, her eyes shining. 'And for another, I lined the entire street where they lived with lanterns, each with a note about—'

'I'm not saying you can't plan an event!' Henry snapped.

This was getting out of hand. Charles's eyes had lit up and Henry could see, with a sinking feeling, that his brother was going to spend more money than he could spare on this ridiculous charade.

It was one question! One day! How hard could it be?

A discomforting pain in his stomach reminded him of the day he had promised himself he would never think of again.

How hard could it be? Oh, he knew all too well.

'—and roses,' Charles was saying. 'All over the place—'

'Do you have any musicians living in the town?' asked Miss Oliver eagerly. 'Professional preferably, but I believe many rural players are quite suffic—'

Henry barked a dry laugh as he leaned back in his chair. 'Rural? We're not just a tourist attraction for city dwellers, you know.'

'We host the Valentine's Day Festival every year,' his brother pointedly out calmly.

Henry glared. That wasn't the point! Couldn't he see that?

Both his brother and the irritating proposal planner roundly ignored him.

'There's a beautiful place, just outside the town,' Charles was saying. 'Really beautiful.'

'Well, that could be the perfect place,' said Ditty, eyes wide. 'Where is it?'

'It can only be found along a woodland trail, and—'

'No.'

Henry had not realised how stern, how loud his voice would be as he said the word.

But he could not help it. Pain was roaring in his ears, a rush like pouring water, and he blinked away stars at the corners of his eyes.

Not there. Anywhere, but there. He had never given his family any of the details, just what Georgiana's response had been.

But he could not bear it if he had to hear the story of how his brother proposed—successfully—to Miss Yorke in the place where he had unsuccessfully offered marriage to a woman he had truly cared for. A woman who had broken his heart.

Not that Charles knew that particular heartbreak had occurred along the woodland trail, of course.

His brother blinked. 'Why on earth not?'

'Just, not there, please?' Henry managed. 'Anywhere else. You're just manufacturing romance!' he burst out, unable to hold it in any longer. 'And you can't! Romance is—it's so much more than dressing up a restaurant or buying a hundred red roses, or, or finding a thousand dogs—'

'Not quite a thousand, about four hundred,' Miss Oliver said succinctly with a wry smile. 'Though it was difficult. Her preferred dog is a very delicate breed—'

'I don't need to be told about dogs, I'm saying you can't just produce romance out of a box! You can't do it on command!'

To his horror, Henry found his breathing was ragged.

How did she do it? This woman, who had swanned into town only yesterday, brought a rise out of him that no one else did.

He could feel the prickles of irritation growing across his chest, flaring to his fingers and toes.

How could she look so calm, as though he was a toddler, throwing a tantrum?

The proposal planner stared curiously. 'Really? I beg to differ. I have successfully planned one hundred and eight—no, my apologies—nine proposals, matching the individuals and guiding the gentleman to the altar. Every single one of the proposals, perfect. Every single one of them leading to an engagement.'

Charles threw out a hand. 'There you go!'

Henry glared. 'I'm not saying you don't get results,' he said stiffly.

'Then what are you saying?' asked Miss Oliver.

He swallowed. *What was he saying?*

There was so much hurt in his heart, hurt he had locked away and promised himself never to unlock. Hurt she wouldn't understand.

How could she? Ditty Oliver spent all her time around people who were madly in love, Henry thought bitterly. People who were about to commit to the rest of their lives together.

Or did they...

'Maybe you don't get the results that are right,' he said darkly. 'Maybe the women feel pressured to say yes after such spectacular proposals, after it is obvious that so much money has been spent.'

Out of the corner of his eye, Henry saw his brother's jaw drop.

'Maybe they feel obliged to accept and then regret it later. Maybe it's a decision made under pressure, not from affection,' Henry said quietly, his gaze flicking to Miss Oliver's face. She looked frozen. 'I mean, how many weddings were you invited to?'

She swallowed.

Was he the sort of man to tear down another person? Why did this woman draw out of him such deep anger?

'I would not expect wedding invitations to all of my proposals. That would be ridiculous,' Miss Oliver said, strength rallying in her voice. 'My clients are fashionable, wealthy individuals, I cannot expect them to make room for—'

'If they are wealthy, an additional seat at a table wouldn't cost too much,' Henry said, pursuing this line doggedly. 'You and your guest, I suppose. Gentleman caller. Fiancé. So how many?' he persisted.

'Henry, you can't ask her—'

'Not 109,' Miss Oliver said, speaking over Charles and not taking her gaze from Henry's. 'But—'

'So what you are saying is,' said Henry, hardly knowing why he was pushing this, 'though you have an excellent track record of getting women to agree to marry your clients…they don't always actually marry them.'

The words hung in the air like bullets, but he could not take them back.

And he wouldn't. It was time, he was certain, for Miss Aphrodite Oliver to be taken down a peg or two.

So why did he feel such a heavy weight of guilt as he saw her bite her lip and glance nervously at his brother?

'I make no promises, no guarantees,' Miss Oliver said finally.

'She did say that,' Charles pointed out fairly.

Henry frowned. Did the man not see he was being entirely taken in?

'I promise romance—manufactured romance, perhaps, but romance nonetheless,' she continued in a soft voice. 'It's not my job to make the relationship perfect. Only the proposal.'

Henry swallowed. There was something so…so intimate about the way she spoke.

Which made no sense. There was no intimacy between them, no affection. He wasn't even sure if he liked her.

He was certain she did not like him.

'Perfect proposal,' he sniffed. 'It cannot be done.'

A wide smile crept across Miss Oliver's face. 'Watch me.'

Chapter Five

January 26: 17 days until the proposal

Ditty halted before the town library and glanced up at the rather elegant building.

Yes, it could work. The columns were impressive, not the sort of thing you would expect in a town this far out in the wilderness—well, not wilderness, precisely. But she hadn't seen a modiste in the two hours she had spent walking around the town, scouting out locations, and what was a town without a modiste?

She hadn't seen a bookshop either. Where did these people get their books?

Ditty opened her notebook.

THE LIBRARY

She wrote the two words at the top of a fresh page, then started to write short points—the sort of things she would need to remember when she was in her room at Mrs Fletcher's.

There were so many pretty little buildings every-where, they were all starting to merge into one. Thank goodness this library looked so very different from the rest.

'Ah, hello there!'

Ditty looked up, pencil hovering over her notebook as though she could not wait to return to her writing.

Which, in a way, she couldn't. This was her job, after all, she thought severely. If she did not plan on doing extremely well for Mr Paisley—for Charles's proposal, then she may as well kiss her reputation goodbye.

She'd be forced to take a job far more menial. Matchmaking was the only thing which had ever brought her joy, the only employment she had ever considered when her father had died. Goodness, it was pleasing: like moving chess pieces across a board. When she was planning a proposal, all involved had to obey her commands. The movement of it, like music, the order that she could bring to a person's life…and, of course, the funds she could earn.

A gentleman beamed as he inclined his head as he passed her—quite opposite to how a gentleman would notice a lady in London. Ditty fought the instinct to glare and instead permitted it to happen. There was nothing untoward about it, after all. It was clear the residents of Brexley had a far warmer approach to strangers than in London.

All except one.

Perfect proposal. It cannot be done.

Ditty's heart twisted painfully as the words of that most irritating man swam through her mind. Worse, there must be many gentlemen and ladies who had read that odious newspaper article slandering her good name. What was she supposed to do, permit that abhorrent son of a lord to pressure that poor vicar's daughter to engage herself to him—when the previous two ladies who had accepted such overtures had been ruined then swiftly abandoned without a thought in the world?

And here she was in Brexley, her own reputation inexplicably under attack, with a man who was fighting against her. What on earth was she going to do with him?

Because do something, she must. She could not permit such a miserly gentleman to be the brother-in-law of her greatest triumph! She would have to win him around to the practicalities of romance before the twelfth—which was, what, seventeen days? Eighteen?

So, back to the library. It was rather like the one in her hometown—at least, what she could remember of it. If her father hadn't died, perhaps she would have stayed. But there was nothing remaining for her in Almsbury and so she had left without a second glance. She hadn't even been back. What was there for her?

Standing here, on King's Street, Brexley, it was in an odd way almost as though she were back there now. The same pattern of houses in the distance, becoming shops the closer you got to King's Street. The same fountain at one end. In fact, in a strange way, it was almost like coming—

No, home was London, she told herself severely. She would finish this match, return to London, and hope to goodness her mother would leave Brighton and her spendthrift habits. Though of course there was far more opportunity for her mother to spend in the capital…

Ditty stood taller as she opened her notebook again and looked at the notes she had made on the town's library.

Outstanding exterior—perfect for the day (is there a portrait artist in town?)
Useful location, right in centre of King's Street (check distance to Cantelli Restaurant)
Must check interior

Well, it was an excellent start. Placing the notebook in her reticule, her fingers brushed up against a piece of paper in her pocket. Strange. She could not recall placing anything in there.

Ah. The letter from Thomas's solicitor.

You are formally given notice of Mr Wright's decision to terminate the romantic relationship between you.

And she wasn't heartbroken. Perhaps she should be.

Ditty swallowed. But she wasn't. She knew Thalia and Calliope expected her to be—expected her to be wailing and gnashing her teeth, probably.

But she wasn't. She hadn't thought about Thomas himself all day. A prickle of irritation over his letter had seared her heart as she had awoken, but that had been it.

So she had to assume she had not truly cared for him, not really. This wasn't what heartbreak felt like, was it?

That was supposed to be…well. Hot and fiery and painful. While she had promised herself that she would never allow herself to be heartbroken again, certainly not by a romantic relationship, she assumed she would feel something akin to upset.

In truth, all Ditty felt knowing she didn't have to go for another mindless walk with Thomas on her return to London…was relief.

Still, it did not make sense. As quickly as Ditty attempted to parse through the feelings which did not correlate with the emotions she was almost certain she should feel…there was no true sadness.

Had she ever cared for him, then? And why did the sensations roaring through her whenever she was in close proximity with her client's brother simply not compare?

'I am not heartbroken,' she said aloud.

Perhaps leaving London and the busyness of the Season and the *ton* was the best thing she could have done.

'In many ways, it's like going back to Almsbury,' Ditty muttered to herself, pressing a hand against the library column. 'Everyone knows each other, everyone cares for each other—'

'And everyone is in everyone's business,' said a deep voice from behind her.

Henry didn't know what made him do it.

It wasn't even as though she had caught his eye, given him the excuse to approach her. No, Miss Aphrodite Oliver had been speaking to herself, facing away from him.

She hadn't spotted him. At least, Henry did not think she had seen him. It was hard to tell under that large bonnet, scarf and thick pelisse.

Despite knowing it was not a good idea, Henry had found himself approaching her.

Foolishness!

Yet he could not help it. The thought of surprising her gave him such a feeling of intense joy that he had felt drawn to her, unable to stop himself approaching.

After all, he hadn't exactly been polite at their last meeting, had he? He probably owed it to her to say something nice and polite now.

Miss Oliver whirled round, cheeks burning, and Henry almost laughed as her jaw fell. 'I— What?' she said, evidently flustered.

Something deep within him stirred, but Henry pushed it aside immediately. He hadn't thought this far ahead in his mischief.

His boots were rooted to the spot as though he had frozen there, the light dusting of snow underneath his feet suddenly ice, preventing him from moving.

Miss Oliver's wide eyes looked up at him. Then she seemed to find her confidence. 'You are just an ill-tempered gentleman who met me at the staging post, criticised me and my job, then tried to make me look bad in front of my client.'

Discomfort rose. When put like that, he didn't come out too well.

Henry's heart skipped a painful beat as Miss Oliver thrust what appeared to be a letter into her reticule. One from the gentleman who was courting her back in London, no doubt.

Not that he cared.

'Well?' Miss Oliver demanded. 'Do townsfolk in Brexley often attempt to listen in on a person's private musings?'

'Only ones made by people trying to fleece my brother,' Henry quipped.

The words had left his mouth before he thought, but it was true. This woman had flounced in here, would undoubtedly charge Charles London prices and would not even—

'A man like your brother has the wealth to do what he likes,' Miss Oliver said sharpy. 'Why, anyone else would think you were jealous.'

Henry swallowed. *How did she do that? Say things that went right to the heart?*

Because he was. In a way.

Not the way she thought, he told himself bitterly. No, she would assume he envied his brother's money, his impressive legal practice. And he supposed some brothers might think that way. They might even complain that inheriting a duchy without a matching income was more a millstone around a man's neck than anything else. Certainly, Charles had never made any mutters about wishing it had been himself who had been the heir to their long-lost great-uncle.

But it wasn't that which Henry envied. Oh, no.

There was something so wonderful and yet so galling about one's brother being so…so happy.

'I thought as much,' said Miss Oliver smugly, entirely misunderstanding his silence. 'Well, I suppose that's the trouble with brothers. You are part of his law firm, right? Junior to him, forced to take orders?'

'Wrong,' said Henry, repressing a smile.

How very wrong she was.

'Oh.' She looked genuinely surprised. 'I just assumed— because it's the Paisley Brothers—'

'Our two uncles, my father's brothers,' said Henry. And wondered precisely when would be the best time to reveal he'd inherited a duchy? Was it ever? 'My own brother took on the place, he was the one with the instinct for the law.'

'Oh.'

Silence fell between them. Henry knew he should walk away—there was no reason to stay here, no reason at all.

No reason except that he didn't seem to know how to walk away.

Or want to.

'So…so you're not a lawyer, then?'

He chuckled. 'You think a lawyer would drive a dog cart like mine?'

For a moment, just a moment, she laughed with him, and Henry found his spirits soaring. He'd been wracked with guilt after their last conversation, had hoped to make amends, but had not expected this. To stand like this with a pretty woman, to hear her laugh at something he said. This was what he had missed. What he had thought he would never share with anyone ever again.

And yet here she was, that dimple appearing once more in—

Miss Oliver forced her face straight. 'No, I suppose not. What do you do, then? Or are you a gentleman of leisure?'

Henry swallowed. She was infuriating, and wrong about so many things…but she was also passionate, and clearly clever.

And she would be leaving soon.

Oh, people enjoyed Brexley for a few days, perhaps two weeks. It was a great place to come for a visit, a chance to leave the smog of London, he was sure…but people like her, they didn't stay.

And although he could not explain it, Henry wasn't ready to open himself up to someone who wasn't going to be here next month.

'I—I am a manager,' he said stiffly.

Why he did not tell her the truth—that he was a doctor, an unexpected duke, that he had far more facets of his personality than she could conceive—he did not know. It would almost be like attempting to earn her praise.

And he would not do that with a title as ridiculous as Duke of Glanyrafon. One he certainly hadn't earned.

'Really?' Miss Oliver attempted a smile. 'How fascinating…'

Her voice trailed away, her mind evidently unable to maintain the conversation any further.

Which did not explain why Henry was so exasperated by her instant lack of interest. Why should it matter? Miss Aphrodite Oliver would soon be gone, getting her coin from his brother in the process, and she would be gone without a second look back.

But none of that explained why the sudden desire to share with her about the Brexley Lodge for Gentlemen and Ladies of a Certain Age, to get her to smile again, overwhelmed him.

It was not the only thing overwhelming about her. She looked delightful, all bristling curves and firm pouting mouth—

Henry swallowed, his jaw inexplicably tight. 'It's actually rather amusing. You see—'

'And what would you say is the best restaurant in Brexley?' Miss Oliver said, cutting across him and showing no interest in what he was saying.

Henry forced down the retort that he had already told her this, and that it was offensive—not to mention upsetting—she had already forgotten.

She wasn't here for you, he reminded himself.

'I think most people rate Reg's place the highest,' he said shortly. 'Though that's not difficult.'

Miss Oliver stared, utterly perplexed. 'What do you mean?'

'It's the only restaurant in town.'

'The only—you cannot be serious.' Miss Oliver's eyebrows frowned.

Henry tried not to notice the thin line that appeared between her puzzled eyes, the way their colour deepened as she considered his words.

'Brexley is a small town,' he reminded her, as a gentleman passed and wiggled his eyebrows at the pair of them. He tried to ignore it. He failed. 'This isn't a big city, you know. We don't have restaurants on every street. We have King's Street. If it's not on King's Street, we don't have it.'

If only he could remove the terseness from his voice. Henry loved this place, and he wasn't doing Brexley any favours by describing it like this to an outsider.

Miss Oliver's frown deepened. 'You are in earnest?' 'Why?'

'I'm doing a survey of the place, looking at potential locations,' she said airily. 'I thought I'd check out Mr Cantelli's place—' Henry almost smiled at how easily she said that, as though she'd lived here all her life '—and compare it to the others. But you're saying… there aren't others?'

Henry tried to smile. 'There's a tavern about five miles out, on the stagecoach road, and there is a tavern for the local working men, but I doubt that Charles has stepped foot in there in his life. Mrs Fletcher does breakfasts for her guests, you'll know that, but there are no other places. Unless you become very friendly with a resident, of course.'

What on earth had possessed him to say such a thing?

Miss Oliver obviously was wondering the same thing. 'I see,' she said carefully. 'Well, in that case, it'll be Mr Cantelli's.'

Sudden realisation dawned. Henry groaned. 'Oh, not a restaurant proposal, I beg you!'

It was the wrong thing to say. Miss Oliver's nostrils

flared and pink patches appeared on her cheeks which had nothing to do with the wintery temperature.

'And what, precisely, is wrong with a restaurant proposal?' she said defensively.

'Oh, it's such a cliché! I am sure it's a clever idea in the city but don't you think it's been done?' Henry could not help but say.

In a way, he was disappointed. After all her impressive speeches at Charles's, he'd rather thought she would come up with something wild. Totally impractical, but at least better than a restaurant proposal.

He could do better than that!

'Oh, indeed, has it?' fired up the woman who never ceased to amaze him. 'I suppose you know better than I do where a lady wishes to hear a proposal?'

Pushing aside the memories of Georgiana and finding much to his surprise that they did not surface, Henry nodded. 'I think I do.'

'Then why don't you find a lady to propose to, then?' she shot back.

The blow, though it did not hurt as he had expected, still landed. Henry's jaw tightened. 'You don't know what you're talking about.'

'I could say much the same to you,' Miss Oliver retorted, smoothing down her gown as though that would soothe her nerves. 'I believe I am the professional here.'

'You may call yourself whatever you like,' Henry said, noting the brilliant sparkling eyes and the flushed cheeks. Was she...enjoying this? Was he? 'That does not make this restaurant idea of yours any good—'

'It's a brilliant idea, and has a 100 percent success rate,' Miss Oliver was saying curtly. 'Why, the last proposal I planned was a restaurant—'

'There you are, then,' Henry interrupted, throwing up his hands. 'Come on, Miss Oliver. I thought you'd be more inventive than that. You'll put yourself out of business that way!'

She stared, face pale now as though he had just insulted all her relatives, living and dead. The colour draining away from her cheeks was startling, and as Henry tried to work out what on earth he could have said to upset her so, she swallowed hard and turned away.

'Aphrodite!' Henry called after her. 'Blast—Miss Oliver!'

She completely ignored him, striding up King's Street without looking back.

Henry bit his lip. Now, why had he pushed her right to the edge…and what had he said to end their conversation so swiftly?

Chapter Six

January 27: 16 days until the proposal

Ditty took a deep breath, and entered the building. She was immediately hit with an overpowering scent of flowers.

Flowers, everywhere. Roses and sweet lilies, orchids and even early daffodils. There were mixed bouquets lined in order of colour and themed arrangements on her right.

Ditty smiled, her shoulders relaxing as she warmed up in the balmy store. There was something about flowers. She'd never met a florist she didn't like, and flowers were always there to welcome her home after a long day if her sisters were out working.

There was nothing like a bouquet of flowers to—

'Well, good morning, Miss Oliver, and how lovely to have you frequenting my little store,' trilled a woman who had appeared from nowhere wearing an apron with secateurs in the pocket. 'I wondered how long it would take you to get here!'

Ditty could not help but smile.

It was something she had learned since yesterday, after the odious encounter with that man who seemed intent on nothing more than her ruin.

Everyone at Brexley had been informed—by Mr Cantelli, or by Mrs Fletcher, she did not know which—that she was here scouting out the place for a ball, secrecy vital. Mrs Fletcher had asked no questions when she had welcomed her back yesterday evening, for which Ditty was grateful. She had been weary, exhausted by her traipsing up King's Street, and full of a delicious stew Mr Cantelli—who had told her sternly to call him Reginald—had assured her would be the best she'd ever tasted.

He had been right. That was the trouble; Ditty had not been able to stop herself from having second helpings, and two portions of a delicious doughy dessert. Her stays were a little tighter that morning and the food had settled like a rock in her stomach by the time she had arrived at the inn, and so she'd had few defences against her landlady's questions.

Yes, a ball, she had told Mrs Fletcher.

Clearly the word had got around…

'Now, I am sure you'll want to see my catalogue, got one of 'em right here,' the florist sang out, pressing a heavy booklet into Ditty's hands. 'But for the right price and with enough notice, I can pretty much create anything, Miss Oliver!'

Ditty grinned. And of course, everyone knew her name.

'Thank you,' she said aloud. 'Miss…?'

'Oh, everyone round here calls me Miss Vivienne,' said the florist with a squeak. 'And you should do the same, too.'

Ditty tried to smile. *Finally, someone I can speak to plainly.* 'I need flowers.'

'Oh, yes, I'd imagine so,' said Miss Vivienne with a grin. 'News travels fast in this town. Now, I've got a lot of roses coming in, for the Valentine's Day Festival, you know. Most of the town decorates its gardens, stoops, doors, shopfronts, you name it. If you want roses, I'm going to have to have your order soon, so I can make sure there's enough for you.'

This was more like it. Practicalities. Ditty nodded. 'I believe I will need—'

'Unless you want to go with a different flower?' interrupted the florist eagerly. 'Roses are so traditional.'

'I find roses work,' said Ditty firmly. She wasn't going to be talked out of her plan—she had it all laid out.

Miss Vivienne nodded. 'Now, why don't we— Oh, hello there! Please do excuse me, Miss Oliver, I shall be right with you. Very important customer...'

She floated away like dandelion seed on the breeze.

Here, it appeared, was a woman after her own heart. Miss Vivienne understood the pressing nature of business, and whoever it was she was off to help, it was clearly an important account.

Here, at least, she could find someone to partner with.

As Miss Vivienne trilled with someone near the door of the store, Ditty wandered. The place was huge, far larger than she had expected from the outside. There were more options than she had seen in a few of the London florists who were on her list, carefully written out in the back of her notebook.

Ideas sparked around her mind, ideas to layer upon her initial spark of genius. A grove—no, a bower! Was Miss Yorke interested in fairy tales? Could she lean into Brexley's natural inclination toward Valentine's Day and create something—

Something out of the corner of her eye interrupted Ditty's thoughts, and she halted her steps. Unsure precisely what had made her feet stop wandering, she returned to her plans. A garland, perhaps. Bouquets had been done, she didn't want to be too derivative. Or mayhap a throne, made from flowers—

All creative thoughts ceased as she realised what had caught her eye. One of the bouquets was wrapped in newspaper...and blaring out in large type were the words 'proposal planner.'

Oh, no. Another mention of her in a newspaper article.

Ditty's stomach clenched. It could be good, she tried to tell herself. It could be complimentary. It could be a lovely review, someone writing to the editor to defend her, something positive...

The trouble was, now she'd seen the words on the printed newspaper, she couldn't help herself.

'Oh, that will be lovely! I am sure she'll love that— and another one, for Avril?'

Ditty did not turn as she lifted the newspaper with a shaking finger. Whoever had just entered the florist, they were clearly courting more than one woman. Bold, in a town as small as Brexley.

Her eyes fell on the article. Even just the headline made her groan.

PROPOSAL PLANNER GONE TO GROUND

It is with great astonishment that we report Miss Aphrodite Oliver, the proposal planner who we reported on just days ago, appears to have disappeared. Cowed into hiding, some would say, after such an awful review in this very newspaper.

Our reporter attempted to find Miss Oliver to discuss the accusations made against her by her latest client, only to discover she is no longer in London. Attempts to track down the 'proposal planner,' as she likes to call herself, have to date been unsuccessful.

'Go away,' said an unnamed woman living at Miss Oliver's residence. 'Go and ruin someone else's life!'

It is of course not this paper's intention to ruin anyone's life, and we are astonished at the accusation—but not as astonished as we were to receive several letters from other men who had been duped into purchasing Miss Oliver's services.

'She told me romance wasn't real, that it was only chemical!' said one unnamed unhappy customer of Miss Oliver's. 'When I told her I loved my lady, now

wife, she laughed and said it was her job to concoct romance, not believe in it!'

Ditty looked up from the printed newspaper. She didn't need to read any more.

Well, when it was put like that, she didn't come across well at all! And to suggest she had purposefully gone missing! Was it not more likely that she had been called away? Ditty tried to lift her chin defiantly, as though the newspaper could see her hiding in a florist in Brexley. She was here, working!

'Go away. Go and ruin someone else's life.'

Ditty could not help but smile. That was Thalia, she was sure. There was only one person who spoke like that in anger.

And it was brave, kind of her sister to defend her, but it did not seem to have changed any of the rumours, did it?

Forcing herself to look away from the offending paper, it was most unfortunate that her gaze fell onto another newspaper—and another mention of her name.

Ditty groaned. Surely not another one? Did London not have better things to do than go after a woman like herself?

This headline was, if anything, worse.

ROMANCE SWINDLER DISAPPEARS WITH CLIENT'S MONEY

Miss Annabelle Oliver, known as Fitty to her clients and friends—if she had any—has been accused of

stealing the money of her clients without deliver-
ing the services she promised.

   Mr Alexander Matthews, 28, told the Gazette...

Ditty did not bother reading any further. Anyone who got her name that wrong evidently had not done their research. And as for Mr Alexander Matthews! Lying to a newspaper! Stealing his money, indeed! Did the man know how much that many rose petals cost in the depths of winter?

Swallowing hard, Ditty tried to put the newspapers from her mind and stuff them behind a periodical examining the roots of begonias, but it was impossible. Her matchmaking services were ruined—her reputation in tatters.

How could she ever return to London now?

She had to make this proposal a success. Ditty blinked away tears, determined not to permit herself to wallow in sadness, even if the last thing she wanted to do was stay here looking at flowers.

Come on, Aphrodite. I thought you'd be more inventive than that. You'll put yourself out of business that way!

Ditty's chest tightened. That was what these people wanted, wasn't it? Be cowed into returning. Admit defeat. But she would not allow her family to fall even further into penury; her mother's grief notwithstanding, the Oliver sisters would not be left stricken and homeless merely because she could not finish a job.

Ditty dashed away a tear forcefully, hating she was

crying—and in public! When was the last time she had cried in public? Not since she had been a small child. She'd learnt, after losing her father that tears got you nowhere.

No, she was going to stay. She was going to see this through.

There would be a perfect proposal in Brexley.

Henry chuckled. 'I know, I know, I shouldn't.'

'And out of your own pocket, too!' Miss Vivienne chided him, pressing a finger into his chest. 'You really should buy them wholesale! I can open an account for you, no trouble.'

Henry hesitated. She was probably right. There probably weren't that many doctors who became dukes and instead of cavorting off to London to luxuriate in the respect their new title deserved, instead decided to open the Lodge in their estate to the elderly of the town who couldn't look after themselves…or many dukes who personally chose and paid for birthday flowers for them all.

But there it was. He was barely certain how he could afford to replace the two saucepans in the kitchen which had worn out. He'd have to hope the third would last a while longer, or else they'd be cooking in shifts.

'And you definitely want the daffodils?'

Miss Vivienne's words brought Henry back to earth. He had only intended to step into the florist quickly on the way back to the Lodge, but of course, he'd forgotten Miss Vivienne's impressive gift for conversation.

'Yes, the daffodils.' Henry nodded.

The florist beamed. 'Wonderful! Let me just go and calculate that all up, won't be a tick.'

She bustled off, just as much a part of the place as her flowers, leaving Henry to stand beside the roses.

He reached out a hand and touched a closed bud. Roses. An overrated flower, in his opinion. Charles had laughed the one time Henry had voiced that, making sure he would never mention it again. Orchids, on the other hand…

Henry stepped along toward another aisle where he knew the orchids could be found, but was surprised to find the aisle was not empty.

A woman stood halfway down it with her back to him. But that didn't matter. Henry would know that pelisse anywhere.

Aphrodite Oliver. Ditty.

His stomach lurched. He had never managed a calm conversation with the woman. They had all been more like a confrontation. It would be a bad idea to have another argument here, right before Miss Vivienne. Another person in Brexley, alongside Mrs Fletcher, thinking he was trying to woo the stranger to the town by arguing with her…

Henry took a quiet step backward and froze as Miss Oliver turned.

But she didn't. Not entirely. She just turned her head slightly as she lifted her sleeve and…wiped away a tear.

A sniff echoed down the aisle.

Oh, goodness. Was she—crying?

Discomfort lodged in Henry's chest. He'd never been

one for accosting strangers, but Miss Oliver wasn't a stranger, was she? He'd driven her about, criticised her, made her life difficult in front of his brother, then berated her on the street for...you know, he couldn't remember why now. And that was only yesterday.

Perhaps it was time the good manners his mother had raised him with came to the fore.

Henry stepped forward.

At the sound of his footstep, Miss Oliver whirled around. She was a picture: red eyes, damp cheeks and absolute horror in her expression.

'You!' she blurted out.

Henry winced. Well, if he had wondered just how much damage he'd managed to do to an innocent woman, he now knew.

'Here,' he said aloud, pulling a handkerchief from his pocket. 'I think you need—just a thought...'

His voice trailed away as Miss Oliver glared, evidently furious he had seen her in this state.

What had caused such a state? She was standing in a florist's, crying. Had she been bereaved? Oh, heaven forbid she had received bad news while away from home.

Henry didn't have to like her to feel sorry for her. It was never nice to feel far from home. The years he'd spent at medical school, over three hours' hard riding from Brexley, had felt like the longest years of his life.

Perhaps if she had a gentleman caller, he would be comforting her.

The thought was swift, fleeting, and Henry tried not

to chase after it. What did he care if Miss Oliver was unattached?

'Here, take it,' he repeated, shoving the handkerchief into her hand.

Much against her better judgement, Miss Oliver accepted the handkerchief and dabbed at her eyes. 'You must think me so silly,' she said in a muffled voice.

Henry shifted uncomfortably on his feet. Well, maybe. It all depended on why she was bawling her eyes out in the middle of a florist's.

Not the sort of question he had ever asked anyone, now he came to think about it.

'Tears are natural,' he said aloud. 'Very healing.'

Ditty snorted as she blew her nose. 'And what would you know about that?'

Henry blinked. Then he remembered that at no point had he mentioned he was a doctor. *Ah*. 'Well, in fact—'

'I am so sorry,' she said, her cheeks flushing. 'You probably don't want this—'

'You keep it,' said Henry swiftly. 'I wanted—'

'I just read—'

They fell silent, awkward tension rising between them.

He was certainly not going to be the one to break it. Something had happened, something powerful enough to make this woman—who had always struck him as being determined, authoritative—to cry. In public.

And it was her bad luck she had to run into him, he thought ruefully.

Miss Oliver blew her nose again, swallowed hard and

forced the handkerchief into her reticule. 'It's probably silly—'

'Nothing that can make a person cry is silly,' Henry interrupted. 'That is something I know a lot about, so you can trust me on that.'

After all, what sort of doctor would he be if he didn't understand grieving?

Miss Oliver smiled wanly. 'I don't think so.'

'Look, Miss Oliver, I may not agree with, well, everything that you do,' said Henry stiffly, 'but I am a man of honour, and…well, as you're all alone here in Brexley—' *and I'm the duke, and I feel a sense of duty and obligation to all in Brexley, and now you're here* '—without a father or brother or…or husband, I mean,' Henry continued, hoping to goodness his voice wouldn't waver. 'If I can be a—a support to you. It's the least I can do. For my brother.'

The smile became a little more watery. 'I suppose you've never read your name in a newspaper?'

Henry considered this. Well. Yes. When he had inherited the dukedom of Glanyrafon, the news had been all over the papers for a time. It had gone fleetingly and it was a relief when it was over, but it was a very stale, factual set of reporting. Most of the time they had not given his actual name, they just spoke of the new Duke of Glanyrafon.

'Well,' he said begrudgingly. 'Not as such.'

'So you've never had to face this?'

Henry's eyes widened as Ditty placed two newspapers, slightly damp, in his hands.

...accused of stealing the money of her clients without delivering the services she promised...

'And you didn't do these things?' he could not help but say, his mouth speaking before his mind could catch up. 'Fleece these people, take their money and run?'

Henry melted under her stern gaze.

'The mere fact you can think to ask the question,' Miss Oliver said icily, wrenching the clippings from his grasp, 'proves you don't know me at all.'

No, Henry wanted to say. *But I'd like to.*

Before today, he would have said the woman who arrived in Brexley and announced she was going to plan his brother's proposal was a charlatan. Out for people's money.

But after their conversation the other day, after seeing her response to his arguably cutting words, seeing her temper flare and the emotions spark under the surface...

Well, now he could not help but be a little curious. A little doubtful that Miss Oliver had come to Brexley to fleece his poor brother, but rather to help him.

After all, a woman who was cold-hearted enough to scam people out of their money didn't break down in tears in the middle of a florist's when accused of such a thing.

Henry shifted uncomfortably on his feet again, wishing he knew what to do with his hands.

'I'm sorry,' he murmured. 'I know that. I knew—I mean, you're obviously not that person.'

Ditty stared for a moment, then grinned ruefully. 'No,

I'm not Annabelle, or whatever other ridiculous names they call me.'

Henry chuckled lightly under his breath, the awkwardness between them not dissipated, but certainly calmer than before.

'No, you're not,' he said lightly. 'You're Aphrodite. Ditty. Sorry, I probably shouldn't—Miss Oliver.'

Their gazes met, and just in that instant, Henry felt the world shiver. As though he had never expected to meet the gaze of someone so different from everything he had expected he would find attractive.

And yet…

'You can call me Ditty, if…if you want,' she said quietly.

Henry swallowed. 'And you must call me Glanyrafon.'

'I beg your pard—'

'I mean, Paisley,' he said swiftly. *Damn.* That was the trouble with being an unwilling duke. One rather forgot one's name.

'I came in here to research flowers,' she said, forcing brightness into her voice. 'I had no idea there would be such variety in such a small place.'

'Oh, Miss Vivienne prides herself in the choice she can offer her customers,' said Henry briskly.

How had she done it? Broken down all his assumptions of her in just one conversation?

'I can see that,' said Ditty softly.

She pulled an orchid from one of the stands and held it to her nose, sniffing.

Henry fought the impulse to buy it for her. *The last*

thing the woman needed was being put in an awkward position, he told himself furiously. The woman was alone in Brexley and clearly had a gentleman courting her in London.

Control yourself!

'It's just… I have to get this right.'

'The flower?'

'No, your brother's proposal,' Ditty said with a dry laugh. 'I've never— Well, this is my first client out of London. I thought this would be a bit of an adventure, I had no idea the newspapers would… This must go well.'

Henry's stomach twisted. 'Ah.'

'And I have so many ideas, good ones, perhaps great once I've put them all together,' she continued in a rush, as though she was trying to convince him. Perhaps she was. 'And I need this to be perfect—your brother deserves it, of course, and so does Miss Yorke, but if I can prove to him, to Brexley, to the world that what I do matters, that it means something—'

'That you aren't a swindler,' Henry added helpfully.

His knees quivered as Ditty shot him a look, but they quivered for quite a different reason when she then smiled, seemingly despite herself.

'Yes, something like that,' she said wryly. 'It's just… can't you see? This is important to me. It must be perfect.'

And he could see it. Henry had never been one for business; Brexley was a small town, and he wasn't in business at all. His work was for the living, and keeping them alive—and happy—for as long as possible. Inheriting a title had not changed that.

But he wasn't an idiot. Articles like those would ruin her. She needed this. She needed his brother's proposal to be…perfect.

Oh, hell.

'Look,' he said awkwardly.

Ditty's gaze flickered up to him, and she waited in silence.

Henry swallowed, tasting his own nerves. 'Look, I won't get in your way. Even if—well, even if I don't agree that romance can be manufactured, or made, or whatever you want to call it. I can see this is important to you, so I won't get involved. I won't ruin it for you.'

His breath caught in his throat as a slow smile crept across Ditty's face. 'Really?'

He nodded, wishing he could think of something clever to say. 'Yes.'

They stood there for a moment in silence. In a way, he rather liked it. It was the first time they had just been in the same place without jumping down each other's throats.

And perhaps it was his imagination that they were somehow standing closer together. Perhaps he was dreaming it, that Ditty was leaning closer to him, her hand near his, her breathing short, her lips so easily kissable just inches away—

'Would—would you like a rose?' Henry cringed as he pointed at the aisle over from them, where the roses were.

What on earth did he think he was doing?

'To cheer you up,' he added, as though attempting to make it perfectly clear that all thoughts of romance were firmly elsewhere. Certainly not in his mind. Or heart.

Ditty grinned. 'Believe it or not… I don't like roses.'

Henry laughed. 'What, a proposal planner who doesn't like roses? You're jesting.'

'On my honour as a proposal planner,' Ditty said, her smile broadening. 'I have just always preferred daisies. That's a strange thing to admit, isn't it?'

Henry hesitated. The sparkle was back in her eyes again, the most natural thing in the world. Of course Ditty didn't like roses. Daisies, that was her preference.

'Well, let me buy you a daisy, then,' Henry found himself saying.

For a moment, he really thought she would accept, but—

'Here you go, two bouquets, one for Mavis, one for Avril,' chirped Miss Vivienne as she bustled over. 'I'm sure they'll both love them.'

Henry watched Ditty's face fall as Miss Vivienne thrust the two bouquets into his arms. *She would think—*

'Far be it for me to overburden your arms,' Ditty said with an awkward laugh. 'You seem to have enough ladies to entertain. Miss Vivienne, if I may borrow you for a moment…'

Henry watched helplessly as Ditty pulled the florist over to the orchid display and started asking pressing questions about flowering time, moisture requirements and wilting under candlelight.

That could have gone better.

Chapter Seven

January 28: 15 days until the proposal

'——and that's as far as I've got!' Ditty said with as broad a smile as she could manage.

Really, she should have been more prepared. There were only two weeks left until this proposal, and in truth, she didn't really have anything much yet.

Other than the restaurant, of course. Ditty had eaten every evening at Reg's and was already wondering how she was going to live without that focaccia bread when she returned to London.

But despite her meagre plans, Charles looked thrilled. 'I love it!'

Ditty blinked. They were in his law office, an impressive one. The seat she was sitting on was very comfortable. The large one Charles was seated on, on the other side of the desk, looked even more luxurious.

'Oh, I would not have thought of half these things,' he continued. 'Really inspiring, you know—but then, that's why I hired you!'

It was good to hear after the week she'd had.

She'd been forced to stop reading newspapers altogether in the mere fear she'd start noticing that every newspaper was mentioning her disaster of a life. No one deserved that, and the very least they could do was get her name right! She'd been Annabelle, Alphabelle—which she wasn't even sure was a name—and for some reason, Delphine. It was ridiculous!

But that was what happened, she supposed, when a mere spinster went up against the son of an earl.

But here, at least, she was starting to be appreciated as she deserved. Even though the proposal was not entirely planned, she had put a lot of thought into it. The florist had been a great help, and now that she could be certain Reg's restaurant could serve up the best meal she had tasted in a long time, half the setting was arranged.

So all she had to do was work on those finishing touches.

'Charles, tell me,' said Ditty aloud, 'is there a haberdasher in Brexley?'

She hadn't seen one in her walk along King's Street, and although she'd ventured into some of the lanes leading from it, she hadn't spotted anything that looked like it sold buttons and ribbons. There would always be custom-made things needed in a proposal, and usually she had three or four places she could go to commission items. But in Brexley?

Her heart sank as Charles considered, then shook his head. 'No, I don't think so. Mrs Fletcher's sister used to have a place, but it closed last year, the village is simply too small. Those who can afford it send away to Marchester, those who cannot, make do and mend. Why?'

Ditty sighed. 'It's nothing, it's just, well, I always like to commission a few things for the proposal. Some keepsakes, sometimes something to decorate—'

'Oh, well, that's different,' said Charles confidently. 'We've got a place for that.'

Ditty blinked. 'You…you do?'

'Oh, yes, if you want something knitted or crocheted or woven or baked, there's only one place in Brexley you go,' said Charles with a smile. 'The Brexley Lodge for Gentlemen and Ladies of a Certain Age.'

Ditty's face fell.

Gentlemen and ladies of a certain age?

The last thing she needed was some old dears getting in her way. This was supposed to be a perfect proposal!

Obviously her scepticism showed on her face, for Charles laughed. 'You'd be surprised—our ladies have won prizes for their embroidery, and there's nothing old Brian can't do with a hammer and nails. Here, I'll give you directions.'

And that was how Ditty was somehow convinced to hike up what felt like a very steep hill just west of the town, up an icy path, in search of old-lady knitters.

Really, was this what she had been reduced to?

Charles had described it as a community in the Lodge of the Glanyrafon Estate, designed for those who didn't want to live on their own, but weren't always unwell.

A community, he'd said. *Not a hospital. Go on up, I think you'll enjoy it there.*

And perhaps she would, Ditty thought as she puffed for breath. *If she ever got there!*

Reaching the peak of the hill, the road twisted to the left. Ditty walked along it for just a minute before a large building appeared with an astounding pair of wrought iron gates.

It was beautiful. If she hadn't seen the sign, Brexley Lodge for Gentlemen and Ladies of a Certain Age: Where Love Comes to Roost, she would have guessed it was a manor house, or some sort of impressive home for a wealthy family.

It was only as she grew closer that she started to notice how dilapidated it was.

The window frames were elegant, but in sore need of repainting. One of the windowpanes was boarded up, which didn't make sense. Why not fix it?

Ditty's eyes scanned over the unimpressive patch jobs that had been done to the brickwork around the door, and the flickering light on the third floor.

What was going on here?

Still, she needed someone who knew one end of a needle from the other. There was nothing to do but go in and see what she could find.

The hall she walked into had seen better days. Wallpaper was peeling from the ceiling, and there was a rundown, almost unloved atmosphere.

No, not unloved. Ditty corrected herself silently as

she stepped to a desk in the corner where a woman sat with a beaming gaze.

There was love in this place, you could feel it oozing from the walls—alongside the slightly damp smell she now registered. Someone had tried to tape the wallpaper back up. Someone had placed a painting on the wall in an attempt to keep the wallpaper from falling down. There were fresh flowers on the desk which smelled wonderful. Daffodils.

'Good day there, how may I help you?' said the woman.

Ditty hesitated. She had never been to a place like this before. Her father had never reached his sixtieth birthday, let alone needed to consider moving to a place like this. Her mother…well, if Ditty could stop her mother gallivanting for more than five minutes together, it would be a miracle.

'Hello,' Ditty said helplessly. 'I was wondering if—'

'Ah, you must be Miss Oliver,' said a cheerful voice behind her. 'I wondered how long it would be before you came.'

Ditty turned on her heels as the lady at the desk said sternly, 'Now then, Mavis.'

'Mavis?' The name sounded familiar somehow, but she couldn't put her finger on it. Where had she heard that name? Sometime recently, in a deep voice that made a shiver rush up her spine.

'I only said I wondered how long it would take before Miss Oliver visited us,' the woman, who was evidently Mavis, said defensively. 'I don't see why that's such a bother. Come on, dear, let's talk properly in the sunroom.'

'The— I haven't actually—'

But it appeared Ditty had no choice in the matter. Mavis had slipped her thin arm into hers and was marching her to the left, down a corridor and into a beautiful large room that overlooked the town.

'You can sit here,' said Mavis sternly, pushing Ditty into an armchair that swallowed her whole. 'Now tell me. How long have you been in Brexley, and why did I not hear about it until this morning?'

Ditty smiled weakly.

Well, old ladies were the same everywhere—not that Mavis could truly be considered old. She could only be in her late seventies, maybe early eighties, with beautiful hair curled and put up in the old-fashioned style of the last century, and was wearing a lovely blue gown with a thick woollen scarf around her shoulders.

A scarf, Ditty could not help but think, she had perhaps made herself?

'Oh, is that her?' Another woman, seated two armchairs down with an empty chair between them, perked up. 'I wondered when she'd be getting here.'

'That's just what I said!' Mavis said triumphantly, giving Ditty a wink that she could not help but smile at. 'But of course, we are a way out of the town. I suppose you had to make your way around the rest of the place.'

'I—'

'I would have thought she'd start with us,' interrupted the woman whose pearl necklace bobbed each time she spoke. 'I'm Avril, dear, but you'll know that. I suppose you've come to—'

'She's my guest, I found her,' Mavis protested.

Ditty's smile broadened. They were rather wonderful—but Avril…why was that name ringing a bell, too? There was something strange going on here, something she did not entirely understand.

Mavis was waving an imperious hand. 'Fine, we'll share her—just don't let that Brian sneak her away, she's not here for him!'

'Brian?' Ditty repeated. 'No, actually I was wondering—'

'A pretty woman like you can certainly do better than Brian,' Avril said decidedly, nodding her head. Her pearls jingled. 'Goodness, *I* could do better than—'

'No you couldn't, dear,' sniffed Mavis haughtily. 'None of us could.'

Ditty gazed between the two of them, completely lost. They weren't suggesting…

'You…you think I'm here looking for a husband?' she said weakly.

She would have laughed aloud if the thought wasn't so ridiculous!

'Well, naturally,' said Mavis smartly. 'Many people come to Brexley for Valentine's Day, hoping to catch someone's eye. You are early—'

'Nothing wrong with being eager,' Avril cut in with a righteous nod. 'I certainly was, when I met my—'

'No one wants to hear that story, Avril, we've all heard

it a thousand times,' Mavis said, rolling her eyes to Ditty as though she was in on the joke.

Ditty tried not to laugh. Oh, she certainly should have come here sooner. If there was one way to push aside the hurt from those newspaper articles, it was speaking to these two!

Mavis and Avril. Why did she have the feeling…

'I suppose you are here for the doctor, aren't you?' said Avril in a mock whisper that carried throughout the entire room.

Ditty grinned. Well, she could play along with two old ladies for a few minutes before she found whoever was in charge here. It wouldn't hurt, would it?

'Why, do you think I should?' she said in a stage whisper of her own. 'Is he very handsome?'

'Oh, I think you'll have to be the judge of that,' said a deep, dry voice from behind her.

Henry tried not to laugh as Ditty struggled to extricate herself from the stuffy armchair, cheeks flaming, almost tripping over her own feet.

He would never have thought Mavis and Avril the sort of people to drop him so firmly into it, but even he had to admit this was kind of perfect.

All of Brexley was always trying to marry him off—saying nothing of how deeply the ladies of the Lodge were desperate to see a Mrs Paisley, and now a Duchess of Glanyrafon—but this? How had they managed to tempt her here?

'H-Henry,' Ditty stammered. 'Mr Paisley, I mean—I didn't—I thought—'

'Ah, there you are,' said Mavis smugly. 'Don't worry, you haven't kept her waiting too long.'

'And we were just about to talk you up, don't you worry,' said Avril in one of her patented whispers which could carry down whole streets. 'In fact, I was going to start with—'

'I'm not actually here to see Henry,' Ditty said hurriedly. 'Mr Paisley.'

Henry was not surprised to see Mavis's and Avril's faces fall. It could not be more obvious they had been hoping she was here to be wooed and wed by their beloved doctor.

No, what was surprising to him was how immediately he was disappointed.

Not here to see him? Why not?

And then he tried to collect himself. He did not care what Ditty Oliver was doing, Henry tried to remind himself. He was not—there was nothing between—

'What do you mean, not here to see Henry?' Mavis said in shock, her brows furrowed. 'I'll have you know he is one of the most eligible bachelors in Brexley!'

Avril was nodding, and Henry could do nothing as she added, 'Even more than my great-nephew, and that is saying something. You must have met him, a lovely chap, he—'

'No one wants to marry your great-nephew, Avril,' Mavis snapped, not taking her eyes from Henry. 'But you—why isn't Miss Oliver here to see you?'

It was an excellent question, Henry thought dryly, and not one he could answer.

All he knew was that Ditty's face had never been redder, and she was clearly mortified to have been found not only in the Lodge, but speaking to his residents about marriage. About him!

'I—I wanted to— Your brother, he said to— What are you doing here?' was all she managed to say.

Henry's gaze flickered to Mavis and Avril. Somehow, and he was not sure how, they had something to do with this. He'd get to the bottom of it—later. First, he had to make sure Ditty didn't combust with embarrassment.

Grabbing her arm, and trying to ignore the sudden heat that flared through his fingers, Henry pulled her to the windows away from the chuckling ladies.

'What am I doing here?' he said quietly. 'I think I should be asking you that question.'

'I—I didn't expect— Your brother told me to come here,' Ditty hissed. 'Is this a trick? Why are you here?'

Henry hesitated. It wasn't like his brother to get matchmaking ideas, so that wasn't it. But why else would Charles send Ditty here, if not to tease him?

The place wasn't exactly the sort of place one proposed in, after all.

'I'm here because I work here,' Henry said, clinging to the facts as the back of his neck prickled. He just knew Mavis and Avril were watching them. 'I own it, too, more to the point. That still doesn't explain—'

'But you said *a manager*,' Ditty said quietly, her gaze

flickering about the place. 'I thought you meant a—a factory, or a mill, something!'

Henry smiled. 'Ah, I thought so.'

But she hadn't thought less of him because she believed he worked with his hands, he could see that. It was fascinating; he had assumed her disinterest when he had told her he worked as a manager was because she did not deem the role impressive.

But he could see now in her clear, brilliant eyes it had nothing to do with where he worked. It had been more his unexpected presence which had so unbalanced her.

'This is where I work,' Henry said, spreading out his arms.

'Here? In the Lodge—for the gentlemen and ladies?'

'For them, I suppose you could say that,' he admitted. 'As I said, I own this place.'

Now, why did he repeat that? Was it in the hope she would be impressed?

Perhaps Henry was fooling himself, but she did look impressed. 'Owner?'

'I inherited it a year ago, yes.'

'You own this place? But doesn't it belong to the Glanyrafon estate? Would it not belong to the Duke?'

Henry watched as Ditty's eyes wandered around the room. It was an impressive building, even he would admit—but it was so run-down. It was hardly worth anything. Well, she'd have to know eventually. 'Well… yes. I am surprised no one has mentioned it, but then, I am still Mr Paisley to so many of Brexley, which I much prefer. But *technically* I am the fourteenth Duke of Glanyrafon.'

Even the words sounded alien in his mouth. Henry tried to hold himself upright as he spoke, tried not to let it become too obvious just how awkward he felt.

It was rather difficult. Ditty's eyes were wide, her mouth open and unspeaking. Perhaps he did not look like the dukes she had met.

'Surprised?' he teased, before he could stop himself.

Ditty breathed a laugh as she met his gaze. 'I mean… yes?'

'You're not here to see the doctor, then?' Mavis's voice was disappointed.

Henry watched as Ditty grinned weakly at the woman behind him. 'No, I'm not. Though even if I found the doctor, I wouldn't know—'

'Found him? You're talking to him!' crowed Avril.

Henry's stomach twisted into a knot as Ditty's gaze moved from the two older ladies behind him and back to his face.

'You…you're the doctor?' Ditty said weakly, her smile growing as her eyes flashed with interest. 'A duke, and a doctor?'

And his heart fluttered, most unexpectedly.

Because it shouldn't. It shouldn't flutter, and his pulse shouldn't race, and his spirits shouldn't soar, and he shouldn't want to pull her into his arms and—

What did it matter to him if Ditty Oliver was impressed he was a doctor?

And so it was entirely unaccountable that Henry's chest swelled. 'I am.'

'But you never said! A duke, a doctor, you never—'

'Was I supposed to?' Henry said quietly, hoping Mavis and Avril had not heard.

The giggles behind him suggested he was not so lucky. It was Ditty, however, who looked mortified.

And Henry knew why. Most doctors didn't drive around in half-rotten old dog carts which had seen better days. Much better. No doctors he knew lived in the small cottage he had managed to scrape enough funds to purchase, and not done a single thing to it since he had moved in. Nor had they inherited a penniless duchy.

Most doctors were happy to overcharge their patients—like his lawyer brother with his own clients.

But not him.

Ditty's cheeks were red but she looked up fiercely, and only then did Henry realise just how delicate she was. Easily breakable. And yet here she was, determined to face him.

You had to admire her.

Not that he did. Not that he could. Not that she wasn't beautiful, and alluring in that almost bluestocking way that so many ladies had these days.

That intelligence, that fiery determination…it made parts of Henry feel—

'I came here,' she said firmly, 'in the hunt—'

'You're on the hunt for a husband, are you?' Avril said eagerly.

Henry watched Ditty's cheeks turn even redder, if possible.

'No—'

'Because we have someone in mind we could recommend,' said Mavis slyly.

Now even Henry's cheeks were starting to burn. *Really, they were outrageous!*

'I was hoping to find some people who could help me craft things. Knit, embroider, that sort of thing. Perhaps even construct a bower? I don't know, I haven't precisely—'

'A bower?' Henry repeated.

Goodness, she really could construct romance. He could see how that could be so romantic. Create an atmosphere, if you will.

Oh, hell. Had she *impressed* him?

'Yes, a bower, preferably one that can be covered in roses,' Ditty was saying. 'Miss Vivienne has assured me she could—'

'Did you say "embroider"?' piped up an elderly woman's voice.

'No one like that here,' Henry said hastily, grabbing Ditty's arm again and wondering why he was suddenly making this sort of thing a habit. 'Let me show you out—'

'Henry Thomas Paisley, how dare you suggest I am not an expert embroiderer!' snapped Mavis. 'I helped bring you into this world, and I can just as soon—'

'I didn't say—'

'You know full well my embroidery was praised by

the old king himself, God rest his soul, when they came here for the waters thirty-odd years ago, and I'll have you know my son's neighbour's daughter sent me a very pleasant note saying she had never seen anything so good in the whole of Brighton!' Mavis said in one breath.

Henry sagged. 'Yes, but—'

'And my knitting is second to none!' Avril said with a wink at Ditty, who giggled. 'If you want crafty people, Miss Oliver, look no further!'

Well, that was true, Henry had to admit—though it was not precisely what had been on his mind.

No, he had been thinking more of getting Ditty on her own. In one of the smaller drawing rooms, where they could talk…

Talk about what? What on earth was he thinking?

'Oh, that's wonderful!' Ditty stepped away and Henry tried not to notice the warmth that left him as she did so. 'I have so many ideas—but you will have your own, and I would love to know your opinion…'

Before he could stop them, before Henry could even think what he could possibly say, the three women were chattering away. Ditty had pulled out the empty armchair and turned it to face both Mavis and Avril, who were excitedly talking about some of their creations.

'And seed pearls all the way down the hem, it was truly—'

'And that was one of my lesser works, you understand! One of my best was…'

Henry sighed, but he could not help but smile. He couldn't remember the last time he'd seen Mavis and

Avril so vibrant. And wasn't that his responsibility? To make sure his residents didn't just keep living, but had a wonderful time doing it?

Even if he wasn't sure how to afford to keep the fires burning.

'—and when young Henry bought me my birthday daffodils, I just knew I had to—'

'That's it! Mavis and Avril!' Ditty said suddenly. She turned and Henry discovered most disconcertingly that her attention made his stomach flip over. 'In the florist's, she gave you two bouquets and said—'

'Mavis and Avril,' he said with a grin.

'It was our birthdays and dear Henry never misses them, such a charming boy,' said Mavis, throwing him a wink.

Henry sighed. *Could they be more blatant?*

'But I thought…' Ditty's voice trailed away, hands twisting in her lap.

He could see precisely what she had thought, and breathed a sigh. At least now she would know he was far lonelier than she had expected.

Wait. Why was that supposed to be a good thing?

'You thought I was courting two ladies,' he said with a laugh. 'At the same time.'

Ditty's flush was doing something criminal to his heart rate. 'Yes. Yes, I did.'

Henry was swiftly realising that earning Miss Ditty Oliver's good opinion was rather heady. She certainly was eyeing him differently, now that she knew he was a doctor, and a duke…and it prompted a warm feeling in his chest that Henry did not like. He'd loved a woman before who had been impressed by his title—but then, Ditty had not simpered, nor curtseyed low to reveal her bosom, nor touched his arm since hearing the news.

Quite the opposite, in fact. She had said she had come to speak to his residents, and so she was with bright eyes and a turn of phrase that made Henry smile.

Ditty gazed over at him, her cheeks still had that pink glow. 'How precisely—'

'Enough about him, we're talking crochet,' Mavis said firmly. 'What we can do is—'

'I've got no hope of controlling you ladies, have I?' Henry said over the chatter, still reeling from the direction of his thoughts. Still wondering what it all meant.

The three ladies halted, turned to him and said in one voice, 'No.'

Chapter Eight

January 30: 13 days until the proposal

'Yes, just under two weeks to go now,' Ditty said with a laugh. 'And you know, I thought I would be able to keep it secret from you!'

Reg chuckled. The Cantelli Restaurant had been closed, only for an hour, while the two of them ran through the menu Ditty had selected for the big day.

Charles Paisley's proposal.

'Ah, a common misconception about small towns,' said Reg grandly, but then he added with a wink, 'Well, not entirely a misconception. Gossip does run about Brexley like nobody's business.'

'Yes, so I heard,' said Ditty, giggling.

It had been a wonderful lunch. Reg had absolutely outdone himself: the risotto, the gnocchi, the prosciutto… It was going to be difficult to choose a menu at this rate. Every dish was sublime.

But it wasn't just the food. No, it was the whole atmosphere. Though she might have called the place rural just a few weeks ago, here in Brexley…it just worked.

'Miss Vivienne has some real beauties in at the moment, doesn't she?' Ditty said, gesturing at the beautiful flowers on every table.

Reg nodded. 'Oh, she only ever sends me the best—roses, of course. Nothing more romantic than roses.'

Ditty smiled, but did not contradict the older man. There was no point getting into that disagreement.

'So, are you going to select the peach or the frangipane parfait?'

Ditty sighed as she looked at the two elegant glass bowls before her. 'You know, I still can't choose.'

'Few can,' said Reg with a glint in his eye. 'Better to have both, I'd say.'

She shot him a grin. 'You strike a hard bargain.'

'I make an excellent parfait.' He corrected her with a chuckle. 'Now, coffee. I know not everyone drinks coffee and many prefer tea, but—'

'Miss Oliver?'

Ditty looked around. A man was standing in the doorway wearing the red of the postal service. In his hand was a letter. 'I am Miss Oliver.'

'Wonderful. Here y'are.'

A letter was pressed into her hand and in an instant, Ditty knew precisely who it was from. She would recognise that handwriting anywhere.

'I do apologise,' said Ditty, hastily ripping open the envelope. 'Sorry, Reg, I've got to read this. Do you mind if—'

'Say no more,' said Reg magnanimously, rising from the table. 'You read that, and then we'll talk coffee!'

Ditty nodded with a smile as she unfolded the letter and breathed out a contented, 'Finally!'

Dear Ditty,

I imagine this letter will take simply an age to find you! The man on the stagecoach had never heard of Brexley! Where on earth are you?

I suppose you have laughed with delight to have escaped London just before the Season, and well may you laugh. It's miserable and grey here, and no matter where one looks, a most despicable newspaper is printing lies about you. Do not read a single one.

I have been completely rushed off my feet. After promising myself that I would go to Brighton to visit Mama, I have found myself suddenly receiving a rush of commissions. Three actual paid commissions! I have cancelled my plans for Brighton and I can already hear you lecturing me, young lady, about not putting our finances first and taking time to relax—but as you are Miss 'Hurtle across the Country for a Client' Oliver, please forgive me if I do not take your advice to heart. Besides, in truth I shall earn but a few shillings after paint and canvas. The cost of paint, you have no idea!

If there are any handsome men, do let us know? I am desperate to paint someone who looks like he

could have walked out of Ancient Egypt. Any ideas?
Just don't fall in love!
I remain ever, your most affectionate and impatient sister,
Calliope

Ditty swallowed. Her first thought was that, though she had never been forced to admit it aloud, Henry was handsome.

Her second thought was that she would absolutely never, under any circumstances, tell him that.

Her third thought was that her first thought should have been about her sisters.

Just don't fall in love!

And at that precise moment, Henry Paisley, newly discovered Duke of Glanyrafon, walked into the restaurant.

Avoiding his displeasure had been difficult, and now avoiding him was downright impossible. The handsomest man she had been avoiding all week. The handsomest doctor. The handsomest duke…

It was a good thing Ditty wasn't taking a bite of the parfait. She would undoubtedly have choked, her brain unable to believe he was here.

Reg approached the man and shook hands with him, handing a tall glass to the Duke and pointing in Ditty's direction as her cheeks flushed with heat.

What was Reg doing?

Ditty stuffed the letter into her reticule and considered her options—but before she could conceive of an escape route—

'Reg asked me to bring this over,' said Henry with a wry smile. 'And I thought my serving days were over.'

He placed the drink onto the table and stood there, waiting.

Ditty tried to smile. She really did. If only she could stop thinking about the teasing Mavis and Avril had given her after she had discovered, right in front of their eyes, that Henry was not just some man in the town, but a doctor…and the local duke.

A duke.

It shouldn't make a difference, she knew. Ditty looked up into the dark eyes and welcoming expression of the man, and knew it did.

There was something about people in the medical field. Intelligent, but caring. They could go out and do anything with their brains, but they chose to do good. And that mattered.

There was also something about gentlemen with titles. Something honourable… Although her experience with Lord Edward had tested that theory.

Yet, try as she might, Ditty could not entirely divorce that fact from the handsome man before her. A duke. The Duke of Glanyrafon.

Why hadn't he said anything? Told her he was titled.

'May I sit down?'

Ditty swallowed. 'Of course.'

It was not what she wanted to say, though precisely what she wanted to say, she did not know. She didn't want to sit with him, that was certain…but his presence was hardly a punishment.

Henry slipped onto the chair and looked at her note-book sprawled out across the table. 'Planning, then.'

Ditty nodded, but didn't elaborate. For a reason she couldn't entirely put her finger on yet, sharing her plans for Charles's proposal with Henry would be...wrong.

'You have served here, in your time?' she said instead.

Henry gave her a lopsided grin. 'I think everyone who grew up in Brexley worked here for a few shillings at some point. A great learning experience, I suppose, and Reg was an excellent boss. You got a solid meal for every four hours of your shift, and you could take left-overs home.'

Ditty groaned. 'Goodness, you'd have to roll me out of this place. Here, save me from myself and eat...'

Her eyes flickered between the two glass bowls.

Henry's laughter made her look up. 'Struggling to decide between them?'

'They are both so good,' she agreed with a nervous smile. 'Go on, you pick.'

'Well, I'll never say no to frangipane,' Henry said, pulling the bowl toward him and taking a spoon from his pocket.

Ditty stared. Now, where had that come from?

'Trust me,' said Henry darkly. 'You wait until Valentine's Day.'

Ditty's eyes widened. *Now, what on earth did he mean by—*

'I just meant, there's a baking competition here in Brexley on Valentine's Day,' Henry added quickly, un-doubtedly seeing her expression. 'No matter where I go, there are sweet treats to be eaten, and eventually it just makes more sense to carry a spoon with you. It's a habit I've got into.'

He took a bite of the frangipane and closed his eyes in appreciation.

Ditty took that moment to examine him more closely. He was…different, somehow.

Oh, still the same Henry who had picked her up from the staging inn. The same Henry who had quibbled with her opinions in front of Charles.

But at the same time…she couldn't describe it. A softness in him, perhaps. A kindness, a warmth.

Sometimes, when Ditty was not keeping an eye on herself, she was tempted to seek out the man and do something wild. And radical.

Like kiss the handsome Duke senseless, then get on with her day.

Molten mortification always cascaded through her at the very thought, but Ditty could not rid her mind of such wanderings. She would not be staying in Brexley, after all. Why not enjoy a passionate kiss—or five—with a man so handsome her toes actually curled whenever she was in his presence?

Which was nonsense. Why was she thinking such things? Surely her head had not been so easily turned by learning he was both a doctor and a duke?

'You love sweet things, then?' Henry asked, opening his eyes and nodding at the peach parfait.

Ditty nodded. 'I love sweet things.'

'Well, I suppose that's why you became a proposal planner,' Henry said with a smile.

For a moment, she hesitated. Was he just teasing her?

Apparently not. 'Yes, I've always liked the sweet things. Biscuits, caramel. Proposals, big displays of affection, huge bejewelled—'

'Don't you think there's more?'

Henry had no idea what had possessed him to say such a thing.

It was ridiculous. It was embarrassing.

It was…just the sort of thing Ditty would laugh at, he was sure.

Henry cringed, waiting for the laughter. But it never came. Instead, Ditty took a delicate mouthful of peach parfait, during which he tried desperately not to look at her mouth, and considered his statement.

'More?' she said finally. 'I… I don't think I know what you mean.'

Henry swallowed, and found his mouth was dry.

This wasn't why he had stepped into Cantelli Restaurant. Reg had once said he knew a few good cheap, delicious recipes he could recommend to the cook at the Lodge. Though Henry had spent the Christmas period keeping to the traditional fare, he could no longer ignore what the ledgers were saying.

He would have to change the menu if he wanted them to keep eating.

But Reg had instead pointed him in the direction of

his newest customer, and all thoughts had disappeared from his mind.

'Well, *more*,' Henry said aloud, twisting his spoon in his fingers as he spoke. 'You know, more than merely spending a whole heap of money.'

Ditty raised an all-too-knowing eyebrow, and a rush of heat inexplicably rushed through Henry's chest. 'Like I require, you mean?'

'Perhaps like you require, yes,' Henry said with a wry smile, trying to force himself to lean back in his chair. Why was he finding this conversation so…so tense? And yet so pleasant? 'But I suppose I meant more that everything in a proposal, and a wedding if it comes to that—'

'Which you have already pointed out to me doesn't always lead from one to the other.'

Henry winced.

Even if it was true. He had pointed that out, hadn't he?

In this moment, looking at Ditty across the table from him, all-knowing smile and raised eyebrow, he almost wished he was wrong.

When had that last happened?

'I suppose I mean, in a perfect world, there wouldn't need to be these huge, grand gestures,' Henry said, striking out for shore. 'You know, these huge, expensive engagement rings that cost more than a monthly salary that Society ladies are starting to expect.'

'You don't think a woman deserves a pretty ring?'

'I think a man deserves to be fallen in love with, not a jewel,' said Henry with a laugh.

He thought for a moment he'd gone too far—but Ditty's shoulders relaxed. 'You know, in some ways I quite agree with you.'

Henry stared, accidentally dropping his spoon onto the table. It rattled, but it was nothing to how rattled he felt.

Ditty Oliver, agreeing with him that romance should not cost the earth? Was he dreaming?

'Oh, not about the big, grand gesture,' she said swiftly, evidently noticing his surprise. 'I like a planned proposal, everything organised, in its place, the woman feeling loved and adored. It's the ring, I mean. If there is to be a ring, I would much rather have a family ring, a vintage piece. These huge diamonds some people of the *ton* wear now—how do they get anything done with those on?'

They laughed together, but Henry's heart skipped a beat.

That was what Georgiana had said. *What is the point,* she had asked sharply, *of you even asking for my hand if a gentleman twenty feet away cannot see the diamond glittering?*

And yet the thought of Georgiana faded far swifter than it ever had. Sitting here in Reg's was pleasant, eating parfait and chattering away about the ridiculous expectations of Society ladies with their diamonds. It was almost like they were…friends.

Which was ridiculous. Miss Ditty Oliver had swept into Brexley and would be sweeping out of it the moment Charles and Miss Yorke were engaged. Ditty would be gone by March at the very latest. It was foolish to think he could befriend her now.

Except he couldn't deny what he was feeling. A warmth, an affection, a curiosity unmatched. And that was friendship, was it not?

'I just think there's more to a proposal than planning,' he said aloud, heat blossoming across his chest as he said so. Thank goodness his high collar hid the colour.

Ditty shrugged. 'Perhaps. But I think you must plan these things, you can't just expect everything to perfectly fall into place.'

'You don't think there's any room for spontaneity?'

Henry chuckled as he watched Ditty's nose wrinkle immediately, as though the peach parfait was poisoned.

'Spontaneity?'

'It's not a disease, you know,' he teased. 'It's not catching.'

'Perhaps not, but I certainly wouldn't want it to spread!' Ditty said with a wide smile.

And that was when Henry's chest lurched.

No. No, don't be so stupid as to think yourself fall—

'Come with me,' he said quietly.

He didn't know what made him do it. Something foolish, something deep within him that hadn't been let out for years. Something he should fight, but it was far more fun to let it out and free, just for a moment. Just for today.

'Why?' Ditty said warily, looking up as he stood, wiping the spoon and popping it into his pocket.

Henry outstretched a hand. 'Come on.'

'I have a proposal to plan!' Ditty protested, looking

at her notebook and, Henry noticed, longingly at the fresh bowl of parfait. 'I have to speak to someone who can build—'

'I said, come with me.'

Henry waited, his heart beating far more frantically than he would have expected. Why did it matter so much whether she took his hand? Why did he care if she came with him or not?

Why was warmth spreading across his chest as she started scooping up her notebook?

'I could do with a breath of fresh air, I suppose,' Ditty said, stuffing the notebook into her reticule after shrugging on her pelisse. 'All that parfait. I really shouldn't have—'

'You would have hurt Reg's feelings if you hadn't,' Henry said with a heavy sigh. 'Trust me, I know. Come on.'

'But I must—'

'Must nothing!' Henry said, grabbing her hand with his and pulling her out of the restaurant. 'Reg will understand, you're a busy woman. We're being spontaneous!'

He could barely breathe as he pulled Ditty down King's Street. Passers-by gawped as they ran down the street until they turned down a lane, and he did not stop running nor pulling her until they'd left the two rows of houses behind and started along the path into Brexley Forest.

'There,' Henry said, panting slightly as he let go of Ditty's hand.

When had he taken her hand? He could hardly remember. All he could think about now was how his fingers still tingled with the contact, even through his winter gloves.

'You…we shouldn't… I need to…' Ditty wheezed, putting her hands on her knees and doubling over as she tried to catch her breath.

Henry grinned. It was rather nice to see Ditty out of her comfort zone. 'There isn't anything you can't do later.'

'Oh, I don't know about that,' Ditty said with a mischievous look as she straightened up. 'I think Reg probably wanted paying for my lunch.'

Her laughter echoed around the otherwise silent woodland. 'But, I'm sure he'll understand—it's not like I'm going anywhere soon.'

'No, I guess not,' said Henry quietly. 'Not for another two weeks.'

Silence fell between them, just for a moment. He tried not to notice her flushed cheeks, bright eyes, the way she stood feet apart, as though she were an explorer adventuring into a new land.

Perhaps she was. When had Ditty last been spontaneous? Henry wondered. *Months. Years?*

'This place is beautiful,' she said softly, looking around them.

Henry mirrored her, his shoulders relaxing as he did so. There was something about this place.

'It's been here hundreds of years,' he said, slowly starting to walk along the path. Ditty followed him, keeping to his pace. 'Sometimes I come here to think.'

It was odd, how the admission changed things between them. Henry was unable to explain it, but sharing with Ditty that this was a special place to him somehow made the forest itself different. He had never shown it to anyone else. Not even—

Henry pushed the thought from his mind. He was not going to allow himself to think about that. *About her.*

'I love old trees,' Ditty said quietly, brushing her fingers against the bark as they passed. 'It reminds me no matter what I do, the world will continue on, turning and growing and thriving.'

Henry glanced over but looked away as she caught his eye.

He hadn't asked her about the newspaper articles. Not after she had thrust them into his hand and made him read them.

Still. Ditty was evidently under a huge amount of pressure if she had to prove herself to these Londoners, Henry thought as their footsteps crunched along the remnants of the winter snow.

No wonder she was so determined to get this silly proposal for Charles perfect.

'It is so beautiful here.' Ditty's voice broke the silence as she coloured. 'Though I can't think when you would have time to come here. I would imagine looking after Mavis and Avril is an absolute dream.'

Henry chuckled. 'Oh, they are—but just multiply their mischief by about thirty, and you have the total residents in the Lodge. That's an awful lot of squabbling from those rascals. You know, I had to ban them from coming out here.'

'Here? Why?'

'Too dangerous,' Henry said with a heavy sigh. 'Oh, it's fine in the summer. Most of them grew up here, they know the forest better than I do. But in the winter it can be treacherous. It's best not to go out alone.'

'I find most things are better if you attempt them alone,' Ditty mused. 'Oh, look at that!'

The path had curved around and up a hill, and came out with a spectacular view that always caught Henry's breath.

'You wait until you come here in the autumn,' he murmured, standing still as they overlooked the picturesque scene. 'It's quite the picture.'

They stood there for a moment, both basking in the wonder of nature.

And then words slipped from Henry's lips he most certainly had not intended. 'You know, if I was ever to propose matrimony again, it would be here.'

The instant the last syllable was spoken, he knew he had made a terrible mistake.

Ditty's head turned. 'Did you say—'

'No,' said Henry automatically.

But she was no fool, her eyes widening. 'You did, didn't you?'

The tension he had half expected in his lungs did not appear, but that did not make Henry's breathing any easier. 'It's—it is a part of my life before—it does not matter.'

It was quite alarming to discover that there was truth in his words. It did not matter. How many months had Henry spent wishing things had been different…and now, he could not recall the last time he had wished for Georgiana to be his duchess by his side.

Not since…well, since Miss Aphrodite Oliver had arrived in Brexley.

She was still looking at him curiously. 'Your Grace, Henry, precisely what occurred when—'

'We'd better get back and pay that bill of yours, or Reg will be storming up to the Lodge for my head,' Henry said cheerfully, forcing down the panic rising in his throat. 'Come on, it's easier on the way back.'

Chapter Nine

January 31: 12 days until the proposal

'**Y**ou will then begin your speech,' Ditty said enthusiastically, running her finger slowly down the colour-labelled schedule she had outlined before meeting Charles in his law office. 'I shall provide you with a template—'

'Oh, good,' said Charles, visibly relieved.

The weather had changed. It was still certainly winter, and Ditty would be wearing her pelisse for many weeks to come, but snow had ceased to fall on Brexley.

In a way, she would miss it. Everywhere looked beautiful with snow, she had always thought. It was why so many proposals occurred at Christmas and the New Year. The world looked fresh, clean, wonderfully ready for a new beginning.

But she had learned a long time ago she could not depend on snow to always improve the surroundings, although in Brexley that was not a problem. She hadn't found a part that wasn't beautiful.

'I shall supply you with the template tomorrow, giving

you a week to compose your speech,' said Ditty, forcing herself to concentrate on the meeting at hand.

It was vital, after all. Thankfully, Charles—unlike his brother—was proving biddable.

'And you'll review it, won't you?'

Ditty nodded, gratified at Charles's trust in her. 'Of course. We shall run through it twice together, once on our own, and once at the rehearsal.'

Charles's face fell. 'Rehearsal?'

'You don't think the best musicians and actors go on stage without a dress rehearsal, do you?'

The blank look the lawyer gave her made Ditty realise perhaps that wasn't the best example. Brexley, almost a five-hours-long stagecoach ride from London, likely did not have a theatre.

Ah. Well, she'd just have to think of another one.

'You wouldn't go to trial without rehearsing your opening statement, am I correct?'

Charles's face immediately relaxed. He leaned back in his chair, the confidence she associated with the man returning. 'Oh, yes, I see. Well, that makes perfect sense. And then I'll present her with the ring!'

Ditty nodded. It was a rather wonderful proposal, she congratulated herself. The embroidered love hearts to cover Reg's restaurant were the finishing touch, particularly if she could help Miss Vivienne source roses close to an exact colour match.

What woman would say no?

'You have a ring, did you say?' A little fashionable, to propose with a ring, but not a problem.

Charles nodded, opening out a drawer. 'I do indeed.'

In his hands was a box, small yet perfectly formed.

Excitement rushed through her. No matter how many matches she made, no matter how many proposals she organised, no matter how many times she heard the word 'Yes!' she would never grow tired of it. 'May I see?'

Ditty's hand was steady as she reached out for the box. When she opened the lid, she smiled to ensure Charles could see her approval.

Now that was a ring. Yellow gold band, and not one, not two, but three huge sapphires. So huge, she wondered the box lid had been able to close over them.

'You like it?'

'I think she'll love it,' said Ditty, sidestepping the question with the skill she had learned over the years.

Never give an opinion. She had learned that the hard way on her very first job, and would never make it again. Whatever you said, it was wrong. Better just to point to the person who was actually going to receive it…

'I am glad it's prepared,' Ditty said aloud, closing the box with a snap and passing it back to Charles. 'It's always a worry if it looks as though something won't be ready in time.'

'Oh, I would never let that happen,' said Charles proudly, as though he personally guarded it with his life. 'So, is that it?'

Ditty recognised the polite—well, almost polite—dismissal. 'If it is acceptable to you, Mr Paisley—'

'I told you, call me Charles!'

'If you are amenable, then, Charles,' said Ditty, wincing slightly. It felt wrong to be on such easy name terms with a gentleman. 'I do not wish to be rude but I must carry on, another appointment—'

'Yes, of course,' said Charles smoothly, rising swiftly. 'In fact I have a client due any minute…'

With polite goodbyes and agreements on when she would deliver the speech template—Ditty would have to ask Mrs Fletcher if she had any more ink—she left the law firm and inhaled deeply. Everything was falling into place.

The fresh wintery air had none of the bite of snow, but it was still fresh. Ditty smiled at Miss Vivienne and two men she recognised as they passed.

'Miss Ditty, good afternoon.'

'Good afternoon Miss Vivienne, Mr Jacks, Mr Martin.'

It was strange, Ditty mused as she meandered down the street. She'd only been in Brexley a week or so, and yet already it felt…well, not like home. Her books weren't here, for a start.

But certainly more like home than she could have predicted. There was something altogether more welcoming than she had anticipated. Everyone here was genuinely interested in her, not just because there was nothing else to do but gossip, but because they cared.

It was a rather disconcerting feeling.

The pangs for Almsbury, always so present, had somehow faded. The busyness of London had appealed to her after her father's death, the anonymity of the large city a welcome relief, a chance to escape the grief…and yet here, in Brexley, there was no need to rush. No need to plan. Just the opportunity to…breathe.

It was Henry's fault, of course. His spontaneity was in some way catching.

She wanted to be caught by it.

Still, she really did have things to do. She'd go up to the Lodge first and pick up that sample Mavis had promised her. If she was going to design the perfect arrangement for Reg's restaurant, she'd need to know—

'There you are!'

Ditty whirled around, heart racing. It was Henry.

Mr Paisley. Dr Paisley. The Duke of Glanyrafon.

Why was it so difficult to know how to address this man?

It surely did not explain why her heart was racing so powerfully. It was because she had turned around so quickly, she tried to tell herself as Henry jogged across the street toward her, grinning.

Not anything to do with the handsome man rushing toward her. The handsome man whose displeasure she had attempted, unsuccessfully, to avoid. The handsome man who made her feel things that Thomas certainly never had. The handsome man who apparently had proposed before…

If I was ever to propose matrimony again, it would be here.

Ditty swallowed. She hadn't asked any more questions. It had been painfully obvious Henry had spoken without thought. He wouldn't ever forgive her if she tried to pry.

Still. It was tempting, she could not deny it, to visit the Lodge not only to see Mavis's sample, but to ask the women a few leading questions.

Like, what happened to Henry Paisley's wife...?

Henry grinned as he stopped before her. 'Here you go.'

He thrust something into her hands, and Ditty took it without a second thought. It was an envelope.

'What's this?' she said, opening it up. 'Oh.'

Working hard to ensure her face didn't fall, Ditty pulled out an embroidered heart. It was evidently Mavis's work; the stitching was entirely different to that of Avril's, though both were exceedingly pleasing.

But why was it here? She had planned to go up to the Lodge herself that very day...

Henry, however, looked very pleased with himself. 'Thought I'd save you a trip, as I was coming down here anyway.'

Ditty tried to smile. 'Thank you. That was kind.'

It was kind, she told herself firmly. So why did she feel so disappointed she wasn't going to spend a lazy afternoon with Mavis and Avril, hearing all about what had happened to break Henry's heart?

Besides, she had so many questions, questions she did not appear able to ask him directly. How was a gentleman like himself—sufficiently dressed but not fashionably attired, working for a living and driving that old dog cart—a duke?

'What are you doing?'

'Wh-what?' Ditty said, blinking.

She really must pay attention! Henry's smile had an

all-too-knowing look after her splutter, and she was determined not to make a fool of herself. Even if her treacherous heart was, for some unknown reason, still fluttering.

'What are you doing?' repeated Henry. 'I thought you'd be harassing the shops of Brexley, ensuring you had everything to put your genius plan together. Most of them will be sold out of all that romantic tat, of course. The Valentine's—'

'Day Festival, yes, I heard,' said Ditty wryly. 'Why does everyone in this town keep talking about it?'

He shrugged, drawing attention to his broad shoulders. 'It's just about the only thing that happens in this place—I mean, Brexley is a wonderful place to live. It's just, this is the one time in the year we get so many visitors. A chance for business owners, I suppose.'

Ditty nodded. It made sense. Whoever had come up with it in the first place was a genius. A purpose-built festival which demanded people come to your town and spend money? Clever.

'But I'm guessing you've got everything tied up in a bow?'

Ditty smiled, despite herself. 'I am happy to declare my ingenious plan is made!'

She tapped her notebook, still tucked under her arm.

Henry raised an eyebrow, then glanced over at the law firm, just down the street. 'Ah. Off to show my brother, right?'

'Already done so, and received what I would consider

the royal seal of approval,' teased Ditty, falling into the tone easily.

Far too easily. Since when had Henry been a friend?

'Here, take a look—just don't read my notes too closely, or you'll give the game away!' Ditty said eagerly, opening up the notebook.

Her breath hitched in her throat as Henry did not take the notebook in his hands, but instead stepped to her side, peering over her shoulder into the carefully colour-coded notebook.

Why was having him so close so…so disconcerting?

It was because the weather was cold today that she was conscious of his warm breath on her neck. That could be the only reason.

'Oh, my goodness,' Henry said with a laugh. 'Are you sure you're not invading another country?'

Ditty looked at her notebook. Well, she could see how someone might make that mistake. On page one was a series of squares, almost like a mural or frieze, showing where people would go and precisely at what times. On the next was a colour-coded map of the restaurant, where people would be stationed, notes on prices…

'I just like to be organised, that's all.' So why was there such a note of defensiveness in her voice?

Henry snorted. 'This isn't organised, this is orchestrated! Have I told you before I don't believe you can plan romance?'

'Yes, you have,' said Ditty, moving just a step away.

Henry Paisley—the *Duke of Glanyrafon's* close proximity was playing havoc with her brain, for some reason.

That was why, Ditty told herself, she could not think of a clever response. The only reason.

'Romance is just biology,' Ditty said, as though she was trying to convince herself as well as the tall doctor before her. The tall, handsome doctor. The tall, handsome, charming and most irritating doctor who was also a duke. *Ditty, get a grip!* 'There's a formula to it, just like there's a formula for everything. Input all the requirements, and—'

'Do you really believe that?' Henry's voice wasn't harsh. Quite the contrary, it was soft, far more gentle than she had heard before.

Ditty swallowed. It seemed ridiculous to have such an intimate conversation on a Brexley pavement. But the street appeared to be deserted. They were alone.

And he was close. So close, she could count his eyelashes. So close she could kiss him, taste his lips, if she leaned forward…

'Do you?' he repeated, his eyes unwavering as they stared into her own. 'Do you think romance can be… can be made, as long as you have the right formula?'

Ditty swallowed.

Henry was tempted to break the silence, but he managed to hold it—as he similarly held Ditty's gaze.

It was painful.

No, not painful. It wasn't pain somehow lodged in Henry's chest, clawing at him like a wild animal.

It was something just as intense, just as uncontrolled. It was taking him over, making him say things and do things that…well, yes, he did want to say them. And do them.

But that didn't mean he should!

'You're determined to be a romantic, then?' Ditty said steadily.

Henry swallowed. 'No one's ever accused me of that before.'

'It's not an accusation. Not really. It's just…most people I know would admit falling in love is a chemical reaction,' she said quietly, dropping her gaze to her notebook, which she snapped shut.

Henry hesitated. 'I'm not saying there's no biological element, but—'

'You're a doctor,' Ditty pointed out with a wry smile. 'I would have thought, of all people…'

Her voice trailed away as she spoke, and she started walking slowly along the pavement. Entirely unsure why he was doing so, Henry started walking alongside her.

A doctor and a duke, he was a puzzle to himself, so there was no reason to suppose that a woman he met a matter of weeks ago would understand him.

Wait—understand him? Did he wish to be understood?

'I am a doctor, and I suppose there is truth to what you say,' he admitted, trying not to swing his arms. Every time he did so, he brushed up against Ditty's pelisse.

Why had he never noticed before just how much he swung his arms?

'Biology,' Ditty said smartly.

Henry chuckled. 'It's not as easy as that.'

'Oh, isn't it?' she said, arching an eyebrow, though he was relieved to see there was a smile dancing across her lips. 'The way I see it, when we meet someone we like, our body changes. Our heart rate increases, our eyes change, our breathing—am I not correct?'

Henry's jaw clenched. To think, he was being given a biology lesson. 'You are.'

Ditty grinned. 'There you go! And you would know better than anyone that the particular mixture within us is highly potent. We become giddy, excited, sometimes even euphoric. It changes our appetite, reduces our ability to sleep. We move into a different chemical state. That's all.'

Henry swallowed. Somehow he had managed to stand closer to the woman who was making his head spin, his mouth dry.

'It is biology,' Ditty said lightly, her pupils dilating as she gazed up at him. 'It's…it's built into how we're made.'

Was it his imagination, or was her breath quickening? Was his? Why were his fingers tingling so?

'You think so?' Henry managed to say.

Ditty's cheeks were pinking, and he could not understand why, nor why she was inexplicably leaning closer to him. 'I have seen it a thousand times. I'm certain I know it when…when I see it.'

Henry swallowed, her gaze darting to his throat, and when her eyes returned to his, there was something in them…something he did not understand.

He should kiss her. He shouldn't kiss her. He should kiss every inch of her and damn the scandal.

'And that's all there is to it,' Ditty said lightly, breaking whatever spell she had put him under. 'The biology of love.'

Oh, hell. It sounded so simple when she put it like that! Yet there was more, he knew. When he had fallen in love with… *No*, he told himself firmly. *He was not going to think about her.*

'It's not that simple,' he said aloud.

Ditty shook her head. 'I've never seen it otherwise.'

'Then perhaps you've never seen love, real love,' he said impulsively. 'When someone falls in love, it isn't that simple. It isn't just biology and chemistry and heart thumping and chest tightening and…'

He couldn't continue as she caught his eye. He looked furiously away.

He wasn't describing himself, Henry told himself firmly. This was different. He felt all fluttery around Ditty because they were arguing. Because they were in a disagreement, yes, that was it.

And that was all.

'It's more than the physical change,' he said aloud, trying to distract himself from the way her hair was pinned in waves around the collar of her pelisse. 'It's the emotional change, isn't it? The feeling that…being with the person is the only place in the world you want to be. Knowing whatever they need from you, you'll give it. Sensing if they fell, you'd catch them, catch them even if it meant falling yourself.'

Henry's mouth was dry. He'd never spoken like this to anyone. Not even—

He continued hastily. 'And those emotions are expressed physically, I'd be no doctor if I couldn't admit that. But I think the emotions, they come from somewhere else. Somewhere deeper. Somewhere more than just biology.'

She examined him carefully as they reached the end of King's Street. Without exchanging a word, they turned on their heels and started walking slowly back up the pavement from where they'd come.

'I was right, then.'

Henry looked quizzically at Ditty, who smiled.

'You are a romantic.'

He chuckled. 'I suppose I am, though I don't know why I'm having this debate with you.'

Well, he had a pretty good idea…

'I think you just like to argue.'

He laughed. 'You've got me all wrong!'

'Oh, I don't think so,' teased Ditty, glancing at him through her lashes. 'I think you've spent too much time here in Brexley with the same people. I think you're looking for a bit of fresh conversation.'

There could be some truth in that, even Henry had to admit. But it was far more likely, in his mind, that there was something about Ditty herself which drew this out of him. Drew it from somewhere deep.

'Perhaps,' he conceded as they passed the floristry.

'I would have thought—I mean, you are a duke. I suppose I should be calling you "Your Grace" or—'

'No, don't,' he said quickly. 'I'd prefer it if you called me Henry.'

Ditty did not look at him as she said, 'My point remains, however, that you are a duke. You should be, I don't know, gracing the floor at Almack's or cheating men at cards at court or—'

Henry could not help but laugh. 'Do I look like that sort of man to you?'

It was the wrong thing to say. She looked at him closely, his chest tightening as her gaze drifted down his body.

'No,' she said softly. 'But then, you don't look like a duke.'

It was perhaps the nicest thing that anyone had ever said to him. Henry grinned. 'Well, I haven't been a duke for very long, and I wasn't raised to be one. My uncle—a great-uncle my mother had never spoken of—died childless, much to our surprise, and my mother turned out to be the granddaughter of a duke, even more to our surprise. And so last year I became something I cannot live up to.'

Damn, he had not intended to speak with such bitterness. When he glanced at Ditty, she was looking at him seemingly with curiosity. He would have to hope it was something like that.

'That explains why you did not introduce yourself to me as the Duke of Glanyrafon.'

Henry snorted. 'The day I start doing that will be a very sorry day indeed.'

'But you do not go to Town for the Season—'

'I like it here,' he said forcefully. 'I like the people here, I like arguing with you about love and romance and biology, but I think I'm fighting a losing battle. I mean, you've clearly built your business on this.'

'This?'

'This formula thing you spoke of,' Henry pointed out. 'You know, your ability to always get a "yes" from any poor unsuspecting woman.'

That was it, meander away from the subject of the duchy and how he did not behave like a proper duke. He tried to put as much teasing into his tone as possible, and was rewarded by a broad smile.

This was ridiculous, he tried to tell himself. He'd only come into town because he needed potatoes and lamp oil for the dining room. More things he couldn't afford. More things he'd have to buy on credit.

Henry's chest, so recently warmed with joy at his conversation with Ditty, iced over. He really had to do something about the dire situation the Lodge found itself in.

If only someone else knew about it. Keeping it a secret that the duchy was penniless was perhaps not the cleverest of moves, but he had done so for a year and could not stop now. Trying to fix the situation all on his own was exhausting.

Henry cast a quick look at Ditty but looked away. No, she wasn't going to help him—and why should she?

She would be gone in two weeks, he reminded himself. Gone, and back to London to her sisters and gentleman caller. Or whoever.

'I suppose I have.'

Henry blinked. 'What?'

'Built my business on the belief of a formula for romance,' Ditty said brightly. 'But then, what sort of proposal planner would I be if I couldn't offer some certainty?'

'But no guarantees.'

'Never any guarantees,' she said with a laugh, her arm brushing against him as they walked.

Warmth spread across his arm from the point where she had touched him. Try as he might, Henry could not ignore it.

'Well, I'm a romantic, and I don't want to think there's only one formula,' he said aloud, as though that could distract him from the pleasurable contact they'd just shared.

They were almost at the other end of King's Street now. There was a bench, relatively dry, and he gestured toward it. They both sat, Henry making sure not to sit too closely to the woman who was already playing havoc with his heart.

Not that it was anything to do with affection—no, surely not. Just something else. Irritation, maybe?

'Look at your Lodge,' Ditty said.

Henry frowned. 'What about it?'

'It's absolutely packed to the rafters with people who have lost the ones they loved,' came Ditty's quiet voice.

His heart skipped a beat. It was true. There were very few married couples who made it to an age to move into his Lodge. Most of the time it was the woman who made it to an advanced age, but there were plenty of widowers there, too.

'Sometimes I think we lose who we are,' he found himself saying quietly, 'when we lose the ones we love.'

'That's exactly what I mean,' Ditty said with a heavy sigh. 'Love, the sort of love you're talking about? That emotional, dependent love—it can hurt you.'

'It can give so much as well.'

'Whatever it gives, it always takes back,' said Ditty, pain clear in her voice. Henry tried not to look at her as she continued, 'I've loved people, people I really cared about. And they're gone now, and I…'

Henry waited. It was clearly difficult for her to speak, and in a way, he was honoured. It did not sound as though Ditty had spoken about this for a long, long time.

'My father…he died when I was young,' Ditty said eventually, her voice thick though her eyes were dry. 'When all of us were young, myself and my two sisters. He died in a carriage accident. My mother has never truly recovered, not really. She…they eloped. He was below her station and so they ran away together. To Greece, actually.'

'That would explain the name,' Henry managed to say as his heart twisted. Oh, to have survived such a bereavement, to live with such grief. He spoke as gently as he could manage. 'I'm so sorry for your loss.'

'In a way, I think I'm still grieving. I certainly did not have much time to consider his loss at the time. My—

my mother fell apart,' she continued, and Henry's heart ached for her. 'I became mother and father to my sisters all in one day.'

'Your time of grieving must end, though—'

'Who are you, who is anyone, to dictate to me when sorrow ends?' Ditty's eyes were still brilliant, still bright, tears wavering and yet unshed. 'Do you think I relish it, the sense of loss? Do you think I wish to feel so alone, so isolated, so…so unsupported?'

Henry could do nothing but look at her, aghast at what he had said, fighting off the instinct to pull her into his embrace.

'I loved him so dearly,' Ditty said, with a false brightness that broke his heart. 'Real love hurts, you know? That's why I thought, still think, it's better to avoid it at all costs.'

Henry blinked. 'Avoid it?'

Her nod was certain. 'Yes, avoid it. I thought, if I ever married, it would be, well, a companionable arrangement. One where I could retain my independence, prevent my heart from… Anyway. And so I thought, why not plan it.'

Henry waited, a gentle freezing breeze tugging at her hair. 'Plan it?'

'Everything. All of it. The whole courtship,' Ditty said matter-of-factly with a sighing laugh. 'I suppose you think me strange, but I would rather have a business partnership with someone, and hope love grows.'

Henry stared. No wonder Ditty Oliver had made a

career by expertly planning, to the very last detail, precisely how a match came about.

If you think you can control love, then it can't hurt you.

Henry could see the logic. Despite his choice to steer clear of it, he still believed in love and romance. For other people. The kind of partnership that Ditty talked of left your heart unscathed and unfulfilled.

'And how is that going for you?'

Ditty coloured. 'Fine.'

Her answer was too quick, in his opinion. Perhaps the situation with the gentleman friend back in London wasn't going that well.

A traitorous spark of hope rose in his chest, quickly pushed down.

'I suppose there are different types of love,' he said aloud. 'There's the romantic kind, of course, but there are others.'

Ditty raised an eyebrow.

'Companionship, I suppose,' Henry said with a laugh. 'I don't know. After my father died, my mother has not remarried, and in a way I'm glad. She's still got a great many friends. They offer her something else, a kind of love that's gentle.'

Ditty met his gaze, and this time she did not look away. 'Companionship?'

'Like, a friendship,' Henry said, his mouth dry. 'But better. Deeper.'

'That...that sounds nice.'

'Something worth hoping for,' said Henry, heart now in his mouth. 'Rather than manufacturing.'

For a moment, he could have sworn they were the only two people in the world. There they sat, on the bench in Brexley, looking at each other, and the longer the moment continued, the more certain Henry was that he was going to fall right there into her eyes. Into Ditty's bright and brilliant eyes, all that intelligence and all that pain mingled together.

Henry moved, his hand reaching out for—

'Well, I'd better get back to Mrs Fletcher's and see if she has any more ink,' said Ditty, leaping up from the bench as though she'd been burned. 'And I'm sure you've got numerous errands. Thank you for the embroidery.'

Henry blinked. Embroidery? What was she—

Then he noticed the envelope in her hand. Of course. She was still holding Mavis's love heart.

'Oh,' he said bleakly. 'Right. Sure. Ditty—'

'I'll see you soon, I am sure,' she said brightly. 'Brexley isn't that large a place.'

Henry watched as she strode along the street toward the inn. *No, it wasn't that large*, he thought ruefully. *And yet you fit here perfectly. Can't you see?*

Chapter Ten

February 1: 11 days until the proposal

'And then you loop it round…like this?'

Ditty stared at the crocheting heart in her hands.

Well. It was supposed to be a heart. She'd never seen anything that looked less like a heart. It was all bunched up on one side, and the threads at the top were nothing like the stitching at the bottom.

She sighed heavily. Whenever she was left alone with a needle and thread, nothing ever seemed to work.

Though Avril and Mavis tried to look kindly at the monstrosity she was holding up in the middle of the table in the Brexley Lodge craft room, Ditty could see what they really thought.

She sighed as she dropped her hands onto the table. 'How do you both do it?'

'Years of practice,' said Avril wisely.

'Years? Decades, more like!' cackled Mavis with a grin. 'You just wait until your children have gone out to play and your husband is tinkering with something daft, and you have twenty minutes to yourself. All those twenty minutes add up!'

Ditty smiled weakly as the two older women laughed together. Of course, she wasn't going to tell them her thoughts. She'd already been far too open with the residents of Brexley as it was.

Well, one of them.

She swallowed, gaze dropping to the misshapen heart in her hands. When had she last spoken about her father? Years ago. Thalia had tried to bring him up occasionally, and she knew Calliope spoke to Thalia about him, but she never joined in.

Until Henry.

'I just wish I was a bit more help,' Ditty said feebly, looking back at…well, she couldn't call it a heart. Not with that shape. 'But I don't seem to have the hang of it.'

'Make a hundred, and by the time you reach the last one, it might even look like a heart,' said Mavis with a grin.

Ditty giggled. 'And if I didn't have such an important proposal to plan, then perhaps I'd take you up on that! But I think it would take me forever, and I'm leaving the day of the proposal.'

Now why did those words sound so strange and foreign in her mouth?

'Humph,' sniffed Mavis. 'You aren't staying, then?'

Ditty blinked. 'Staying?'

She must have heard wrong. There was absolutely no chance of her—

'Oh, you've got to stay, Brexley has been brought alive

again by your presence here,' said Avril, slowly cutting the material for the next heart. 'Every shop in town says you've purchased from them.'

'I have to get back home, keep building up my career,' she said with a brief smile. 'You wouldn't want me here—'

'Oh, yes, I would greatly miss you if you decided to go back to that big city of yours,' said Avril, her eyes narrowed as she waved the pinking shears at her. 'And I can think of one other person who would miss you a great deal, as well.'

Both the ladies glanced to their left.

Unable to help herself, and utterly perplexed as to what they could mean, Ditty looked in the same direction they were pointedly gazing at.

And flushed.

It was most unfair her body would betray her in that way. It was only Henry, after all. Henry in a greatcoat, standing outside the wide window and evidently looking up at something.

Ditty could feel her cheeks burning, and they only increased in temperature as Avril and Mavis giggled.

'You're as bad as a pair of schoolgirls,' Ditty chastised with a raised eyebrow. 'And you couldn't be more wrong.'

'Tell that to your cheeks,' said Avril with a wink.

Ditty flushed and looked once more at her ridiculous attempt at making a heart.

She couldn't make a heart. She couldn't even open

her own. What was it Thomas had said in that idiotic letter of his?

He understands this may come as a surprise, but he has given much thought to the matter, and after consideration has concluded there is nothing more to be gained from the relationship.

'Why don't you go and see what that nice duke is up to?' Avril said sweetly.

Ditty rolled her eyes. 'You know, you could at least attempt to hide what you're doing!'

'No, we couldn't—and when you get to our age, you'll know there is absolutely no time like the present,' said Mavis severely, though there was a twinkle in her eye. 'Now go and talk to the boy. See what he's up to. Report back.'

'But not too quickly,' said Avril with a wink.

Ditty sighed but rose, as though she could not disobey.

Something was drawing her to him, something she had never felt before. Something strange, that pattered in her chest and refused to stay still. Perhaps if she just went out there and asked what he was up to, Ditty reasoned as she pulled on her pelisse, then this hot feeling would be gone. Whatever it was.

Smiling at the other residents as she walked down the corridor to the hall, Ditty was surprised at how many names she had learned in her short time here. She found Henry still outside the large Lodge, though farther along, to her great relief. At least Mavis and Avril wouldn't have a clear view.

'Hello,' Ditty said, shyness suddenly overwhelming her.

Henry turned and beamed, and that strange fluttery feeling in her chest increased.

What on earth was going on?

'Hullo, Ditty,' he said easily, his tall frame just covered with his greatcoat.

Ditty could not help but notice it was short in the arms. What was a duke doing, wearing a greatcoat with frayed cuffs?

She glanced up and immediately saw what he was looking at.

'Now, I'm no expert,' she said, 'but that looks like damp to me.'

Henry sighed. 'Don't need to be an expert to see it.'

Indeed, Ditty was rather surprised she hadn't noticed it as she had arrived earlier that day. It looked from the ground as though the drainpipe had cracked, allowing a small but steady trickle of rain down the side of the building. Over time, it had created a damp patch which had to be at least four feet wide.

Ditty shrugged. 'Shouldn't be too hard to fix.'

Just for a moment, she thought he was going to say something, sadness in his eyes she had never seen before.

And then it was gone. Henry smiled. 'Yes, I suppose it is not complicated. How's your heart?'

Ditty swallowed. What the—what did he think he was doing, asking a question like that?

'Mavis said you were learning to make one today, but she didn't hold out much hope for you,' he continued in a low, conspiratorial voice. 'Avril stood up for you, if it matters.'

Ditty forced herself to laugh. 'Oh! Oh, of course. I'm afraid my ability to make a heart just isn't that impressive.'

The words tasted strange on her tongue, but surely it was the cold in the air.

Henry was nodding. 'I suppose you came out here to escape them.'

It wasn't really a question—at least, it didn't sound like one. Ditty nodded, not entirely sure what else to say.

She knew what she wanted to ask, but the very beginning of their…whatever this was, had been more than a little fractious. And what she wanted to ask was far too intrusive a question, she knew. Even so…

'What is it?' Henry said, pulling a hand through his hair. 'What, have I got something on my face?'

Ditty's gaze was pulled inexorably toward his handsome features. 'N-no.'

'Then what is it? You're looking at me like I've grown another head.'

Her stomach swooped, but there was nothing for it. *She had to know.* 'When we took that walk in the woods, you—you said something about proposing matrimony again.'

Henry's smile faded, but he did not look angry or upset. 'I did.'

'So you have proposed to someone before?' Ditty prompted, her heart racing.

Why was it so important to ask? She still couldn't quite put her finger on that.

Henry glanced up at the building once more, as

though if he didn't, it would fall down. Or perhaps that was just her imagination. Perhaps he just didn't want to look at her.

'Yes. Yes, I was almost engaged about two years ago.'

And a rush of jealousy, a powerful rush of envy Ditty had never known before, soared through her, overwhelming her carefully planned reply.

'Why almost?' she said quickly. 'Why didn't she—how did you plan your proposal?'

Henry laughed.

After all, what else could he do? There was absolutely no chance he was going to let that slide, even if Ditty looked almost as red as a beetroot.

And attractive, at the same time. How did she do that?

Still, there was a sting in her words. He had damned well planned the proposal, and look where it had got him?

'Now then, don't you blame the fact that she said no on the fact that I didn't plan it properly!' he teased.

At least, he tried to tease. It was difficult while his entire chest was frozen like ice and his heart wasn't beating.

Ditty's gaze had dropped to her hands and for that, he was thankful. Now Henry could try to collect himself before he spoke any more about that day in his life to which he had promised himself he would never return.

It had been a mistake taking Ditty along that path. He had known it at the time, especially when his mouth had slipped. He shouldn't have even mentioned Georgiana.

Henry swallowed. The hurt inside was not what he had expected, though.

After Georgiana had declined his proposal, he'd been sure he would never think of her, speak of her, even return to that place without the sharp agonising pain which had cut his heart in two.

And for a while, that had been true.

But it was strange…speaking about it with Ditty, even in vague terms, didn't bring back the same agonising pain. In fact, there wasn't even a dull ache.

'I did not say you didn't plan it properly,' said Ditty defensively. 'I—'

'I'm sure you didn't, I'm just teasing,' Henry said softly.

'She declined your proposal, then.'

He nodded. 'That she did.'

And in no uncertain terms, he could not help but think. Goodness, just a 'no' might have been bearable. He could perhaps have laughed about that with Charles, told their mother he'd done his best but his best, for some reason, had not been sufficient.

But instead…

How can you even think to ask me that? After everything I've been saying to you for months, telling you that you need to improve this cottage, explaining just how important it was that you increased your income—and you ask me to marry you? You're a joke!

For a moment, just a moment, Henry closed his eyes. Georgiana hadn't been the woman he'd thought she was.

He knew that now, hindsight making it easier to spot. But at the time…

'Just, no?'

'I mean, she did not exactly have a speech prepared,' said Henry warily. 'Not that it stopped her. But yes, she was clear in her decline.'

All too clear.

'But you'd offered marriage,' said Ditty quietly. 'I mean, you must have thought your courtship was tending that way.'

Henry breathed out a heavy sigh, watching it blossom in the cold air. 'Yes, I had thought so. I thought we both were. I mean, I was courting her, it was just…' His voice trailed away.

He'd never done this before. Explained it to another person. He'd had enough difficulty explaining it to himself.

But his mother had never pressed him, and Henry thought Charles would rather pull his own arm off than have a heart-to-heart. So he'd never tried to articulate it all.

'I wanted to marry her,' he said finally, noticing Ditty perking up as he started to talk. 'And she wanted to marry me, just not the me I was. I mean, she declined my proposal because I was a poor doctor and she wished to live in town.'

'London?'

Henry chuckled. Only a Londoner would think it was the centre of the world. 'No, Marchester.'

He grinned as Ditty's jaw fell. 'You call that "Town"?'

'Well, around here, it is!' he pointed out. 'It was where she was from, we met while I was training to be a doctor. When I returned here, we continued to court. I thought she would wish to join me one day.'

Ditty nodded and a lurch crept up Henry's chest. She understood, of course she did. Would not a lady such as Miss Oliver have a gentleman caller of her own—would she not be eager to return to him, in London?

At least that simplified matters. She was not going to get the wrong end of the stick here, Henry tried to tell himself. Ditty wasn't interested in him, certainly not in that way. She was curious, but she had her own suitor. That was the only reason she was asking.

'I bought an expensive ring from a jeweller out in Marchester, on credit,' Henry said, trying to inject a laugh into his voice. He couldn't. 'This huge emerald, you had to see it to believe it.'

'And I'm the one who says you can manufacture romance,' Ditty said dryly.

He shot her a glance but there wasn't any malice in her words. Quite the contrary, she had an understanding wry smile on her lips.

'You didn't want to use a family ring? Or not offer a ring at all?'

Henry's jaw tightened. 'It never occurred to me. I suppose I wanted to impress her. And part of me didn't want her to have one of my mother's rings. Perhaps that should have been my first sign I wasn't as committed to her as I thought. Perhaps I was forcing things.'

He'd never thought of that before. Strange.

'I suppose I thought she would always be happy to move here, to Brexley,' he continued. 'And it turns out… she wasn't. This place wasn't enough. My income wasn't enough. I wasn't enough. And then,' he said with a dark laugh, 'a duchy fell into my lap. Suddenly I was no longer Mr Paisley as I had been when we first met, or Dr Paisley as I had become, but the Duke of Glanyrafon. All of a sudden, Georgiana was very interested in making my acquaintance again. All of a sudden, Georgiana was hopeful of receiving my addresses again—at least, receiving the addresses of His Grace, the Duke of Glanyrafon.'

Ditty winced, wrapping her scarf a little more tightly around her. 'Ah.'

'Ah, indeed,' Henry said with a heavy sigh. 'She was not the woman I thought she was. Perhaps that is what hurt the most. Without the title, I was not enough.'

He looked over at Ditty.

'I don't think it was that you weren't enough,' she said quietly.

Henry did not understand why hearing her say that meant so much. 'You think so?'

'Some people just aren't suited,' she said calmly, as though she were some sort of expert. Which, Henry reminded himself, she was. 'I see it all the time.'

Now, that was surprising. 'You do?'

She nodded. Henry tried not to notice the way her lips quirked into a smile. 'You know those 109 proposals I've planned, that I told your brother about?'

Henry grinned. 'How could I forget?'

'Well, there's a reason that number isn't higher,' Ditty said covertly, lowering her voice. 'I—I've actually turned down about fifty clients or so.'

Now, that was surprising. Henry didn't understand it; she was a proposal planner, she needed the customers. She had said so herself, this proposal of Charles's had to be perfect.

'Why on earth would you do that?'

'You can tell, just by meeting someone, whether the relationship is right for matrimony,' said Ditty with a wry smile. 'Just meeting one of them is usually enough. I have a sense for it, this knowing sensation in the pit of my stomach. I will not put a lady in a tricky spot, especially if the gentleman is not even courting her. If I worked with everyone, my percentages would be far lower.'

'Bad for business.'

Ditty nudged him in the arm and Henry grinned, loving the closeness that gesture created. 'You know, I don't just say all this for the effect. I truly mean it, I live by it!'

Henry examined her for a moment. 'Is that a fact?'

Well, she had asked a rather personal question of him, hadn't she? Evidently their friendship, or whatever this was, had grown to such an extent where he could do the same.

Even if it hadn't, Henry was sure his curiosity couldn't be held back any longer. 'What about your own gentleman caller?'

There was absolutely no chance he could have mistaken that—a flash of hurt, or something like it, swept across Ditty's face. 'What did you say?'

'Your gentleman caller,' he persisted. *Well, in for a penny...* 'I thought—I suppose I presumed—a woman such as yourself—'

'You thought wrong,' said Ditty shortly.

Henry swallowed. All the camaraderie in the air had gone, and it was his fault. How had he managed to spoil such a—

Ditty sighed heavily. 'He… Thomas, I mean. He sent me a relationship cessation notice just before I came here.'

It took Henry all his self-control not to allow his jaw to drop. He must have heard incorrectly. Though the wintery air was silent, there was no possibility he could have heard right.

'I'm sorry,' Henry said weakly. 'Could you say that again?'

A slow smile crept around one corner of Ditty's mouth. 'A relationship cessation notice,' she repeated. 'He ended our courtship.'

'I'm sorry, with a—'

'A relationship cess— You're just making me say it again,' Ditty protested, nudging him with a laugh.

Henry resisted the temptation to pull her into his arms for a comforting embrace. She looked like she needed it.

A relationship cessation notice? 'That sounds like the sort of thing Charles would draw up for two business partners.'

'I suppose it was like that, in a way,' Ditty admitted,

her cheeks pinking slightly. 'It was notarised by his solicitor. I told you, I live what I preach. When I said the other day a relationship should be more businesslike, and you hope love comes—'

'So that is your idea of romance?'

Henry could hardly believe it. This vibrant, passionate, creative woman being given *a relationship cessation notice*? The idea of anyone deciding to cease courting Ditty was bizarre, but doing it in such a cold manner?

'Did he sign it and just—just hand it to you?' he said, trying to wrap his head around the whole thing.

Ditty hesitated, and Henry immediately wished he hadn't asked. 'He sent it to me by post.'

'No!' He almost laughed, it was so ridiculous. 'You cannot tell me you miss that idiot.'

Why did it matter how she replied?

Because it did matter. Try as he might, Henry could no longer deny to himself that Ditty was…important. Precious. Her hurts mattered in a way like no one else's, not even his residents.

His hands started to clench into fists before he forced them to unclench. He wasn't going to get anywhere by getting angry at this gentleman, this Thomas, whoever he was.

'I suppose we were more like business partners,' Ditty said quietly. 'I don't think you can miss something that isn't there.'

'Business partners?'

She looked, not uncomfortable, but rather, a little surprised at what she was saying. 'Yes, I… I knew that love hurt. That it was painful, that loving meant accepting grief, and so—so I proposed something more akin to a business arrangement. I organised the courtship. It all sounds so cold now I say it aloud.'

Henry's heart broke for her. 'Not cold. Detached, certainly.'

Ditty's smile was rueful. 'Detached, but safe. Safer than… I feel with you,' she finished softly.

Henry had reached out before he could stop himself. His hand enclosed around Ditty's, his cold fingers intertwining with her own. Their warmth, or perhaps the warmth of their contact, Henry didn't know, sparked heat up his arm.

Ditty looked up at him.

She was close. Standing right beside him, their hands together, he realised her breathing seemed to change, though he could not describe how. His own did not appear particularly regular, now he came to think about it.

Henry looked into her eyes. There was so much he wanted to say, but he hardly knew where to begin. He hardly knew what he would say once he opened his mouth.

'Thank you for telling me,' Ditty said softly. 'About your proposal.'

'Thank you for telling me about that blagg—idiot,' Henry amended hastily.

She chuckled under her breath. 'Is this what you call companionship, then?'

Companionship. Connection. Warmth.

He had thought he'd known those things, understood

those things, but Ditty Oliver was incomparable to Georgiana.

This was different. This was comfortable, and yet his whole body was on fire whenever he was near her. This was a connection that he did not understand and yet yearned to become an expert in.

This was warmth; of growing familiarity, to be certain, but that could not fully explain the warmth in his chest, in his loins, in that part of him that he had never truly given to another before.

Henry swallowed. *Oh, this was far much more.* 'Why not.'

Chapter Eleven

February 2: 10 days until the proposal

'You must be joking,' said Ditty, horror in her voice.

She had to be dreaming. No, not dreaming; she must be having a nightmare.

Because what she had just heard, it couldn't be true. Not with ten days to go before the most perfect proposal she had ever planned.

The proposal that would restore her reputation. The proposal that would show all the newspapers back in London that what she did was worthwhile, not a scam. The proposal that would keep allowing her to provide for her family.

The proposal that would show Henry just how romantic it could be...

Ditty swallowed. She should not be thinking of Henry at a time like this.

As she sat within the inn's breakfast room, surrounded by the shapes of hearts and a pink lamp with wings, she could not believe what she was hearing. She had thought it bad enough that the fireworks she had ordered were yet to arrive, but this?

On the opposite side of the table, Reg sighed. 'I am not joking.'

'But it must be a mistake. It cannot be as serious as all that,' Ditty said eagerly, as though she could persuade him.

'Ditty, I'm telling you, the roof has fallen in,' said Reg gently, as though it was her restaurant destroyed in the night. 'With all the snow melting… I've been meaning to get it looked at for a while—'

'But the whole roof? The entire restaurant? Are you sure there isn't a part that—'

'Ditty, the restaurant is closed.' Reg sighed heavily. 'I don't know what to say, except that I'm sorry. I won't be able to host your planned proposal—I won't be able to host anything for a while.'

Ditty leaned back against her chair as she heard the resignation in Reg's voice, as panic threatened to overwhelm her.

The roof, the restaurant, it was all ruined. She'd never find a place suitable in time, and all the preparations had been made with Reg's place in mind, how could she—

She was being selfish. A wave of guilt overcame her, and she bit her lip as she tried to think what to say.

This wasn't about her.

Well, the urgent meeting Reg had requested was. The distraught man had wanted to let her know the moment he had arrived at Cantelli Restaurant that morning and discovered the destruction.

Wanted to give her enough time to replan the proposal, he had said.

But though this was a blow to her plans, it was a far greater blow to Reg. His restaurant, his precious business—he loved welcoming people into that place, seeing them well-fed, enjoying their enjoyment, gaining joy from their joy.

And now it was all destroyed.

She couldn't be selfish and pretend this was her tragedy. It was Reg's.

'I am so sorry, Reg,' she said softly.

When Reg spoke, Ditty could see he was holding back tears. 'Oh, what's a restaurant in the grand scheme of things! Nobody died!'

The crack in his voice said otherwise.

Ditty clutched at the table. 'I know, but it's still sad, and once I've sorted out this proposal I'll work out a plan to help you, Reg. You've been so kind to me, welcoming me to Brexley.'

Ditty embraced Reg before he left the inn. She closed her eyes for a moment and tried to take it all in. The Cantelli Restaurant was closed. The perfect proposal was no longer perfect.

And she had only ten days to make it so.

Besides, it was not only her problem. The loss of the only restaurant in the place was going to play havoc with their plans for their Valentine's Day Festival.

She swallowed. All those visitors coming here for the festival; all the preparations the town had been doing, all

the flowers Miss Vivienne had brought in, all the decorations Mrs Fletcher had added to her inn.

It would all be a disaster without somewhere for all
the tourists to eat.

Ditty twisted her hands together as she tried to think,
forcing the panic at bay. There had to be a solution—but
really, she needed to think of Charles's proposal first.
That was the reason she was in Brexley in the first place!

And she wanted to show Henry, really show him,
what she could do.

If she was at home, she'd have all her books out on the
carpet by now. How would she order them this time? By
her enjoyment rating? By age of the author? By average
length of chapter?

Ditty rose from the chair and pulled on her pelisse.
She had to see Henry. He would help her.

The walk from Mrs Fletcher's inn to the Lodge was
not a long one, but the brisk fresh air did wonders to
Ditty's state of mind.

Her determination only increased as she entered the
Lodge.

'Ah, Ditty! I didn't expect to—'

'Henry,' she said, the name of the one person she
wanted most in the world in that moment spilling from
her lips. Swallowing, she said, 'Dr. Paisley. The Duke
of Glanyrafon—I need—where is he?'

The woman blinked. 'Oh. Oh, I think he's in his study.'

Ditty waited for directions, but as none seemed forth-
coming, prompted, 'And that is…?'

The woman flushed and pointed to her left. 'Dr. Paisley doesn't like being disturbed in his—'

'Thank you,' Ditty said swiftly, striding in the direction that the woman had pointed. This part of the Lodge seemed to be…well, she wouldn't say it aloud, but even more decrepit. There was a flickering lamp at one end, and the carpet had definitely seen better days.

The door before her said, in gold letters: D CT R.

'It used to say "Doctor,"' said Mavis with a sigh. 'But that was a few years ago now. I don't know why Henry doesn't have that fixed, but there we are. Have fun, Miss Ditty, but not too much fun.'

'Mavis!' said Ditty, shocked.

The older woman winked, then returned up the corridor.

Ditty swallowed as she turned to the door suddenly hesitant. Henry was a busy man. Doctor and duke, it was a wonder he'd had time to speak with her so much as he had. *And why was that?* she wondered for the first time. He had been very kind, but—

'Ditty?'

She blinked. The door before her had opened and there stood Henry, thick greatcoat on and heavy scarf wrapped around his face. He looked as though he had stepped in from the outdoors, rather than from his study.

'Henry,' Ditty said weakly.

'What are you— Is everything quite well?'

'Yes,' she said instinctively. Her shoulders slumped. 'No. I need your help. Can I come in?'

For some reason, Henry looked over his shoulder

and glanced back into his study. 'Erm…yes. I don't see why not.'

Deflated, Ditty turned to go. 'Sorry, I shouldn't have come. Do not concern yourself with my—'

'Ditty, wait!'

She froze. No, that wasn't the right word—because heat was washing up her arm, through her pelisse, where Henry had grabbed hold of her.

She turned back to face him and saw…what was that, in his eyes? Eagerness? Something more?

'I just didn't want you seeing my study in such a mess,' he said ruefully. 'But come on in. I… I want to help.'

Ditty tried to think about his words as she stepped into the study. He wanted to help? What did that mean?

Unfortunately, she was unable to consider it any further as she looked around her.

Well, at everything not covered by paperwork. She had never seen such a mess; every square inch of the place was covered with paper, teacups without saucers scattered everywhere, their rings left staining anything they rested on. There was a box of what appeared to be bills sitting in one corner, and the desk at one end of the room could have been light or dark wood but it was impossible to tell. Notebooks filled with spidery handwriting—*a doctor's handwriting*, Ditty thought wryly—were all over the sofa, along with envelopes, which from the look of them, hadn't ever been opened.

'You…you work in here?' Ditty had not intended to speak, but couldn't stop herself.

Henry gave her a wry grin as he pushed some papers from a sofa and indicated she should sit. 'Not really. I escape it as much as possible, I've never really been a dab hand at paperwork.'

Ditty's eyes widened as she sat. 'Yes, I am getting that impression.'

Yet her heart warmed. This was a man who clearly focused on what he thought was important: his residents. Paperwork could always wait. Clearly.

'So, what's wrong?'

Ditty took a deep breath as all the panic she had pushed down from Reg's conversation soared. 'Reg's restaurant—'

'I heard, the roof's fallen in.'

Ditty frowned. 'How do you—'

'Brexley is not that big a place, I told you,' Henry said with a laugh as he leaned against his desk. There wasn't enough space for him on the sofa—something Ditty noticed with a tinge of regret. 'That rather scuppers your proposal plan, doesn't it?'

How could he speak so calmly? 'I thought you could help me.'

'I'm not sure what I can do,' said Henry, popping his hands in his greatcoat pockets. It was remarkably cold in here, now Ditty came to think of it. 'I mean, I'm not a roofer.'

'But I had the perfect plan!' The words exploded from her.

'Sometimes you don't need a plan.'

'I need a plan,' said Ditty, glaring, wondering why on

earth she thought she could come here for help. It could not be more clear he was delighted her perfect plan was over! 'I had a plan, and now it's ruined. What am I supposed to do now?'

Henry swallowed.

He hadn't meant it to sound like that.

Sometimes you don't need a plan.

It was just…well. She'd had a plan, Henry knew. The plan now couldn't work, so she would have to make a new plan.

How hard could it be?

But he looked at Ditty—really looked. He saw her hands, fingers twisted together in her lap, constantly moving as though if she stopped, the world would end. He saw her wide eyes, as though desperately seeking a solution somewhere in his study.

Henry almost laughed at that. If there had been solutions to anything in his study, he would be the one desperate to find them. As it was, he hadn't found anything in his study for a while—except a sandwich, once. In his filing cabinet.

But most of all, he could hear in Ditty's voice that she was frantic. It was so unlike the Ditty he had grown to know over the weeks; the strong, determined, capable Ditty.

This was Ditty in real distress. And she had come to him.

Focus on her, Henry tried to tell himself. *Not yourself.*

But there was something instantly warming about

the idea she had come straight to him. She had been in trouble, and she had sought him out.

Despite himself, a smile crept across his lips.

'Why on earth are you smiling?' Ditty demanded.

Henry cleared his throat. 'No I'm not.'

'Yes, you are—well, you were,' she amended, scowling at him and looking damned pretty while doing so. 'What on earth am I going to do?'

It was indeed a challenge, Henry could see that. Brexley was not large, and though he loved the small town which had always been there for him, there were few options for a romantic...

A romantic...

No. No, he could not share that place. It was his, his and... But even as Henry thought that, his gaze flickered to Ditty. To the woman he was starting to care far too much about.

'What is it?'

Henry froze. 'What?'

'That smile—you've thought of something, haven't you?' Ditty's expression was still marred by tension.

Oh, God, he was going to do this. 'I... I have a solution for you, but I don't know if I should share it.'

Ditty perked up immediately. 'A solution? A new plan?'

Henry hesitated. He had been speaking the truth when he said he wasn't sure if he should share it—but probably not for the reason she would assume.

Taking her there...where he had proposed to Georgiana...

He hadn't been there in a while. A long while. In fact, now he came to think about it, had he been there since the disastrous proposal?

'Henry?'

Henry's jaw had tightened, but he tried to loosen it as he rose. This would hurt, but it was the right thing to do. 'Come with me. Let me show you the next best place—no, what am I saying? *The* best place for a proposal in all of Brexley.'

There was just a moment of hesitation in Ditty's face as she considered his words. Henry's heart skipped a beat. Was she willing to trust him? Was he willing to open this part of his life to someone who, he knew, would be gone in just under two weeks?

'Fine, but this place had better be good,' said Ditty in a warning tone, rising to her feet. 'A better menu than Reg's—no, what am I saying, how would that be possible?'

Henry snorted as he pulled on a pair of gloves and opened the door to the corridor. 'There's no menu at all.'

'No menu? How does one order?'

'It's—it's easier to show you,' said Henry with a dry laugh, closing his study door behind them and striding down the corridor. 'Just follow me.'

It was pleasant to have Ditty by his side once more. He had never noticed just how lonely living in a place like Brexley could be, especially around Valentine's Day.

Especially around— What was he thinking?

'The path to the woodland?' Ditty wrinkled her nose. 'In the woods, really, Henry?'

He laughed, breath billowing as they stepped outside the Lodge and toward the forest. 'Can you just trust me for, I don't know, more than two minutes?'

Ditty caught his eye and grinned. 'I suppose I can try. For you.'

A flicker of warmth spread across Henry's chest as he laughed with her, though his was slightly forced.

For him? It was starting to get ridiculous just how much he wanted her to look at him, smile, trust him.

Worse, he was going to feel even more ridiculous once she left Brexley and returned to London. Went back to her life.

Because this is not her life, Henry tried to tell himself as they walked along the path, deeper into the Brexley Forest. *This is your life. She just happens to be in it for a few weeks. And then she'll be gone.*

His trepidation about showing her the place grew the closer they got, and Henry found his footsteps slowing.

'Are we almost there?' Ditty asked quietly. 'This special place of yours?'

Henry swallowed. 'Yes.'

After a moment of silence, she said, 'It's the place where you proposed, isn't it?'

Stopping dead in his tracks, Henry felt his cheeks burn as Ditty looked up with calm and compassionate eyes.

She was not teasing. She was certainly not laughing. Instead, she looked concerned.

'You don't have to take me there,' Ditty said softly.

'I can find somewhere else, perhaps look at going to Marchester—'

'No. Charles would want to get engaged here, in Brexley,' Henry cut across her, his chest tightening. *He could do this. For her. For his brother.* 'It's just…'

His voice trailed away as his gaze flickered to the path ahead of them. He had not expected coming back here to be so odd.

But when he looked back at Ditty, all the hesitation seemed to melt away.

'I want to show you—and you should use it for my brother's proposal, if you think it'll be suitable,' Henry said in a stronger voice, striding forward. 'It's just around the corner.'

Just a few more steps, and they would be there.

He heard Ditty gasp as they stepped around the corner and she saw it. The most beautiful part of Brexley.

'It's…it's…' Ditty gasped.

Henry grinned. 'I know.'

The waterfall was hundreds of feet high. Water soared down from the edge of the cliff across the chasm from them—but a trick of the light made it look as though they could reach out and touch it.

Rainbows glittered in the air. Birdsong echoed beautifully in the naturally made chamber, and it was at least ten degrees warmer than the rest of the woods, the curve of the cliff protecting them from the wind.

'It's…magnificent,' Ditty breathed, staring around her.

Henry's chest swelled with pride, as though he had

carved the place himself. 'It's amazing, is it not? People always think it'll be too loud, but—'

'How on earth can we hear each other?' Ditty said in wonder. 'I thought waterfalls were loud.'

'They are—this is,' said Henry. 'But it's a trick of the eye, the chasm is much farther out than you think. So you can look out at it, but still have a conversation. Still propose marriage, as it happens. That I can promise.'

He tried to put as much teasing laughter into his comment as possible, but Ditty was not so easily fooled.

'So it *was* here…'

'Yes,' said Henry with a nod. 'It was here.'

Only now of course did he realise, with a shock, that though his heart had been broken here, it was also now being mended.

In the very same place, but with a very different woman.

'I… I am just astonished!'

Henry chuckled. 'When the visitors arrive for the St Valentine's Day Festival, we always make sure to keep this place quiet,' he said, watching Ditty walk around slowly, gazing all about her. 'It's a special place for us Brexley residents, we don't like sharing—'

'And it's not too much of a walk, is it?' Ditty said eagerly.

Henry saw the light of passion in her eyes, her creativity rising to the challenge, and adored what he saw.

Who could help it?

There was something so intoxicating about seeing Ditty at work. She was a marvel. Just as much a marvel, in truth, as the waterfall he had known all his life. The same rush of power.

She was so beautiful—inside and out.

'So I could get all the supplies up here myself, probably,' Ditty said, eyes gleaming. 'And the musicians—and perhaps even… No, that would need thinking about, the flowers…'

Her voice trailed off and Henry watched with a smile as her mind continued to work it out.

No matter what she did, he could plainly see, she would come up with a plan. A plan that would work. A plan that was, in some small way, because of him.

Ditty turned and beamed. 'Thank you.'

Before Henry could say a word, she had rushed toward him and pulled him into an impetuous embrace.

His arms closed about her and for a moment, just a moment, they stood there.

He swallowed, breathed in the scent of Ditty. She was small and warm in his arms, clinging onto him in evident gratitude—and relief.

And that is all, he tried to tell himself. *This attraction, this affection you have for her—it's all one-sided. She's here to do a job, and that is all.*

Still, he could not help but wish the embrace would never end.

Ditty pulled back and laughed with bright, shining eyes. 'I have a lot of planning to do.'

Henry rolled his eyes as he tried not to pull her back into his embrace. 'I thought you'd learnt recently the dangers of trying to plan?'

'It's not a plan,' she corrected him with a smile. 'It's… it's preparation.'

Henry smiled in return, and that twisting ache returned to his stomach.

Oh, he was in deep trouble.

'I would have thought you'd learn not to plan too much,' he said quietly, refusing to release her, knowing that he should. 'I thought you had avoided that since arriving here.'

'I tried to avoid you and your displeasure since arriving here,' she shot back in a low voice, gaze unwavering.

'And how is that going?'

Ditty bit her lip, and that was what did it. The restraint of weeks could no longer be held in—it was impossible. How could he prevent himself from tasting those luscious lips?

Henry had hardly realised he had done so until he was doing it. Leaned forward, pulled Ditty back into his arms and placed his lips on hers.

She did not fight him. If anything, she pulled him closer. Lips parting and a light moan in her throat, Ditty gave herself to him in a way he could not have predicted.

This was what he wanted—who he wanted. From the very moment she had stepped off that stagecoach, Henry had been fighting this instinct, these desires awoken that he had believed dormant.

But Georgiana had never made him feel like this, sink into a kiss like this, want to pull pins out of cascading curls like this, cradle a woman's jaw and tilt her into him like this.

Desire throbbed in his body as Henry teased pleasure in her mouth, aching as he felt her respond. This kiss between them had been needed for so long, his fingers entangled in her hair, her palm splayed against his chest. She tasted wonderful, like fire and honey—

'No,' Ditty whispered, pulling back.

Henry stepped back immediately, heart pounding, hardly sure if he had heard correctly. 'I—I beg your pardon?'

Her cheeks were pink and for the first time in their acquaintance, Ditty refused to meet his gaze as the roar of the waterfall continued behind them. 'I… I just think… it was a mistake, that was all. A mistake.'

A mistake? How could she say that? Could she not feel how he wanted her?

Henry swallowed. But he was no rogue. He would not force her. He was not about to start arguing with her. He stepped back. 'A mistake.'

'Yes, w-we got swept up in the moment. I should go and tidy myself up before returning to Mrs Fletcher's,' Ditty said hastily, backing away from him. 'Before it gets too dark.'

'I could take you across town in my dog cart—'

'No, no, the walk will do me good,' Ditty said with a brief smile before slipping down the path, round the corner and out of sight.

Henry breathed out a heavy sigh as he staggered back to lean against the trunk of a tree.

Hell.

Chapter Twelve

February 4: 8 days until the proposal

When Ditty woke up for the second morning in a row with a slow and slightly confused smile on her face, she knew precisely why.

Henry.

The way he had kissed her had been hungry and all-consuming, and for a moment she had been willing to give herself up to it.

But then…

She would not lose herself to love, to any great emotion. That was how one became completely lost.

That was why she'd told Henry it was a mistake. Yet, now she winced at the memory, the look on his face. And had it really been a mistake?

Curled up under the coverlet in Mrs Fletcher's best room, Ditty knew she was getting distracted. But who could blame her?

Henry Paisley, Duke of Glanyrafon, was an excellent distraction.

And besides, she tried to reason with herself in the quiet of the early morning, her friendship, or whatever it was with Henry, had become the solution to her biggest problem.

Ditty smiled, hugging the spare pillow as she remembered that moment. She had been filled with warmth, a sense of knowing, a sense of being known. A sense of belonging. A need to stay with him.

Those feelings had transmuted when he had kissed her. He had kissed her with passion and with purpose and with a clear sense of what he wanted.

Her.

She had never allowed herself to feel so wanted. Never put herself in a position to let her emotions overtake her. That was what had made her pull back.

Those feelings had not faded after she had returned to the inn, and Ditty had spent an evening trying to untangle precisely what it was she felt for this man. The doctor. The duke. The gentleman who had made her first few days here so difficult.

But now…

'You are not falling in love,' Ditty whispered in the quiet of the room. 'You've got a job to do, a match to make! Remember?'

Stretching out an arm into the chilly air, she reached for the stack of letters that had been waiting for her last evening, her eyes too tired to read.

A note from Calliope, who demanded an update— adding that if she and Thalia did not start hearing from her more often, they were both going to jump on the next stagecoach to Brexley.

That made Ditty smile. It was so wonderful to know, even though they were miles away, she had her sisters worrying about her.

And there was a letter from Thalia—with something else inside it. Her eyes roved over the short missive.

Ditty—
I did not know what to do, and so I hope you can forgive me when I send on this letter. I thought you would wish to read it immediately, rather than wait until you return to London. If I am in error, I do apologise.
Your loving sister (please don't be angry),
Thalia

Ditty blinked. It was a rather worried tone from her sister. Her gaze moved to the enclosed thing—a letter from Thomas.

She sat up so quickly that the coverlet fell and she had to pull it up to keep warm.

Thomas? What on earth was he writing to her about? From the little she could remember of the cold relationship cessation notice he had sent her just before she had come to Brexley, he had not wished to have anything more to do with her.

So why was he sending her a letter?

With a certain amount of trepidation, but more than a little curiosity, Ditty opened it.

Dear Ditty,

It's strange not to have heard from you in such a long time. Weeks, I think.

As it turns out, I grew so accustomed to having you I hardly realised what it would be to do without you.

I went by your lodgings and saw your sisters who aren't overly impressed with me anymore, for some reason. They said you'd left London for a match-making client. It's not over, then? You've managed to salvage your reputation enough to secure a client?

Some of the things in the newspapers... I will be honest, at first I was glad I was no longer courting you. It would have been embarrassing at the bank to be tied to someone in the newspapers—and in such a manner.

But I can see now how they were wrong. I think on reflection, I was wrong, too.

With that in mind, I am contacting you with a proposal.

Ditty gasped. The letter slipped from her hand and for a few heart-stopping moments, it got tangled into the bed sheets.

When she had finally managed to find it again, it had folded itself. Ditty hesitated a moment, trying to catch her breath before she opened it again.

She couldn't have read that right. Could she?

There was absolutely no possibility that Thomas was going to propose. Propose? Thomas?

Still, Ditty pondered, if he was going to do something like that, a letter would be just the way he would do it. Clean, calm, clinical. No ability to misunderstand his intentions. A firm yes or no in response.

Just like Thomas. Just like their relationship had always been.

Which did not explain why her heart was hammering so fast…yet she felt no excitement, no joy, no relief. In all honesty, Ditty couldn't remember the last time she had thought about him.

Taking a deep breath, she unfolded the letter and kept reading.

With that in mind, I am contacting you with a proposal. I suggest we resume our previous courtship, with the following caveats:

1. We wait to see what the newspapers say about you and your career before announcing this to our friends/relations, etc

2. We will meet no more and no less than once a week (I have a place in my schedule already marked out)

3. During these meetings

Ditty put the letter down.

She should be happy. She knew she should; it was a return to the plan, a step back into the schedule she had arranged months ago, all to guard her heart.

But none of that sparked any excitement, any joy, in her.

When had that changed? When had her mind meandered away from rules, regulations, a safe and content future with Thomas…to the spontaneity, the surprises, the unsettling sensations in her stomach whenever she was with Henry?

She didn't need to read any more. She might not want to dive headfirst into the feelings that Henry invoked, but her heart had already told her what she thought of Thomas's suggestion, and it just wasn't interested.

Ditty had been momentarily upset on receiving the relationship cessation notice, and it was galling to have him reach out like this, as though he was doing her a favour…

But in a way, he was.

Ditty looked around the room she was in. This room had everything in it she would associate with romance. Love hearts, the colour pink, cupids, bows, flowers…

I want more.

It felt strange thinking that, but Ditty knew it was the truth. More than what Thomas had to offer her.

Oh, he would be the perfect husband for someone, she had no doubt. But he was not for her. She wanted the fluttery feelings in her heart she felt whenever she looked at Henry Paisley, Duke of Glanyrafon.

Admitting that to herself felt strange after all this time. It wasn't *safe* in the slightest. It wasn't that she was imaging that Henry might be the perfect husband, but she did know he was showing her there was more out there, more to feel. *If* she gave herself permission to.

'The only trouble, of course,' Ditty muttered with a sigh, 'is you're leaving in just over a week.'

Eight days. Eight more days in Brexley, that was all she had.

A knock on her door made her jump. 'Yes?'

'Breakfast is ready, dear,' came Mrs Fletcher's voice through the door. 'And a man called to say the fireworks you ordered—'

Ditty scrambled out of bed, swiftly pulling on a shawl and almost stumbling to the door as she opened it. 'They're here?'

Mrs Fletcher's eyebrow raised at the sight of her guest in her night things—but then, Ditty's travel nightgown was so thick and woollen, there was no hint of impropriety.

'Sadly not,' she said. 'The man said they'd be delivered here tonight, by special courier.'

Ditty sighed. That was all she needed—more things to go wrong. 'You were absolutely sure he said—'

'I took down the message here, dear, I thought you'd want it written down. He wouldn't stay, said he had other deliveries to make,' said Mrs Fletcher cheerfully, handing her a piece of paper.

Ditty glanced at it. Mrs Fletcher was right; it was much better to have it in writing, though that didn't change the fact the fireworks were now three days late. Another day wouldn't matter, perhaps another two days, even three…

But after that?

'In that case, I'll take my breakfast with me, Mrs Fletcher,' she said impulsively.

Her hostess's other eyebrow rose. 'With you?'

'Yes, I think I'll go for a walk on this beautiful morning,' Ditty said.

'My word. "With you." Well, I'm not sure how I will manage the porridge, or the tea, or the eggs, or the—'

'Toast will be absolutely fine,' interrupted Ditty hastily, certain she was about to be treated to a monologue of all the different delicious breakfast items Mrs Fletcher's inn could offer, and whether each of them could easily be transported. 'Really. Toast.'

Not half an hour later, she was striding out of Mrs Fletcher's and along King's Street with a piece of toast cut into a heart.

It's the look of the thing, dear, Mrs Fletcher had said fondly. *You know how it is.*

And it was delicious, Ditty thought as she munched happily, greeting the people of Brexley as she went. There were fewer and fewer faces she did not recognise now, and each time there was a look of recognition and a smile in someone's eyes, that warm glow in her chest seemed to brighten.

She didn't have a particular direction in mind. At least, that was what Ditty told herself. It was easier than admitting she had been intending to go to the Lodge all along.

When she arrived, there was a loud noise coming from the drawing room.

'Morning,' said Ditty easily. 'What are they getting up to in there?'

'The waltz,' said Mavis, who was wandering through the hall. 'I keep telling Henry it's not good for them, at that age, but—'

Ditty opened the door, and the sight she beheld was quite astonishing. About twenty people, all in their seventies or above, were marching about in pairs as a woman who had to be at least ninety was playing a dainty waltz on a pianoforte.

'—push forward with your arms, yes, perfect, Emmeline, and turn. What did I tell you, Brian, about getting ahead of yourself?'

Ditty closed the door as quietly as she could without being seen.

'Ah, you're here to visit your young man, aren't you?' Mavis continued blithely. 'Oh, that Henry will be such a catch for someone and I hope it's you, dear. I do wish in a way you were here for us, but you're not, are you? It's your young man.'

Ditty flushed. 'He's not—'

'He's in his study, at least he was the last time I checked,' said Mavis, as though it was her job to continually review Henry's movements. 'Along with you.'

It did not appear Ditty was to be given much choice. Besides, she could not deny—even if she did not say it aloud—that she wanted to see Henry. If only for a minute.

No matter how long he pored over these numbers, Henry knew he was never going to understand them.

He groaned. 'If only you were a wound I could suture, or a fever I could bring down!'

Then he might have some idea how to understand these terrible ledgers.

'There has to be an answer,' Henry muttered under his breath, picking up a bank statement and sighing as he saw a plethora of others underneath, all just as incomprehensible.

That was the trouble with the strange way he had inherited the duchy. Most people would love to be a duke. A title, prestige, a manor, wealth…it was an honour to inherit. That was what the solicitor had said anyway when he had handed a befuddled Henry the keys and a pile of bills.

And Henry knew in a way, he was right. But didn't most dukes with manors have heaps of money?

There had to be a way to save money. He could cut the waltzing classes, except they were run by one of the residents. He couldn't cut any more desserts, they were down to weekends as it was, and there had been a small yet polite riot over that. If it hadn't been for Mavis calming everyone down and promising to bake twice a week, things could have got awkward. But how would he buy her the ingredients?

Henry wracked his tired brain, trying desperately to think of a way to find a few more coins. If he wasn't careful, he was going to have to reduce the coal order again, and he was certain it was morally reprehensible to allow the elderly to freeze.

But what else was he meant to do? They were in arrears with everything—it was thanks to the kindness of the townsfolk of Brexley they were still given credit for repairs at the boot-maker. *How much longer could this last?*

'Planning?' came a voice from the door.

Despite his troubles, despite his frustrations, despite the concern he had for each and every one of his residents, Henry could not help but smile as he saw Ditty leaning against the door-frame. He hadn't even noticed her open the door.

'You were so lost in your thoughts, I could have left you there for hours,' she said conversationally.

Henry tried to smile. 'I'm glad you didn't. It's good to see you. Any fireworks?'

He cringed inwardly the moment he spoke. What had he been thinking? *Any fireworks! She might think—*

'No, they're delayed again,' said Ditty with a sigh. 'But I have the courier's assurances from Mrs Fletcher that they'll be here by tonight.'

'And that's enough time to get them all set up?' asked Henry. 'Come in, by the way.'

Ditty's smile danced as she did so, shutting the door behind her. 'Do you not ever get tired of the place being so untidy?'

Untidy?

Henry looked around him. It was untidy—he hadn't wanted Ditty in here just days ago, he was so conscious of how it would look. A doctor, a duke, unable to keep on top of his paperwork!

'I had a personal clerk,' he said, by way of explanation, and shrugged with a grin. 'And a steward, and a man of business. But after they left—'

'You didn't want to replace them?'

Henry hesitated as Ditty lowered herself onto the sofa. If only it had been that simple. He'd thought at the time it was an easy way to save them seventy pounds each month. After all, how hard could it all be? Write letters, post letters, file letters. He could do that.

It had only taken two weeks for the place to get like this, and then he hadn't the heart to do anything about it.

'There's always…something else more important to do, I suppose,' he said aloud.

Ditty grinned. 'You'd never find my study like this— if I ever had a study, that is.'

Henry laughed as he stepped out and around from his desk and unceremoniously tipped a pile of paperwork off the sofa and onto the floor before sitting beside her on the sofa. 'I wouldn't think so. Yours would be organised, colour-coded—'

'You say that like it's a bad thing!' Ditty protested, though she was smiling as she twisted on the sofa, pulling a foot underneath her to look at him.

Henry smiled. How did she do it? Her mere presence was enough to calm him, to remind him there were more important things in life than money. After all, it wasn't going to be as simple as finding a few shillings behind the back of a sofa.

'I don't think being organised is a bad thing,' he clarified. 'I'd love to be more organised.'

He watched Ditty cast an expert eye over his study. 'You know, I could get this sorted for you in, say, an afternoon.'

Henry tensed, the taut awkwardness rising up his spine and across his shoulder blades. 'No,' he said quickly.

Too quickly. Ditty looked at him with a curious expression. 'Why?'

How could he explain? There was so much he wanted to tell her; Henry had never met anyone he wanted to be so open with.

Did he fear her discovering the truth of the financial state of this place? Or was he more afraid because the more time he spent with her, the more he…cared about her?

Ditty Oliver might have arrived at Brexley just weeks ago, and he may have accidentally berated her about her very reason for doing so, but so much had happened since then. So much had changed.

And yet in a very real way, nothing had changed. He was still the doctor here at Brexley, still the penniless duke of a place he knew he never wanted to leave.

And Ditty Oliver would complete her matchmaking here, help his brother get engaged, then disappear back to London. They'd never see each other again.

She had likely been right to call their kiss a mistake…

'I just…it's my job, you know,' he tried to say with more ease than he felt. 'I may be His Grace if I ever bothered to step into London, but here, I'm Dr. Paisley. I can't have you doing my job when you've got your own to worry about.'

Ditty's smile was so innocent, so eager. 'I don't mind! It'll keep me from worrying, to be honest. I can't stop thinking of all the things that could go wrong, and I haven't thought of a way to help Reg yet…'

Henry nodded as she chattered on, feeling the tension in his bones melt away.

Because it was true. It wasn't a lie, he would have felt awful letting Ditty do something that was his responsibility.

But it wasn't the only reason. If Ditty started to help him clean up, it would only be a matter of time before she realised the numbers on these balance sheets were low. Dangerously low.

Henry had managed to keep this fact from his brother, all the residents here at the Lodge and everyone in town. He wasn't about to give it away now just because of a pretty face.

'—must be something I can do, I just haven't thought of it yet,' Ditty was saying. 'What? You're smiling.'

Henry hadn't noticed he was, but it seemed to be an occupational hazard whenever he was around her. 'I am?'

'You are,' she said with a grin of her own. 'Go on, tell me what you're thinking.'

Not on your life. 'I was just wondering why you always feel the need to help people. Solve their problems for them?'

Ditty blinked, as though she did not understand the question. 'What do you mean?'

'Well. Proposal planning,' Henry said, hardly knowing where he was going with this, but absolutely certain he wasn't about to reveal the dire state of his finances. 'You're helping people, solving problems—it speaks so highly of you, Ditty,' Henry said, unable to stop smiling. 'You're…you are a really good person.'

Would it be so bad to let her help him?

She was only inches away. Henry hadn't noticed when he had sat on the sofa just how small it was for two people. Usually it was only himself, when there wasn't paperwork covering it. He only ever sat there when his desk chair got too uncomfortable.

But with two people, their knees were almost touching.

Henry tried to breathe normally, but something funny seemed to have happened to his lungs, and all he could do was think of her. Of Ditty, and how close she was. How it had felt to have her in his arms, his lips on hers.

'You're not too bad yourself,' she said gently.

Henry coloured. 'What do you—'

'Well, this place,' Ditty said, gesturing around them. 'The Brexley Lodge for Gentlemen and Ladies of a Certain Age. You think I haven't noticed how much work you put into it, how your whole life is consumed by it?'

Now that was not something he had expected her to

say. The heat in Henry's cheeks burned. 'It's what any-one would—'

'No, I don't think it is, actually,' she said gently. Her voice was low, soft, melodious. Henry itched to reach out and take her hands in his own. 'I think you go above and beyond what is expected of you here, and you're doing two jobs—more than that, from what I've seen.'

Henry's stomach lurched at the thought of Ditty see-ing him in such an honourable light. Goodness knew he hadn't thought of it in that way in a long time.

'I think you're doing great work here, and I'm not the only one who thinks so,' Ditty said.

It was all he could do not to beam. Henry knew he worked hard, but the idea someone else had noticed, and that it had been Ditty...

'No one really ever says thank you,' Henry said gruffly. 'And don't get me wrong, I don't need them to, it's just, well. It's nice to hear.'

He caught Ditty's gaze and saw something in her eye he thought he recognised. Was it affection? Or was he simply fooling himself, making him believe there was something between them?

'You should celebrate, you know,' she said softly, and to Henry's astonishment, she actually reached out and squeezed his hand. 'Why not do something nice on Val-entine's Day?'

Henry's head spun. *She couldn't mean—*

'Obviously I'll be gone by then, but I'm sure you could do something nice here, at the Lodge.'

Ditty's hand left his and her words made his heart

sink. *Of course. She was just being polite*, Henry tried to tell himself. *There was no more in it than that.*

'Yes, maybe,' he said, as briskly as he could. 'Why don't you go and see how Mavis and Avril are doing? I'm… I'm very busy here.'

Chapter Thirteen

February 5: 7 days until the proposal

Ditty looked out across the tens, no, the hundreds of champagne flutes, and sighed.

'Don't despair!' said Charles cheerfully.

She glanced over and tried not to smile. In many ways, he and his brother were very different, but there was something deep within that was very similar. Their ability to look at a problem and just see the possibilities for solutions was second to none. Their ability to get people on side, to see the best in people.

She certainly did not share his enthusiasm.

'It's a lot of work,' Ditty said helplessly.

'And I have complete faith in you, though now I come to think of it, I need to head back to the law office,' said Charles, glancing at his watch. 'What a shame.'

What a shame indeed. Ditty would never have agreed to doing this if she had known she would be doing it alone.

On the dining table of Charles Paisley's house, every

single surface was covered in champagne flutes. Every. Single. Inch. It was a good thing Miss Yorke had decided to extend her trip, Charles had explained. His fiancée wasn't going to be impressed by the state of his home.

'How many did you say there were, again?' Ditty asked weakly, her head spinning.

'Oh, at least three hundred, but to be honest I cannot remember ever bothering to count them,' said her client nonchalantly. 'Whenever we needed more for larger events, the Valentine's Day Festival, other things, I just bought more, and—'

'Here we are,' completed Ditty.

Well, it was her own fault, in a way. She had included in his proposal plan that after he had successfully completed his proposal, the townsfolk would come out and celebrate with them. That had made a lot more sense when the proposal was going to be held at Reg's, of course. He had his own glassware.

'I like the pink ribbon, very fine,' said Charles approvingly.

Ditty perked up a bit. She didn't think of herself as a particularly proud woman, but it was nice to be appreciated for one's hard work. 'You really like it?'

'Miss Yorke's favourite colour,' he said confidently. 'She'll love it.'

A warm glow flickered in Ditty's stomach. *And that's why I do this*, she reminded herself. Even when it was hard, even when fireworks still weren't delivered, even when people wrote untrue things about her in the newspaper.

It was for moments like this—or at least, the moment it would be once Miss Yorke realised how much her new betrothed cared about her.

'And you have been practicing your speech?' she said, leaning against the back of a chair.

For some unknown reason, Charles was suddenly unable to catch her eye. 'Speech?'

'Your proposal speech,' Ditty said severely. *Surely he had not forgotten!* 'I sent you the template, you should have filled it in by now. To be honest, I was expecting you to show it to me for approval.'

As Charles stammered, trying to tell her he had been very busy at the office, Ditty felt…strange.

She had said those words before. *I sent you the template, you should have filled it in by now.* Had often said them; men were not often very good at considering how they would like to tell the love of their life precisely how much they cared about them.

But somehow it felt…wrong. As though she was a schoolteacher scolding her class. As though she was holding rigidly to a rule that didn't really work.

Ditty shook her head, brushing that thought away.

Honestly! She had a system, and it worked. Why would she want to deviate from that?

'Well, I'd better go—'

'Charles, wait,' Ditty started.

But it was too late. Her client had slipped out of his own dining room, strode across his hall in what sounded like two steps, and—there was the sound of the front door closing.

Ditty sighed, shoulders drooping. Charles had servants, but they were all otherwise engaged, she had inquired the moment she had arrived. That meant she had around three hundred champagne flutes before her, a large roll of ribbon and a pair of scissors. *All* she had to do was cut off a length of ribbon about ten inches, wrap it around the champagne flute stem so it was completely covered in ribbon, then tie it with a bow.

Over, and over, and over again...

Well, there was no point complaining about it, Ditty thought as she rolled up her sleeves. This was part of the matchmaking life. It wasn't all exciting colour coding and time schedule mapping.

Sometimes, you had to be a little bored.

And it was boring. The dull repetition of measuring out the ribbon, cutting it carefully on a diagonal to prevent fraying, and the slow delicate winding of the ribbon around the champagne flutes was, in truth, rather hypnotising. Ditty wasn't sure how long she had been at it before she heard a noise, but it made her head jerk up— and the source of the noise made her mouth fall open.

'Well,' said Henry slowly, a broad smile on his face. 'You're robbing my brother's house, fine...but decorating first?'

Ditty had to laugh. 'Me, a burglar?'

'Yes, I didn't have you down as someone who would be so blatant,' he said, shrugging off his greatcoat and throwing it to the floor.

He hadn't been raised to be a duke, Ditty reminded

herself. In many ways, he was just like her. They would have been equals—

But not anymore.

'You were the one who accused me of being, what was it, a charlatan? Trying to steal money from your brother?'

A flicker of excitement rushed through Ditty's chest as she saw Henry bring a hand to his heart and mimic being wounded.

Why was it she felt so—so alive whenever she was with this man?

'I would have thought I'd be the one offended!' she teased, finishing off a ribbon bow on a champagne glass. 'I'm the one whose character has been besmirched!'

'Well, I was wrong,' Henry said simply, stepping toward her. 'What are you doing?'

But Ditty couldn't reply to the innocent question. She was too astonished. 'Did you just apologise to me?'

Henry's forehead wrinkled into a frown as he stood on the opposite side of the dining table. 'No.'

'Yes, you—well, you admitted you were wrong,' Ditty pointed out.

Was that why her heart was beating so fast? Was that why she couldn't stop looking at Henry? At the way the whole room seemed to soften now he was in it?

Do not think about that kiss, do not feel hot, do not feel your knees quiver—

He shrugged, and she tried not to notice just how broad his shoulders were. 'I suppose that's a compromise. I won't apologise, for I thought what I was doing was right, but I was wrong.'

Ditty looked at him, and he looked back, frown gone and smile dancing on his lips. Her stomach lurched, but it was not an unpleasant sensation.

The champagne flute slipped from her fingers.

'Careful!' Henry lunged across the table and caught the precious glass-ware, placing it delicately down as Ditty's heart pounded.

'Thank you, that could have been— I am not a burglar,' Ditty said in a rush.

It was astonishing; that single moment of panic, when she thought she would be handing over hundreds of pounds to pay for the replacement of the champagne flutes—she was certain Charles would want a matching set—did not seem to have disappeared.

Quite to the contrary. Her heart was still beating wildly, a strange fluttering moving down her chest and across her back, right to her fingertips.

Ditty swallowed. She needed to say something. It was, after all, strange to be found in someone's house with their glass-ware all over the place.

'Champagne flutes,' she said helplessly.

Henry's lips quirked into a smile. 'Yes, I can see that. Finally getting into the Brexley spirit and helping out with the Valentine's Day Festival?'

Ditty's stomach twisted. She wouldn't be here for the festival. 'No, I'll be gone by then.'

'Oh, yes,' Henry said nonchalantly, as though he'd completely forgotten.

How had she managed to forget?

'So what are all these for?'

'For the proposal. Charles's proposal, your brother's proposal.'

For some reason Henry looked surprised. 'Oh… I see. How many people are you expecting at this thing?'

Ditty could not understand why he did not look excited. It was in a week exactly, after all! 'Well, your brother said something about the whole town—'

'And…you trusted him to invite people?' Henry said cautiously.

Ditty opened her mouth, hesitated, then closed it.

Well, yes, she did. She had. Charles was the client, he was the one who had lived in Brexley almost all his life. He was the one who knew everyone, who might wish to avoid inviting certain people over others.

Was it not entirely natural for her to leave it to him?

But just one glance at Henry's face told her in unequivocal terms, she had made a mistake. *Another one to add to the list…*

Ditty groaned. 'No one has been invited, have they?'

'Well, *I* certainly haven't,' said Henry with a broad grin. 'You'd think I'd be the first to know, would you not?'

Ditty raised a hand to her face. 'You're jesting with me!'

'I'm afraid I am not!' For some reason the man looked too cheerful. 'But I wouldn't worry about it.'

Dropping her hand, she looked at him as though he was delusional. 'Don't worry—I have less than a week, still no food to serve at this proposal, the fireworks aren't here and now hundreds of invitations—'

'Leave the invitations to me, I know everyone in this town,' said Henry smoothly.

Ditty blinked.

It was odd, to allow part of the planning to leave her hands, but she could not deny Henry was right. He did know everyone, far better than she did. He could arrange it all without much fuss, without getting Miss Yorke suspicious. If she started to suspect…

'You're sure about this?' she asked slowly. 'I, well, I would have thought you had enough to be getting on with, at the Lodge.'

There it was again. The same odd expression she had noticed the last time they had spoken, in his study—the same panic, and then repression of that panic. *What was going on?*

'Leave it with me. It will be nice to have something to distract—to take my mind off—' Henry cleared his throat. 'Leave it with me.'

She hesitated. She was never one to burden someone with her problems, and though Henry hadn't shared his own, it couldn't be denied that he seemed to have many. Something was weighing on him, something he clearly had no wish to tell her.

Unless…unless that was why he was here. Her heart leapt. *Had he come here looking for her?*

Almost as though he had read her mind, he said briskly, 'Now, where's that brother of mine?'

Ditty tried not to notice just how disappointed she

was. After she had rejected his advance, she shouldn't really have expected Henry to want to continue as they had been. Besides, she would be gone in a week, she reminded herself. This was not a town where she could build a life—not enough people to arrange their proposals, for a start!

'He's back at his law office, pretending to be working on his proposal speech,' she said with a mischievous grin. 'But as you are at a loose end, and I happen to be buried in ribbon…'

Ditty looked pointedly out at the myriad of champagne flutes.

Henry chuckled. 'You are not going to—'

'All I'm asking for is half an hour of your time,' Ditty declared, excitement rushing through her at the thought of spending another half an hour alone with Henry. 'Please?'

He met her eyes, then groaned. 'Fine! But I warn you, I'm going to be about as good at this as you are at being spontaneous.'

'You are fortunate there are champagne flutes and a table between us, Henry, for I do not take kindly to that remark,' Ditty said with a laugh that was accompanied by a rush of desire.

A desire she should definitely not be feeling.

'Like this?' Henry held out what he considered to be a perfectly ribboned champagne flute.

Ditty glanced up from the bow she was making on

one of her own. 'That's—that's perfect. How did you
do that?'

'You spend a term at medical school learning how
to sew up patients, I promise you'll soon be a master at
tying ribbon,' he said dryly.

Her laughter filled the dining room, but more, it filled
Henry's heart.

It was so simple. Two people in a room, not even
touching, completing a task together.

So why did it fill him with more joy than he could remember sharing with another person? Why did he not
want this half hour to end?

In truth, he had intentionally not looked at the long-
case clock or his pocket-watch. He didn't want to be reminded he was due back at the Lodge in a few hours.
He wanted to spend the time with her. Ditty.

As the chance for more hours with her slipped away,
he had to make the most of each one.

'Well, I should have asked you to help me with this
days ago,' said Ditty with a grin. 'Who knew you'd be
such a master?'

Henry grinned, her praise doing something strange
to the tension in his chest. When he was with her—
especially when he and Ditty were not at the Lodge—
he could forget all the troubles he'd left there.

Well, almost. The tension in his body never seemed to
completely disappear, but for moments, he could forget.

'And I really must track down some fireworks,' she
said vaguely.

Henry looked up. 'Fireworks?'

'I placed my order days ago, but apparently unless you live in London, nothing can be done swiftly or on time,' Ditty said with a wry smile.

It was difficult to return it. Yes, Brexley was a little out of the way. But it was home. It was everything he had ever wanted. For a time, he had hoped—thought that Georgiana had understood it. The last few days had made him hope that Ditty would.

But would the lure of London always tempt away a woman like Ditty?

'Now, why don't you tell me what's eating at you?' she said calmly, placing her beribboned champagne flute onto the dining table.

Henry was about to do the same with his own, but his hand halted and he looked up at her with concern.

What had she heard?

'I don't know what you mean,' he gambled, hoping it was a lucky guess.

Ditty examined him calmly; no judgement, no anger, but also no willingness to look away.

'Don't give me that guff,' she said quietly. 'You've helped me, and I would like to help you. I don't need to have lived in Brexley my whole life to know there's something wrong up at your Lodge.'

Henry swallowed. How on earth had she noticed?

'Perhaps it's because I haven't lived here for an age that I see it,' she mused aloud, almost directly answering his question. 'I would hazard a guess that most people here haven't noticed the place getting more and more run-down, haven't wondered why you've not repaired anything.'

Panic started to rush through Henry's chest. She had noticed—and if she noticed, it wouldn't be long before others did.

What would they say? Would they think he was a bad doctor, a bad duke? Would they criticise him, demand he—

'It's only literally this moment I realised,' said Ditty, a sad smile now creasing her lips. 'Oh, Henry. What happened?'

He glanced at his hands. They were doctor's hands. His tutor had said one of the benefits of being a doctor was that they'd always be warm, always be whole, cared for. They'd never know true hardship.

Look at them now. Calluses, a small cut where a splinter had to be dug out. These were hands that worked an honest day's job, and he was proud of that.

But he couldn't keep doing this on his own.

Henry took a deep breath. 'It's… You're right. I don't know how you managed to see it, but there's no money.'

Ditty frowned, as though what he said didn't make any sense. 'What do you mean, no money?'

'I mean we're in debt up to our eyeballs, and I don't have any money to buy food for next week,' Henry said blandly. In a weird way, it was almost a relief to be saying it out loud. 'We seem to owe everyone money, and the place is getting more damp and decrepit with every passing week. I've not replaced five members of staff as they've left and yet I still—'

'I don't understand. Is it—is it truly that bad?'

He cringed at the empathy in her voice. She would never see him in the same way again once she knew, he thought dully.

She had respected him, perhaps even admired him. Admired not just the title of duke, but the man he was. Not as much as he admired her, he was certain, but just having her respect had been something to buoy him up through the hard days.

But now she was looking at him in dismay. 'But how did this happen?'

Henry swallowed. It was difficult, he was discovering, being vulnerable.

Usually other people were vulnerable with him. It was part and parcel of being a doctor; people told you their greatest fears, shared their symptoms with you and sometimes had to hear bad news.

But now that it was the other way around, he was finding it rather difficult.

He looked up at Ditty and saw nothing but compassion in her eyes. His fear subsided. No matter what, she would not judge him. She might even be able to help. But no. No one could help. He would have spotted a way if it were possible.

'I don't honestly know,' Henry said truthfully. 'Well, you've seen what I'm like with paperwork,' he then quipped, trying to add a little lightness.

A wry smile slipped across her lips. 'I have indeed.'

'But that happened after—I mean, I wasn't able to replace my clerk before the paperwork started piling up, so it's not like the answer is in there,' he said defensively.

Ditty stepped away from the dining table and to the doorway leading to the drawing room. 'Come and tell me all about it.'

Henry hesitated. And then he did.

The two of them on the sofa, he poured out all the fears, the panic, the bills unpaid, the tabs building up with Brexley townsfolk, all of it. How when he had inherited the duchy he had opened the Lodge in grand expectation of riches, waited for the solicitor to dazzle him with the new income that would be his own now that he was the Duke of Glanyrafon…and the shock he had experienced to discover the duchy was instead in grievous debt.

With each sentence he uttered, it was as though he was drawing poison from a wound. Everything he shared seemed to lessen the weight on his own shoulders. Every detail he recounted seemed to relieve him of the burden.

And Ditty sat there, sympathetic and listening carefully, as he had never imagined anyone would.

The few times he had considered trying to tell someone about the mess he had inherited, the only thing he could imagine was judgement. In his very worst nightmares, his residents would all have to be separated, leave Brexley…and the town would turn on him.

But looking into Ditty's eyes, seeing her compassion and her genuine concern calmed him in a way he could never have imagined.

'…and that's about it,' Henry said heavily, coming to

the end of what felt like the most despairing of mono-
logues. 'And if I don't do something soon—'

'Why are you telling me this now?'

He swallowed. It was a reasonable question. 'I didn't
feel like I knew you before.' It was more than that. If it
was simply about knowing her then he could have con-
fided in anyone in Brexley.

Ditty's cheeks flushed. 'And…and you do now?'

'I do,' said Henry, a strange feeling cascading down
his spine. 'And what's more, I like what I've found. I
like you, Ditty.'

The words seemed to echo around Charles's drawing room, sounding foolish, almost childlike. He braced
himself for a rebuttal, for Ditty to awkwardly pull away,
to move from the sofa and make it entirely clear she had
no wish for him to think of her in that way.

She did not move. She did smile, and her cheeks dark-
ened in colour. 'I… I like you, too, Henry.'

They stared at each other for a moment, facing each
other as they sat twisted on the sofa, and he wished
he knew what to do next. Did she understand what he
meant? His 'like' was far more than the pedestrian like
of a friend, even if this affection he felt could not go
anywhere.

Did she mean the same thing?

'You need to balance the books,' she said firmly. 'If
there's one thing I've learnt about business, it's that if
you don't have enough coming in to cover what's going
out, you're in trouble.'

'I've been in trouble since I have inherited the blasted

thing,' said Henry wearily. 'That's the problem—I've tried to cover it up for so long, I forgot how to ask for help. But even so, I can't just ask Brexley people to forgive my tab, or the coal merchant to hand over coal without payment, or—'

'No, I don't suppose you can,' said Ditty, biting her lip.

He watched her with a growing appreciation. She had that look about her, that creative, problem-solving, excited look she had when ideas were coming to her.

There was something to really admire about the way Ditty thought. He watched, fascinated, as she carefully considered all he had said, and then started to put her mind to work.

'I don't suppose you could ask your residents for an increase in fees?' she suggested hesitantly. 'If I know anything about you, Henry, you barely charge them a thing.'

He grinned. 'Hardly a bean. But most of my residents couldn't afford to stay in Brexley, where they've lived all their lives, if I put up the fees. Besides…'

His voice trailed away and she gave him a mock severe look. 'Henry Paisley, you're not charging all of them, are you?'

'What, me?' he said innocently.

'Are you charging any of them?'

Henry grinned. He was unceremoniously hit with a cushion. 'Ouch!'

'Henry Paisley, you are far too wonderful for your own good!' Ditty said with a laugh.

He caught the cushion she was hitting him with, and

his fingers brushed against her own. 'Do you really think so?'

For a moment, he thought she was going to lean forward and—

But the moment passed before it had really arrived, and she was shaking her head. 'You are a good man, but you cannot just home people for no money, forever!'

His shoulders sagged. Finally letting himself feel the weight of it all. 'I've tried everything, Ditty. Everything. I promise you, if there was anything that could be done, I would have done it already. I just have to accept—'

'Ah,' she said with a broad smile, pulling her notebook toward her. 'But you haven't had me here, though, have you?'

Chapter Fourteen

February 6: 6 days until the proposal

Ditty almost buzzed with excitement. 'Yes, please, carry it on through—no, those need to go to the kitchen, not the card room!'

It was absolute pandemonium and she was discovering, rather to her surprise, she wouldn't have it any other way.

'What are your orders, Admiral?' asked Brian, saluting before her.

Ditty giggled. 'You don't have to salute, Brian.'

'Wouldn't dare not give the respect deserved by my superior officer,' said Brian, though he winked as he spoke. 'Where do you want me?'

As it happened, Ditty could use an additional hand unpacking in the card room, so she sent him on his way.

As she stood in the Lodge's hall, everyone bustling, laughter and chatter filling the old place, Ditty realised three things she had never expected.

Firstly, she liked ordering people about.

Well, she probably should have known that. She ordered people about as a proposal planner, but most of the time it was a huge effort to get her clients to do what she wanted, and she was constantly juggling the stress of the musicians, artists, restaurants, locations…

But this? This was easy. Every single resident had loved her idea and immediately asked how they could help. That was why Mavis was organising the kitchen and Avril the craft room, all getting ready for the big day.

'Over here, was it?' asked Jim, holding a huge wooden love heart.

'Oh, Jim, that is beautiful!' Ditty sighed.

It was magnificent. Woven with willow, the heart was about two feet wide and looked stunning.

'In the drawing room, please,' she called after him.

The second thing she'd realised was that it was pleasant to organise something that wasn't about matrimony.

Not that this wasn't about love. Ditty had never felt more love in one place. When she had told Henry he had to tell the people at the Lodge the truth, she had never seen him look more horrified. But he had conceded that she was right.

For a horrible moment when he had made the announcement, Ditty had thought she had been wrong to think that the residents would rally around him. There had been a mutinous silence. But then—

What can we do to help? Mavis and Avril had asked together.

Yes, there was love in this place. The Lodge absolutely

buzzed with it, everyone wanting to play their part, to help their doctor. Their duke. Their friend.

Ditty beamed as she watched a pair of elderly gentlemen slowly carry through bunting. It might not be romantic love driving this place, but it was most definitely love.

And the third, and perhaps this was the most important revelation—

'There you are,' said Henry, grinning as he carried a heavy box. 'Who would have thought, eh?'

Ditty grinned. 'I did.'

It had all seemed so simple when she started to think about the practicalities.

So Henry had this huge Lodge and manor house elsewhere on the estate, and couldn't pay for the upkeep. Fine. Every town needed somewhere to gather for balls, celebrations, splendid occasions, and Brexley itself was crying out for a large location for its Valentine's Day festivities. It all felt so obvious when Ditty had tried to explain it to Henry.

'Host a ball—at the Lodge?'

'Not a ball—well, kind of a ball,' Ditty had admitted. 'A Valentine's Day–themed ball, for the whole town.'

She had seen the panic in Henry's eyes. 'But the place is falling apart!'

'We don't have to use the wing which is more dilapidated,' she had said hastily, trying to reassure him. 'The hall, the drawing room, the craft room, the card room— that is more than enough space.'

Henry had not been easily convinced. 'Why on earth

would anyone from the town want to come up to the Lodge—and before Valentine's Day? Everyone will be getting ready for the visitors.'

But Ditty had already thought of that.

'Ditty, we're almost done,' said Avril smartly.

Both she and Henry turned to her.

'You—you are?' Ditty said in surprise.

She had expected, in truth, for that part of organising the ball to take forever.

Avril beamed. 'Never underestimate a woman over the age of sixty, my dear. Yes, all the crafts are done.'

Henry looked between her and Ditty. 'You're really going to make this work, aren't you?'

Ditty glowed. It was foolish of course, to be so delighted she had impressed him; but if she were truly honest with herself, a huge part of her plan was designed to do just that.

Impressing Henry felt important, kisses or no kisses.

Even if she was spending today getting entirely distracted from the proposal she should be planning…

'I'll put them all together on the table Jim's set up in the craft room,' said Avril confidently, evidently not needing to be instructed on the subject. 'Come on, ladies.'

Ditty watched with an amused smile as Avril bustled forward, a trail of at least eight women, some holding knitting needles, some holding darning mushrooms, following her.

'Walk with me,' murmured Henry in Ditty's ear.

She shivered at the sudden close contact, but to her

great disappointment it did not last. He buttoned up his greatcoat as he stepped outside the Lodge and with only a moment of hesitation, she followed.

It was freezing outside, but she was warmed, either thanks to her pelisse or by the smile Henry gave her. She wasn't sure which.

'You are a marvel, you know,' he said warmly as he started to walk around the Lodge.

She fell in step with him. 'Well, I don't know about that.'

'I do, and I will be forever grateful to you,' came his quiet voice. 'I don't know where you get your ideas from. To be honest there's so much to take in, I can hardly think straight.'

Ditty laughed as their footsteps crunched on the frozen ground. 'It really isn't that difficult. A Brexley Lodge for Gentlemen and Ladies of a Certain Age Valentine's Day Ball.'

'Isn't that a bit of a mouthful?'

She shrugged. 'Memorable, though, isn't it?'

He grinned. 'And you really think we need to go the whole hog?'

'Most definitely,' she said firmly. Based on what Henry had told her, they had to make money. And fast.

'I like the theme.'

Ditty beamed. 'The Last Century?'

'A time my residents remember, or just about,' Henry said with a laugh. 'You'll be bored silly by Emmeline's memories, I'm afraid. She's got an almost encyclopaedic recollection of Brexley from that time.'

Ditty stepped closer to Henry. She could not help herself; he was so tantalisingly close. As they walked, their hands almost brushed against each other. Her pulse quickened.

'Musicians, dancing, favourite treats from that time—Mavis has promised marvels in that kitchen of yours,' she said as they turned around the west side of the Lodge and started along the south side, where there used to be kitchen gardens. 'And that reminds me, why don't you use the kitchen gardens anymore?'

Henry stared as though she had lost her mind. 'What?'

'These kitchen gardens,' she said, waving toward them. 'They'd be perfect for growing your own fruit and veg, then you wouldn't have to buy them.'

It had seemed an obvious idea, but evidently Henry had never considered it before. 'Well, we had a gardener, but when he accepted a job with the Marquess of Jutland, we—'

'Never replaced him,' chorused Ditty with a grin. 'I don't understand you sometimes—you've got a lodge full of people!'

'We can't put them to work,' Henry protested.

She nudged him, warmth spiralling up her arm as she did so. 'I'm not saying that! I'm just saying, there must be people who loved gardening in their own homes. They may enjoy having the challenge of a vegetable patch. You could make it a competition—a community project, really bring them together.'

Excitement suffused through every word, but Ditty

could not help it. There was so much potential here, so many opportunities.

'You're just made of ideas, aren't you?'

She glanced up but Henry was not teasing her. He seemed in earnest.

'I mean, this ball—a raffle, love heart biscuits, donations, a dance, all to raise funds for the Lodge,' said Henry softly as they continued on to the southeastern corner. 'Ideas just spring from you like a fountain, don't they?'

She flushed. 'It is how I earn a living for myself and my family.'

Her family. When was the last time she had written to her sisters—and wasn't their mama due to return from Brighton? She had become so easily distracted by this duke.

'You're a proposal planner, not...not whatever this is,' Henry pointed out. 'I'm surprised you didn't think of doing that, to be honest. I am sure St James Court needs someone about the place to organise balls and the like.'

'I suppose so. I suppose dukes do, as well.'

Henry's cheeks burned. Perhaps he had never thought of that. Most dukes would have a housekeeper who would orchestrate events like this—dukes who had been raised to it from the very day they were born. Dukes who inherited an income, not just debts and responsibility.

She shrugged, hoping he would think she had missed his moment of discomfort. 'I gain happiness from seeing people who love each other come together, make promises to each other.'

Why did those words feel so heavy with meaning? She tried not to catch his eye, but it was as though Henry was trying to catch hers.

Warmth rushed through her. Oh, she liked him. She more than liked him.

And what's more, I like what I've found. I like you, Ditty.

I... I like you, too, Henry.

He wasn't to know she meant that in an entirely different way. Ditty couldn't bring herself to reveal all, it would be too excruciating to hear his embarrassed stammers that he had not meant it like that. She enjoyed his company, yes. Her heart leapt when she was with him, yes, and some of the dreams she'd been having lately...

Well, she knew the practicalities of lovemaking, but had presumed she would likely never know them after Thomas had ended their courtship. Yet, if her dreams lately were anything to go by, she was missing out on a great deal.

'There's a lot of love here, I suppose,' Henry said, gesturing around the Lodge.

Ditty smiled weakly. After so long, she could never have thought a small town would once again capture her heart. She had fought it at first, but it had snuck up on her. The feeling of belonging. 'Yes, and I think it's time the town of Brexley showed our elders just how much they are loved. We're nothing, after all, without each other.'

As she said these words, her hand brushed up against his accidently. At least, it was accidental on her side.

Ditty tried to push away the hope that it was purpose-ful from him.

Henry wouldn't do anything silly like try to take her hand in his. He wasn't foolish like that.

'Well, I am very impressed,' he said quietly. 'And grateful. Thank you.'

Henry swallowed. He'd had to speak, it was impossi-ble to keep this much gratitude inside. He watched Ditty smile with pleasure at his words. Not because *he'd* said them, but because they were a compliment.

Was he fooling himself, wishing she could be happy it was he, Henry Paisley, who was grateful to her?

'I didn't think you'd be here so much,' he found him-self saying.

A crease appeared between Ditty's forehead as she halted in her tracks. 'Would you rather I wasn't here?'

'No! No, not at all,' he said hastily. *He was such an idiot!* 'No, I just meant—well, with my brother's pro-posal coming up—'

'Oh, that's almost completely planned,' said Ditty with a smile. 'I've still got to work out one problem, but I'm sure it'll sort itself. When the time is right.'

When the time is right. Henry looked at her, stand-ing right before him, perhaps only two feet away, and swallowed.

With each passing day, he had started to wonder whether the time would ever be right. Right for him to try to explain what Ditty was starting to mean to him. Right to explain that the kiss they had shared had not been a mistake, but was instead precisely what he wanted. Right to tell her how he felt.

If he could ever untangle that for himself, of course.

But whenever he thought maybe this was the right time, the words simply did not come. Nothing seemed to make sense except Ditty, and his heart fluttered, and his stomach lurched, and his fingers tingled because he wanted to take her into his arms…

He swallowed. He had never given much thought to this proposal template of hers. Charles had only mentioned it a few times, and each time, Henry had scoffed.

It did not seem so foolish now. Having a template sounded ideal.

'You aren't worried about it, then?' he forced himself to say, continuing the conversation. 'Charles's proposal, that is?'

She chuckled as she shook her head, her hair fluttering in the light breeze. 'No, not in the slightest. I am a proposal planner, I know what I'm doing.'

'I didn't say you—'

'And besides, the only loose cannon right now is your brother himself,' she added. 'If he doesn't show me his proposal speech based on my template soon, I'm going to have to march over there and demand it!'

She laughed, and Henry tried to laugh with her.

He was running out of time. A week, that was all Ditty had to spend in Brexley.

A lot could change in a week, Henry knew. But could it change enough? Could he change enough, have the bravery to say something…to ask her to stay in Brexley?

You know how well that went last time, a voice in his head reminded him. *Do you really think you have anything better to offer? Except more bills?*

He cleared his throat. 'It's a good idea. The kitchen garden.'

Ditty beamed and turned to look at the abandoned garden. 'I think you'll find some real treasures in that Lodge of yours, people who would love the idea of a challenge.'

His gaze flickered over her as she looked out at the kitchen garden. Once again he could see her creativity rising to the fore, her passion for planning and organisation creating ideas in her mind.

'You could organise it.'

She turned in astonishment. 'What did you say?'

Henry half wished he had not said anything at all, but he could not back down now. Even if he wanted to. 'I mean, it wouldn't take long to organise, would it? I know you're only here for a few more days...'

And that was when his bravery ran out.

All the light in Ditty's eyes vanished. 'Oh. Oh, yes, I had forgotten I'll be back in London in a week.'

She sounded almost surprised, as though she truly had forgotten, and it caused hope to rise in his chest.

Perhaps she wasn't entirely wedded to returning to London? Perhaps, just perhaps, she could be persuaded to stay.

'I'd better see what's going on in there,' Ditty said into the awkward silence.

She took a step forward to return to the hall, but then she suddenly halted.

For an instant, Henry wasn't sure why. Then he realised his own hand had reached out and grabbed her arm, stopping her in her tracks.

She looked slowly at his hand on her arm. He looked at it, too. Why did this feel so special? This small intimacy, this tiny show of affection? Did she understand what he was trying to tell her, to show her?

'Henry?' she said, uncertainly.

He swallowed. 'I—I just wanted to say, before we went in…'

His traitorous voice hesitated, leaving him abandoned as Ditty stood so close to him, his hand still on her arm. Was it his imagination or had her breath caught in her throat? Was her breathing short?

'Yes?' she whispered, looking into his eyes.

This is it, Henry tried to tell himself. *This is the perfect moment to tell her. To say something, anything, about how much you admire her. How much you like her.*

How you think that 'like' might be growing into—

'I just wanted to say…to say how impressed I am. With what you're doing, I mean. Here at the Lodge—in such a short amount of time. It's impressive. I'm impressed, with you.'

He couldn't do it. If she didn't feel the same, he'd never recover. Not a second time.

He hastily dropped Ditty's arm. His fingers burned where they had touched her pelisse, and it might have been nothing, but he thought she stretched her arm as though she had been similarly burned.

'Thank you,' she said softly. 'I think.'

Henry tried again. 'I really think you're very good. At what you do, I mean. Matchmaking. Planning.'

There was a mischievous sparkle in her eyes. 'I thought you said I shouldn't plan.'

'Preparing, then,' he said, returning her smile. 'I'm impressed. With you.'

Why oh why did he have to keep saying that?

But there was something in the air. He could not describe it, even if he had the time to think with Ditty standing before him, making his knees weak and his heart sing.

Something to do with Valentine's Day, perhaps, or the approach of spring. Something fresh, exciting, vibrant in the air that made him feel as though anything was possible. As though all he had to do was reach out and—

'Well, what else are proposal planners good for?' she said with a self-deprecating smile. 'Creating romance from a formula.'

'It's so much more than that, and you know it,' said Henry fiercely. 'What you're doing here—it's wonderful.'

In truth, he had not quite believed her plan would be possible when she had talked him through it the first time. A huge ball with music, food, dancing, craft sale, raffle—

It was almost finished, and in a day. Ditty Oliver was a precious gift, and the fact she didn't know it confused him greatly.

Not that he had managed to tell her with any sort of coherence.

'Well, it's what I'm good at. What I'm good for.'

Henry took a step forward. He knew he probably shouldn't, knew closing the gap between them would only lead to more heartache later, but he couldn't help it. He had to be near her.

'You are good at so many things, you know,' he murmured. 'You're good for so many things, and you…you deserve to find love yourself.'

The words had poured from his lips without any thought but Henry did not care. She had to know. Whether she realised just how deep his affections were, or whether—far more likely—she returned to London and found someone there to love her…

What mattered was that Ditty was loved.

Henry swallowed. 'I mean it.'

'I know you do,' she said softly. 'But you're just saying that because—'

Henry held his breath. *Well, this was it.* He should have known being so open, so honest, would mean Ditty would realise what he was truly trying to say.

He was an open book to her, after all. Had she not worked out the secret money troubles he had managed to keep from the rest of the town for months?

'—because I'm saving the day,' Ditty finished, with a grin.

He laughed. It was more a sigh of relief than a laugh, but he managed to make it sound natural. Almost. 'I suppose so! But still. Thank you.'

She leaned forward and for a moment, just a moment, he thought she was going to embrace him. A cherished moment that would have been, but instead she rested her palm on his cheek.

Henry's chest tightened. It was such an intimate gesture, a closeness he had not shared with her before, it quite took his breath away.

His eyes met hers. And the world shifted, the ground underneath him lurched, and the world was spinning, the only thing in it staying still was Ditty. She was looking at him in a way that made him sure they were going to—her lips were moving forward—they were going to kiss. He couldn't stop it even if he had wanted to, and Henry most certainly did not want to. This time their kiss was slow, reverential, glorifying in every moment, the pressure of her lips strong on his as she returned the ardour that he poured down onto them.

Henry tugged her into his embrace and she whimpered, and the noise flared fire down his body as his manhood stiffened, ready, eager to—

'Henry? Henry, where are you?'

He and Ditty sprang apart.

'I've been looking all over for you,' said Mavis severely, her hands thrust into her apron pocket. 'I am entirely out of sugar and I need one of you to—'

'Yes, I can do that,' said Ditty hastily, stepping toward the irate baker and leaving Henry standing there. 'What kind do you need?'

He tried to collect himself. He'd kissed Ditty. She'd kissed him in return. And yet once again there was no conversation about staying, not from her and not from him.

Chapter Fifteen

February 10: 2 days until the proposal

Ditty took a deep breath.

When she had joked about making a stage for the musicians, she hadn't actually expected Brian, Jim and other residents of the Lodge—including Emmeline—to create one in under a day.

What this place needs, she couldn't help but think, is a woodwork club.

And it was definitely a stage outside the Lodge. And she was definitely standing on it, with what appeared to be most of the town of Brexley before her.

Faces, all crowded together, looking up at her. All those eyes, focused on her.

Ditty swallowed. She wasn't really a public speaker. Her work was always with an individual, just one client. He was the one that made the speeches.

Besides, she so rarely wore a gown of this quality. Mrs Fletcher had insisted, as Ditty had left her formal ball gowns back in London, that she lend her lodger one—

and Ditty had to admit, the bodice swept far lower than she had expected, colour far richer than she normally wore.

Someone cleared their throat, obviously waiting, and she flushed. She looked at her hands, where her notes for her speech were held, then back up at the people before her.

At Henry.

He was standing right at the front of the crowd, wearing a cravat with a pin and a matching waistcoat, and he was smiling. His smile made warmth rush through her, and before Ditty knew what she was doing, she grinned back.

He was here.

Of course he was. This was his event—well, *their* event.

'Ladies and gentlemen!' Ditty called out, ignoring her notes and just letting the passion for this event fuel her. 'I am delighted to welcome you to the inaugural Brexley Lodge for Gentlemen and Ladies of a Certain Age Valentine's Day Ball!'

Henry led a roaring cheer which was swiftly taken up by the crowd. Ditty grinned, heart fluttering, and forced herself to look away. She couldn't just stand here gawping.

As she did so, she caught sight of faces she recognised: Miss Vivienne the florist, Mrs Fletcher, the man from the bookmakers, the grocer, the baker and his wife, Vicar Melview, who looked delighted. They all grinned, and Reg put two thumbs up.

Ditty beamed. It was strange. There was something about Brexley; the town seemed to sweep you up into its arms and offer you a place to belong, in a way London never had done. Even the small town where she and her sisters had grown up had not felt like this.

'This place is a symbol of everything good about this town,' Ditty said, her voice carrying over the lawn as the crowd quietened. 'It's full of love, and laughter, and wisdom. This day is to celebrate that love, show each other how much we love being a part of Brexley, and raise a donation to help Henry—help His Grace—help Dr. Paisley continue his great work.'

She caught his eye and grinned at the obvious discomfort he felt by having his name mentioned.

But it was impossible not to. Even if she didn't feel this way about him, Ditty knew it was due to the town's affection for the doctor that they were all here.

'Hear! Hear!' cried a voice that sounded remarkably like Mavis.

'Couldn't agree more!' called Avril, evidently not willing to be outdone.

'I know you have always rallied around and supported each other,' said Ditty, feeling a twinge of envy. 'Though Henry has tried to carry this burden on his own...'

Just for a moment she smiled, and he smiled back, and the whole world seemed to quiver. He had done so much alone, but *she* had been the one he'd reached out to for help.

For a strange reason, that made her feel awfully warm inside.

'Today's ball is a chance to enjoy the day, but also raise some well-needed money to help the Brexley Lodge for Gentlemen and Ladies of a Certain Age,' she continued.

Another cheer rippled through the crowd and she could see people nodding, their children pulling at their arms to enter the Lodge and discover where the delicious smell was coming from.

Her stomach rumbled.

'There is plenty to enjoy and explore inside,' said Ditty, sensing the crowd's eager anticipation. 'So there is nothing more for me to do but declare this Brexley Lodge for Gentlemen and Ladies of a Certain Age Valentine's Day Ball...open!'

Right on cue, Brian and Jim dropped the large ribbon—Henry had advised no scissors be given to either of them—and the crowd cheered once more.

'You know, I can't remember when the town had something like this to look forward to,' said Miss Vivienne as Ditty descended from the stage. 'Excellent work, Ditty!'

'Is that music I hear?' Mrs Fletcher perked up as she entered. 'Oh, I love this piece. Goodness, this takes me back!'

Ditty glowed as she watched the crowd enter. The oohs and aahs of those discovering the musicians stirred her heart.

They had done it. And in only a few days, too—and while she was trying to finish off Charles's proposal.

'You are a triumph.'

Ditty turned and flushed at Henry's praise. 'It's not all me.'

'It was all your idea,' he pointed out with a grin as children scampered past to eat Mavis's goodies. 'All the decorations, the music, the dancing, the food, the raffle—all your vision.'

She shrugged, slightly embarrassed by his praise as the crowd thinned outside the Lodge. 'I just…well, it was just obvious.'

He chuckled. 'Not to the rest of us.'

'I suppose I am just lucky in that way.'

'I think it comes from hard work, and being such a talented proposal planner, and having created so many wonderful matches,' he said quietly.

Ditty glanced up but had to immediately look away. There was something so personal, so vulnerable about how he said that. Was he thinking of his unsuccessful proposal? Was he thinking of their kiss—their kisses, now, which still made her pink whenever she saw him. Was he thinking of his brother's upcoming proposal?

Or was it possible, and her heart quickened at the very thought, Henry could be thinking of…a different proposal? A new one?

Surely not…

A month ago she would have decried it. A year ago she would have told him firmly that she had abandoned romantic love as something too likely to injure.

And now…now Henry had quite altered her hopes for the future, without her even noticing.

A delighted shriek echoed out of the main doors. 'Oh, look at these darling love heart ornaments!'

Ditty giggled. 'I thought Mrs Fletcher would like them. They'd be perfect to put around her front door, really go with—'

'My vision!' came Mrs Fletcher's voice.

Henry shook his head with an expression of awe. 'How on earth do you do it?'

'Do what?' Ditty had not intended to sound defensive as she walked forward into the hall.

Why was she starting to feel so on edge around Henry? It wasn't anything he had done. No, it was her, all her fault. She wanted more, though she didn't have the words to ask.

In just two days, her work here would be complete and Brexley would continue without her. As if, Ditty thought with a lump in her throat, she had never been here.

'How do you do this?' Henry said, throwing out his arms.

Ditty smiled as she took in the sight. The musicians in the drawing room were being enjoyed by people tapping their feet and dancing, and the craft room was doing a raucous sale of all the pretty things the residents had made. She could just about glimpse Mavis telling a child they could have as many biscuits as their parent said, and no more, while Avril fluttered by with a trail of women from the town behind her.

She watched the lively crowd with delight. The ball was going better than she had hoped for, better than she could have planned. Because it wasn't just her efforts which had made this day possible. It was everyone else. It was being able to depend on them to contribute something just as wonderful, if not better, than what she could do herself.

This felt better than every proposal she had ever planned. Combined.

'There she is, the woman of the hour!' Mavis had suddenly appeared by her side and was pulling her away from Henry. 'Miss Ditty Oliver, everyone!'

A great crowd of Brexley residents, both from the town and the Lodge, turned away from the musicians and broke out into applause as she entered the drawing room where the dancing was taking place.

Ditty flushed. She was accustomed to being thanked for her work—well, paid, at the very least—but had never received a round of applause before. It was rather pleasant, though it was Henry's face she sought out. She couldn't see him—where was he?

'It's all thanks to Miss Ditty that today is happening,' said Mavis loudly, pulling her to stand before the musicians. 'And that is why we would like to give you the honour of picking the first winner of the raffle.'

Ditty blinked. 'What?'

'The raffle, young lady,' Mavis said severely, holding out a box which had scraps of paper all folded within it. 'First prize is a dance with our very own Duke of Glanyrafon or our heroine of the hour, Miss Ditty Oliver!'

Cheers went up, mainly from the women in the room,

and from somewhere Henry was pushed to the front to stand beside Ditty.

Her cheeks flushed and she tried not to look at him as she hissed, 'But, Mavis, the event has only just opened, I didn't think we were going to choose the raffle winners until—'

'For some reason, all tickets have already been purchased,' said Mavis blithely. 'Go on. Pick the lucky person who will dance with the Duke.'

And Ditty knew then. She absolutely knew, without a shadow of a doubt, what had happened.

She glanced at Henry, who coloured. So he knew— or at least, had guessed. Oh, those scheming ladies! Did they know no bounds?

'Pick a ticket, Ditty,' said Mavis with a grin. 'I wonder who our winner will be?'

I don't, thought Ditty wearily, and she was quite right. After stuffing a hand into the box and picking out a scrap of paper at random, she showed it to the crowd.

'Eighty-four,' said Mavis, pulling out a notebook from one of her apron pockets and riffling through the pages. 'Would you look at that! Ditty is our winner—she'll dance with the Duke!'

Henry tried to smile, but it took a great deal of effort.

It could not be more obvious Ditty had not even bought a single raffle ticket, and if her hurried whispers to Mavis were any indication, she was not happy about it.

'—can't be seen to be unfair,' she was hissing under

her breath, though it looked like she was being entirely ignored by Mavis. 'I can't draw out my own name!'

'Thems the luck of the draw, my dear,' said Mavis happily.

Henry cleared his throat. 'I didn't actually offer myself as a raffle prize, Mavis.'

'There you are, then!' Ditty said, jabbing a finger at Henry but still not looking at him. 'We can't just start giving away people as prizes if they haven't agreed to it.'

'All for a good cause,' said Mavis calmly, but Henry could not help but notice there was a steely look in her eye.

He sighed. There was no point in arguing with Mavis; he had learned that lesson well. Indeed, it was often easier just to agree with her than try to spend your breath arguing with her.

Besides, it was not exactly a hardship. Ditty had looked pretty the moment he had first clapped eyes on her, but in that gown—it did something peculiar to his loins, that gown, drawing his attention to her swelling bust and the curve of her hips. And the pearls, so elegant and refined, elevating Ditty in a way he had never expected.

Her beauty was unchanged, but seeing her like this was a reminder that she did not belong here. No, Brexley could not contain such a woman. She belonged, Henry thought with a clench of his heart, in the ballrooms of London.

'Now, then, Henry, I'm sure you are delighted to dance with Ditty, aren't you?'

He swallowed. Well, it would be rude to disagree— and truth be told, he was more than a little delighted.

A dance with Ditty was something he could never have hoped for in his wildest dreams, though admittedly his dreams were a little more sensual in nature. It was difficult to think of anything unsensual, after the kisses which had started an affection within him he had no chance of quelling. Those scheming women were far better at trying to find him a wife than he was.

'I would be honoured, Miss Oliver, if you'd accept me for this dance,' said Henry.

Her cheeks pinked. 'You would?'

He nodded as the crowd backed to the walls, leaving a space for them to dance.

'I'll request a waltz,' Avril said cheerfully before bustling away.

'I haven't danced in a long time,' Ditty murmured as she took his hand and stepped with him into the centre of the room, evidently unconcerned.

At least, that was what Henry thought she said. It could have been something else, but it was hard to tell. His heart was beating so loudly in his ears, his pulse roaring, she could have said anything and he would have nodded just the same.

The musicians struck up. It was a slower waltz, thank goodness, not one that would require him to gallivant at speed about the place, but at the same time it made Henry's stomach twist.

He was about to dance. In public. With Ditty.

He wasn't sure which part of that he was most nervous about.

'Don't worry, after the first minute I'll invite everyone else to join us,' she whispered as his hands placed themselves delicately on her waist.

Henry tried to smile. 'Just like at a wedding, I guess.'

Why on earth had he thought this was a good time to mention weddings? Ditty's smile faded, but she rallied and nodded, as though that was the most obvious comparison to make, and not a completely foolish thing to say.

'Exactly. Just like at a wedding.'

Just concentrate on the dancing, Henry tried to tell himself. *Or your attempt at dancing.*

An attempt was probably a more accurate description of what they were doing, but at least that reduced the pressure to do anything impressive. Ditty's hands were clasped on his arm and around his hand, and Henry was doing his best not to notice every minute shift of her fingertips, the way her thumb brushed against his own.

Why was his heart beating this loudly—surely she would be able to hear it!

'You know, I have to hand it to you,' he said quietly, under the noise of the music as people watched them dance gently to the rhythm of the waltz. 'I didn't think it would be possible to do all this.'

'What, put together a spectacular ball, in just days, two days before your brother's proposal?' Ditty said with a smile.

He chuckled, tension seeping from his shoulders. 'No,

not quite. I mean, yes, that, too. But, well, I told you once I didn't believe you could manufacture romance.'

The words were tripping off his tongue and he couldn't stop them, but in a way, Henry did not want to.

He was running out of time. Ditty would be gone the day after tomorrow, after Charles had successfully proposed marriage to Miss Yorke, then all those chance encounters, moments together, opportunities to speak, would all be over. He had to say something today, and now appeared as good a time as ever.

Even if he was momentarily distracted by the movement of her body as they danced.

'And I told you there was a formula,' Ditty said softly.

Henry looked deep into her eyes, and knew the words which had to come next. 'Perhaps you were right. Perhaps in the right circumstances, surrounded by good food, and laughter, and talented musicians…you can manufacture romance. Or maybe something more.'

He held her gaze just long enough to feel the discomfort melt away, though he was never truly awkward around Ditty, was he? She drew something out of him, something deeper and better than he was before.

Ditty swallowed. 'More?'

He nodded. He didn't trust his voice to speak, it would be so thick with repressed longing. Longing to tell her how much he appreciated all she had done for his Lodge; how much she had done for Brexley.

How she had changed him. Healed his heart, taken his hurt from his failed proposal and made him believe in something again. Something like love.

'More,' Henry repeated softly as they continued to dance to the music. 'You've…you've changed something here, Ditty, you have to know that.'

She grinned. 'Brexley is eternal.'

'But you've brought something new to it,' he persisted. *She had to understand.* 'Here, right now in this room… I can feel more love than I ever have before.'

His breath caught in his lungs. He had said too much, probably revealed himself to be an absolute fool. Because she didn't feel that way about him, did she? She didn't feel a rush dancing here with him, as he did.

He watched her swallow again, her gaze dropping from his own and staring instead at his chest.

'It's not me,' Ditty said quietly. 'It's you.'

He almost fell over. 'What do you—'

'You have brought the love here,' she continued in a quiet voice, barely audible under the waltz. 'You have friends here, Henry, people who care about you, respect you.'

He tried to calm himself. She wasn't saying what he thought she was saying—at least, he didn't think so. It was so difficult to think with all this emotion rushing through him.

'The love was already here,' Ditty said with a smile to his chest. 'I just brought it out into the sun, that's all.'

'And,' Henry whispered, 'is there…more?'

And she looked up. Ditty's bright eyes, glittering with intelligence and compassion, gazed up at him.

'Henry,' she whispered, 'I…'

'Yes?' he said eagerly.

Perhaps far too eagerly. Ditty's smile was, after all, a little too knowing. 'Come with me.'

Ditty did not know what made her do it. Something in her, something that recalled the fiery intensity of a kiss they should not have shared by the waterfall, no doubt, but she could not help herself.

Grabbing Henry's arm and pulling him, through the now crowded dance floor, out of the drawing room and out of the Lodge, down the path as her mind whirled and behind the gardener's shed where they could not be seen.

Well, she would be leaving anyway. Any hint of a scandal would remain here, in Brexley. And if she were never to know the touch of a man as a wife...

'Ditty, what on earth—'

He could not continue. It would have been rather difficult, Ditty thought as she lost herself in the kiss she pressed against his lips.

For a moment, she thought she had been wrong, that she had entirely misread the situation. That unlike her, Henry had not been thinking of those kisses over and over again, hoping their intimacy would return, desperate to know that they shared the same longing.

And then Henry pulled at her, crushing her breasts against his chest, a low groan in his throat as he kissed her passionately, his tongue sliding down the slit of her lips and parting them none too gently.

She whimpered. This was what she wanted—the passion, the need she had never realised was missing with Thomas. Oh, he had kissed her hand once or twice, but there had been nothing like this animalistic need to be close to each other, the crushing ache within to touch, to be touched, the heady knowledge that nothing would be like this, nothing would—

'Ditty,' he growled under his breath and she felt her body respond, knew she wanted more, all of it, all of him.

Her hands started tugging wildly at the buttons of his greatcoat and his hands were cupping her buttocks, pulling her close to something that was hard and pressing into her hip and she wanted, she needed—

'Ditty? Where is she, does anyone know?' They heard people moving about the garden.

Pulling away and trying to catch her breath, she looked up at Henry shyly. He grinned silently, brushing a curl of her hair back, and nodded.

Her heart soared. He understood. They didn't need to speak to share this thought.

They must not be found together.

'Every time I try to seduce you,' Henry breathed, his forehead pressed against hers as he spoke with a laugh, 'something holds us back.'

Ditty's thighs quivered at all the promised pleasure which she had not gained. 'Then perhaps you should try harder.'

His gaze caught hers. 'Do you want me to?'

Chapter Sixteen

Her heart was not beating frantically. Her lungs were not tight. And she certainly could say words. She knew plenty of words.

Ditty blinked. Henry was still before her, a lilting smile on his handsome face, making her body heat with just a glance.

'I said, do you want me to,' he repeated, as she stood mute, utterly unable to marshal her lips into saying anything.

'Want you to?' Ditty said in a rush, desperate to say anything that wasn't the request spinning through her mind. 'I—I never planned to—'

Henry nodded, his gaze flickering up her body in a most disconcerting way as the cold chill of the evening stroked at her skin. 'Don't plan. Don't think, just ask.'

Help me rid myself of this ache inside. Help me know what it is to love, freely and unrestrained. Help me to throw aside all plans and just be.

Ditty tried to smile. 'I… I don't know how to.'

She had never asked for what she wanted; she was

the eldest of three daughters, she did what she was told. Her father's death had left a hole in the family that her mother had been unable to fill, and in truth, Ditty could not recall the last time she had asked for anything.

'I had better escort you back to the inn,' said Henry lightly. 'Help you back there.'

And Ditty was not entirely sure what made her do it. Something ridiculous of course, perhaps blameable on the champagne she had sipped—but she had barely finished her glass, and it was a different kind of soaring recklessness that was filling her now, as they stood out here in the dark evening.

'Perhaps,' Ditty found herself saying, 'you could help me.'

The words were spoken before she could take them back but she did not want to. She had been good her entire life, always doing what was right, always doing what was practical.

She wanted this moment now to be different.

He had lifted an eyebrow in that irritating, seductive manner of his, and Ditty knew she was about to make herself ridiculous; but she didn't care. How could she care, when it was Henry and herself, and no one else, precisely as the world was supposed to be.

'It…it's madness, I know,' Ditty said, trying to pull enough air into her lungs to speak and keep her voice low at the same time. 'Respectable young ladies do not ask dukes to ravish them, and yet that's all I want—and I'll lose my reputation but that hardly seems to matter now, because I want you, I want—'

Precisely what she wanted, she was not able to elaborate on. That was because the lips of Henry Paisley, the Duke of Glanyrafon, were pressed against hers.

They were not pressed for long. He pulled back but just an inch, his gaze searching for hers, and when Ditty gave a nod to his unspoken question he groaned and pulled her into a tight embrace, his lips crushing her own.

She melted into his arms. This was where she belonged, this was where she wanted to be. His tongue teased along the slit of her mouth and she welcomed him in immediately, moaning at the taste of him, the raw power of him, the way his kisses sparked joy in her heart and heat between her thighs.

Somehow her fingers had tangled in his hair and somehow his hand was cupping her buttocks and Ditty gave herself up to it, the longing, the passion which had been pushed down for far too long.

When the kiss finally ended, she whimpered softly at the lack of contact.

Henry chuckled, and she felt it through her breasts pushed up against his chest. 'I keep a bedchamber upstairs. No one will spot us through the side gate.'

There was no need for hesitation.

'Lead the way,' she whispered, cheeks burning only slightly.

It was a wanton thing to say indeed, but it did not feel so. Ditty would certainly have chastised her sisters for saying such a thing, she could not help but think as she and Henry crept up along the building, through a side gate and into the back corridor in the gloom of the night, then up the stairs and quietly along the landing and round the corner to a corridor kept separate from the main house by a heavy door.

'I have my own wing in the Lodge,' Henry murmured as he closed the door behind them and led her down another corridor. 'Though I rarely sleep here.'

'An ever expanding Lodge,' Ditty could not help but murmur.

His chuckle could be felt through his arm and she felt as though she were floating—no, flying, for there was so much exuberance in her mind this could not merely be a gentle meander.

Henry opened a door to their left and they entered a bedchamber. And it was most definitely a bedchamber.

Ditty swallowed hard as Henry closed the door behind them. Before her was a large four-poster bed. A very large bed. The coverlet was a dark rich damask red and the bed had been made roughly, clearly by someone in a rush. There was something so intimate about being welcomed into this space…intimate, and yet charming.

When she turned to the man who still held her hand, it was to see Henry flushing.

'It's perhaps not the luxury that one might expect from a duke. It felt foolish to spend funds on it when—'

'Henry,' she said firmly, placing a finger on his lips and shivering at the flare of need that blossomed in his eyes. 'Less talking. More kissing.'

For perhaps once in their entire acquaintanceship, the Duke of Glanyrafon obeyed her direction without a single correction. Pouring kisses down her neck and burying his lips in her décolletage, Ditty gasped and tried to remember how to stand up as pleasure roared through her body. His doctor's hands, always kind and so clever, were making light work of her gown and she could not help but revel in the way the fabric fell to the floor. This was wrong, this was right, this was what she needed, what she wanted, what she craved—

Henry's fingers brushed past her shoulder as he slowly lowered her chemise. 'So beautiful. So perfect, Ditty.'

Heat burned her cheeks. 'Y-you are not such a bad specimen yourself.'

It had cost her dear to be so direct and though he chuckled, there was no teasing in his voice, just joy. 'I want to see all of you. I want to lay you out on my bed and kiss every inch of you.'

Ditty's eyes widened even as he pressed a kiss on her lips and tugged at her stays. Every—every inch of her? Surely he could not mean—

All other thoughts disappeared as her stays fell to the carpet. She was nude.

The instinct to cover herself flashed in her mind for a moment, but it faded without any sense of shame. Why should she hide who she was? She would never marry, she was sure of that now, and here was the chance to experience pleasure with a gentleman who would never tell a soul. Besides, out here in Brexley, who could he tell who was of any consequence?

When Ditty looked up, it was to see hunger and desire and something akin to reverence in his eyes. Soon, her innocence would be gone—but what good had it ever brought her? 'You're looking at me.'

'That I am,' said Henry quietly, stripping off his own clothes with rapid fingers without taking his eyes from her. 'And I like what I see.'

There was no time to be ashamed, not when the man she knew she loved had swept her into his arms and actually carried her to the bed.

Before Ditty could say a word, Henry was kissing her, his naked scalding body pressed up against hers, and dear God there was nothing like it, nothing at all. She clung to him, kissing him passionately as her need built, and he was kissing her, his hands stroking, his fingertips caressing—

Ditty gasped in the kiss and he chuckled.

'Do you want me to stop?'

Stop? Stop the wonderful feelings that was sparking through her body as Henry slowly slid a finger across her secret place? Stop the jolts of bliss that shot through her, tingling in all the right places when he slowly slid a finger within her, brushing across a nub of pleasure?

Ditty blinked. He was looking down at her with such adoration, it was all she could do not to spill out her affections.

'I'll stop,' he repeated quietly, 'if you want me to.'

She reacted instinctively. 'Don't you dare.'

His moan of appreciation was transfigured into a kiss that scalded her to her very toes. Though that could have been the way his fingers were now stroking her to a rhythm that her whole body seemed to know. Her breath shortened as sensual delight shivered through her, and before she could say a word his kisses were suddenly absent.

'Henry, what—Henry!'

It was a good thing that the other residents of the Lodge were mostly hard of hearing, Ditty managed to think as she arched her back and thrust her hips into the face of the mouth who was now kissing her, actually kissing her right there!

And yet it felt so right. Henry's tongue darted within her, deeper this time and slowly twisting around as Ditty moaned, desperate for more but hardly knowing what more there was to have.

'Yes,' she whimpered, her fingers fisting in Henry's hair as though she could bring him deeper, deeper. 'Yes…'

It was an onslaught, but a most welcome one. The man seemed to know precisely what she wanted, what she needed, his tongue licking and his eager and satisfied sounds of delight somehow raising her own.

She could not bear it. She was being pushed to a precipice that she had never known before, and yet she wanted more, more, and she ground her hips forward in her desperate silent request.

Henry understood. While his tongue continued to lap at her sweetness, he pressed a thumb into her depths before swirling it around that nub and Ditty fell apart.

'Henry!'

Ecstasy roared through her, every nerve in her body jangling as she gave herself up to the pleasure that could not be contained. He was merciless, continuing to worship at her secret place as Ditty's body spasmed in powerful roaring waves.

And then it was over; well, except for the shuddering aftershocks that threatened to make speech impossible.

She blinked up at the four-poster canopy. Henry's face appeared.

'I didn't hurt you, did I?' His expression was anxious, something inexplicable as far as she was concerned.

Hurt her? Such pleasure, she had never imagined it could be found. Hurt her?

'We can stop here,' came Henry's soft yet clearly eager voice. 'We don't have to— I mean, if you don't want to.'

Ditty knew precisely what she wanted, and she was going to have it, Society and its rules be damned. 'I want it all,' she said quietly, looking up at the man she loved. 'I want you, Henry. I want you now.'

It was hard to believe this was happening, and yet even in his wildest dreams Henry could not have imagined this.

Ditty, asking him to make love to her.

Ditty, naked in his arms, in his bed.

Ditty, coming apart thanks to his ministrations, tasting the pleasure in her as it captured her.

Ditty, telling him that she wanted him.

It healed a part of him he had never known was broken. It swept through him, taking over his senses, taking over his sense. What need had he for logic when the woman he adored was asking for what he so wanted to give her?

'I've wanted this for so long,' he murmured, grabbing a preservative from his bedside table and pulling it on with fumbling fingers before moving between Ditty's legs and trying not to think how wet she was, how he had just brought her to climax. 'I've wanted you for so long.'

'Really?'

There was such incredulity in her voice, it almost broke his heart. Could this woman not see how desirable she was? How entirely wonderful she was? How he was honoured to even touch her, let alone taste her?

The only answer Henry could think to give was to lean forward and kiss her, a reverential slow kiss that relaxed Ditty beneath him.

That was when he entered her.

The way she gasped into his mouth told him that she had not expected it, but the way she immediately angled her hips told him she wanted this just as much as he wanted her, and for that Henry could have wept. To be so eagerly welcomed, to plunge himself into her warmth, her wetness, to feel her stretch and accommodate him—

There was nothing else like it.

'Oh, Henry,' she moaned, throwing back her head as her eyelashes fluttered shut.

Gritting his teeth and hoping to God he didn't come in an instant, he slowly lifted his hips until he was almost completely out of her, then slid forward a little faster this time.

It was in the catch of her breath that he knew he was hitting the spot. Ditty's eyes opened. 'Again.'

He hardly needed the encouragement. Between kisses mingled with sweet nothings, Henry built a rhythm, trying for her sake to remain slow, knowing that this first time with her—for surely it could not be the last—would be rushed.

It was not possible to hold himself back.

Soon she was writhing underneath him, her whimpering moans of pleasure filling the room and Henry could have roared with possessive desire as his hips started to thrust, to pick up the pace, to pound into the woman that was surely so close to her peak—

'Oh, Henry, yes, yes, yes!'

Christ but he felt it, he felt her pleasure as it rippled through her, and the way her body contracted and tightened around him made it impossible to hold off what Henry was frankly astonished he had managed to avoid so far.

Roaring her name and crushing her lips with his own, Henry abandoned himself to the pleasure of their coupling as his body poured out his seed. The climax was sudden and swift, but it remained longer than he could have imagined, his hips jerking into her until there was nothing more to give.

Slowly, slowly, Henry withdrew from her. Ditty's eyes were closed as though she could not take in another sense, and he carefully rolled onto his back beside her.

Well. That was…that was…

And the trouble was, he was completely in love with

her. That was not usually an issue, he thought wryly, but now that he had made Ditty his own, possessed her entirely, he had to do the impossible and find a way of telling her.

'Ditty?'

'Mmm?'

He smiled as he stared up at the canopy of his bed. It was so familiar, and somehow so different. Something had changed. Perhaps it was him.

'Ditty, I... I did not know how to tell you this before. Perhaps I should have done, but I did not.'

She said nothing, but that was to be expected. He had just brought her to pleasure twice. She was undoubtedly weary, and perhaps a little shy. Perhaps it was best this way.

Henry cleared his throat. 'I...well, I never thought I would again. I never thought I could, after— And yet meeting you, knowing you, seeing the way you see the world...'

Damn it, he wasn't making any sense. *Pull yourself together, man!*

'I love you,' he said simply. There. That was better. 'I love you, and it's a love I've never known before. I—I love everything about you! Not just your beauty, though you are beautiful. Not just your kindness, though you are kind. I love the way you wrinkle your nose when you're about to disagree with someone.' Henry thought for a moment. 'Usually me. I love the way you see any problem as a puzzle. I love the way you love daisies, and the way you plan because you want the world to be better than it is. I love the way you care for your family and you know that they care for you in a different way. And I thought you should know. You should know how loved you are, Ditty. I love you.'

It was perhaps not the most impressive of speeches, but to be fair, Henry thought muzzily, he had not had much time to prepare. And so he waited.

And waited.

'Ditty?' he said, turning his head.

Ditty had fallen asleep.

A slow smile crept across his face. Well, so she had not heard his declaration. That did not matter. There would be plenty of time to make his confession.

Chapter Seventeen

February 12: the day of the proposal

Ditty held her breath as she hid just out of sight.

Everything was perfect.

At least, as far as she had seen when she had performed her final check, just ten minutes before Charles and Miss Yorke were scheduled to arrive at the waterfall.

Though her heart had been beating frantically, that hadn't distracted Ditty from her purpose: ensuring this proposal was the absolute best it could be. And she had done it. She was almost certain.

Now all she had to do was trust that Charles had learned his approved speech properly…

Ditty pushed a curl behind her ear as she leaned close against the cliff face. It was imperative Miss Yorke suspected nothing. It was just a walk in the woods. That was all.

Were those footsteps?

Her ears pricked, trying to take in every sound. It truly was a miracle the waterfall did not dullen all sound—

a trick of perspective, Henry had called it, and he was right.

Henry.

Ditty's heart skipped a beat, but she tried desperately to push it from her mind. This was not the time to be thinking of how he had made love to her; how he had known her, fully known her, and loved what he found; how she had crept out from the Lodge that morning and prayed no one had seen her as she made the walk back into town, creeping into her room at the inn and thanking her stars that Mrs Fletcher had not locked the front door…

A flutter of something white, just out of the corner of her eye. Was that from her reticule? Surely she could not have been so stupid as to—

Fumbling in her panic, Ditty grasped at the two pieces of paper that had escaped from her reticule and thrust them back inside, clicking the clasp more firmly into place. She did not need to look at them. She had already memorised the notes which had arrived that morning.

It will be perfect. Can't wait to have you home to tell us all about Brexley's menfolk…

Deep breath, I know you did a great job. Get ready to celebrate another success and your matchmaking reputation saved…

Ditty tried to smile. Her sisters meant well; their kind wishes warmed her heart, and helped to reduce her worry. Nothing could remove it until the proposal was successful.

But Thalia's written words kept echoing in her mind as she ensured her reticule was well and truly closed.

Can't wait to have you home to tell us all about Brexley's menfolk...

Ditty swallowed as the waterfall continued to cascade. She hadn't exactly been keeping Henry a secret. Not really. She hadn't told her sisters about him in the sparse letters she had sent back to London, but they knew her well enough to know it was in her silences that the real story could be found.

But she couldn't think about him now—it was a different Paisley brother she needed to focus on! And once he had proposed, there would be no reason to stay in Brexley, and she would have to return to London, pay the bills, keep providing for her sisters and pay off any debts her mother had racked up—and, if possible, prevent her from generating any more.

Footsteps. Ditty stiffened, holding herself back against the cliff face as best she could. This had to be perfect.

Cowed into hiding, some would say, after such an awful review in this very paper.

...accused of stealing the money of her clients without delivering the services she promised.

As the cruel words from the newspapers back in London circled in her mind, Ditty held her breath. The footsteps were getting closer. *This was it.*

At her signal, the three musicians began to play. The string trio played the most exquisite music, echoing around them as it bounced off the waterfall, creating an ambience of magic and beauty.

Ditty swallowed, forcing herself to breathe. *Well, that was the first step.*

'Oh, Charles!'

And she relaxed. She didn't need to look to know precisely the expression on Miss Yorke's face. She had seen it countless times—created it countless times.

Who could look upon the splendour she had created and not be amazed?

The scent of roses lingered on the air. Ditty smiled. Miss Vivienne had absolutely outdone herself—she had never seen so many roses that the term *festoons* actually applied. The love heart biscuits had been strung about the place, all thanks to Mavis and Avril at the Lodge. And as the sun set slowly over the mountains, golden orange light streamed through the waterfall, throwing cascades of rainbows about them.

'Oh, Charles,' came the emotional voice of Miss Yorke, her throat evidently full.

Ditty smiled, her heart slowing, as the proposal speech of Charles started to fill the air over the beautiful music.

'Miss Yorke, I knew from the moment I met you— Stop crying will you, I've got a speech to do. Are you ready? Right. I knew from the moment I met you…'

Ditty stifled a laugh. Well, it wasn't precisely the script she had worked out with him rapidly last night. She wouldn't have left it so late normally, except she'd been so caught up with Henry. That was, the Brexley

Lodge for Gentlemen and Ladies of a Certain Age. Saving the Lodge. Saving it for Henry.

Her stomach fluttered as warmth suffused her chest at the thought of him.

'—and if you would do me the honour of—'

'Yes!' squealed Miss Yorke's voice.

Ditty stifled another laugh.

'Miss Yorke, you're supposed to wait until I've finished my—'

'Oh, my goodness, is that a ring?'

Joy spread through Ditty as she heard the muffled sobs, the thick emotion in Charles's voice as two people promised to love each other for the rest of their lives.

A wistful smile quirked Ditty's lips. If only that were the end of the story for everyone.

She straightened as she heard Charles's voice.

'I am so glad you said…*yes*!'

And right on cue—

'Congratulations!' Cries rang out as well-wishers, family and friends from the town of Brexley joined the happy couple.

They'd been waiting just down the path, as Ditty had instructed them. She stepped out herself, shy now her main purpose was achieved. Oh, the party would continue into the evening, she was sure, especially as the musicians continued to play and the food and drink was brought out into the clearing. Fires were swiftly lit in the pyres which had been made to keep the place warm, and children laughed as they tugged at the love heart biscuits, warnings from parents that they could only have one each echoing around the place.

But her contribution was done. It was over. The proposal was a success.

There stood Charles, beaming with a boyish grin Ditty had never seen before. Hanging on to his arm, beaming just as broadly with an elegant ring on her finger, was a pretty woman Ditty had seen at the Brexley Lodge for Gentlemen and Ladies of a Certain Age Valentine's Day Ball. Goodness, it was a miracle no one had let the proposal plans slip. The entire place was covered in the reminders of Valentine's Day: hearts, pink decorations, beautiful music, heartfelt words…

But there was something more.

It was not just the love of a man for a woman, and a woman for a man. It was the love of a town.

Charles's hand was wrung countless times, friends demanded to see Miss Yorke's ring, and everyone accepted glasses of champagne in the beribboned flutes she and Henry had created.

A lump formed in Ditty's throat. It truly was a perfect proposal. But not because of her. Or at least, what made the proposal so special was something she could never have planned for. It was the way people had rushed to be involved, to help her pull everything together, even when it had been falling apart.

Because the town of Brexley loved Charles and Miss Yorke.

'You did an excellent job!'

Ditty turned and grinned at Reg, who was carrying

two silver platters of what smelt like the most delicious food ever made. 'You think so?'

'I've never seen a more romantic setting—and timing the proposal for sunset, through the waterfall? Inspired!' said Reg enthusiastically. His eyebrows wiggled. 'Giving me the chance to serve food cooked up in my kitchen, when I can't seat people in my restaurant? Even more inspired!'

Ditty giggled as the man winked and started offering the platters to celebrating guests.

'A little of this? I promise you, you won't be disappointed, something of my own devising.'

It was an excellent idea, even she had to admit. It wasn't Reg's kitchen that was damaged, it was where diners would sit. That was where the roof had leaked. So why not make the most of a captive audience?

Happiness flowed through the place as people started laughing and talking, eating with gusto, and enjoying the music. The roses were resplendent and the candles she had stationed all over the place were being lit by—

Henry.

Her heart skipped a beat, and this time she didn't need to wonder why.

She was in love with Henry. In love with a man who never thought of himself, who would rather drive a dilapidated dog cart than even consider taking money from those who needed it.

A doctor, a duke, but also a man who'd had his heart broken and still believed in romance.

A man who had chastised her when she had first arrived in Brexley, Ditty thought with a wry smile, but had supported her and helped her and encouraged her when she had needed a friend.

But she wanted more than a friend.

Henry caught her eye and grinned. She tried to grin back, though it was difficult, now her time here was over, to think what she could say.

'You are a complete success,' Henry said quietly as he stepped over. 'You know, I never thought someone could pack as many romantic things into one place as possible, but you did it.'

She beamed, conscious of just how close he was. It was perfectly normal he was standing that close. Probably.

'Musicians, a romantic evening,' said Ditty as cheerfully as she could manage, ticking things off on her fingers. 'Roses, waterfall, sunset, emotional speech, a ring—'

'Not on Valentine's Day, though.'

Ditty waved away his interruption. 'That's what Charles asked for, he wanted to go and visit Miss Yorke's family for Valentine's as an engaged man. Family and friends here to celebrate, champagne flutes with pink ribbon—'

'Love heart biscuits,' cut in Henry with a grin. 'I've already eaten one, I hope you don't mind.'

Ditty nudged his arm, glad for the excuse to touch him and trying not to notice the tingling sensation rushing up her arm. *Do not think about how the last time you saw him he was naked, and lustful, and—* 'Those were supposed to be for the happy couple, to take home and enjoy—and for the children!'

'Mavis and Avril baked hundreds of these, you can't expect Charles and Miss Yorke to eat them all,' protested Henry with a mischievous grin. 'Besides, old Reg's food is doing a roaring trade. I don't think he made dessert, but then Mavis and April's biscuits are hanging about the place. It's all gone well.'

Ditty gave a theatrical sigh, but couldn't help but privately agree. It had all gone so well. *Perfectly*. A perfect proposal.

'You did it.'

She looked up into Henry's dark eyes. He had spoken more seriously now, more quietly, words for her ears only.

Not that she should be thinking this way. Ditty swallowed. 'I suppose I did.'

'The perfect proposal,' he said, as though he had seen into her mind. 'Your career is saved, though I don't think it was in need of saving to begin with. Everyone knows how hard you work.'

Ditty tried to smile. Did he know how much it meant, those words coming from him? 'Thank you.'

'You…you must be really pleased.'

Was she? Ditty hardly knew. She was pleased, at least in an abstract, distant way. She knew she would feel more pleased once she returned to London, to her rooms with Thalia and Calliope, but right now…

Right now, all she could taste was bittersweet. 'Yes. Yes, I'm pleased.'

But how could she be? Ditty knew nothing would ever be the same again, now her time at Brexley had come to an end.

You...you must be really pleased.
Yes. Yes, I'm pleased.
Then Ditty needed to tell her face, Henry could not help but think. She looked...well, not pleased.

Could he dare hope it was because she had also realised that, after Charles's successful proposal, there was nothing to keep her here?

Expect perhaps you.
The thought rushed through his mind before he could stop it, but Henry couldn't lie to himself any longer.

She was beautiful. She was the most beautiful woman he had ever known, and she was lit up most charmingly by the fading sunset and the countless candles he had lit on her behalf. When he had whispered those words of affection, of love, he had never dreamed that she had already fallen asleep. And now he had to say them again.

Henry swallowed. If he wasn't careful, words of devotion and admiration would flow from his lips and he would not be able to stop himself.

Who could when in Ditty's presence?

'Your brother seems happy.'

Henry blinked. She was pointing just over his shoulder. He turned and saw Charles, now hand in hand with Miss Yorke, who had pink cheeks, conversing with Mavis.

'Yes, he really does,' he said, trying to keep his voice

free of emotion. It wouldn't do to lose control. 'I'm glad you were able to bring him such happiness.'

'Oh, I'm not sure I can take much credit for that,' said Ditty, who was flushing when he turned back to her.

He frowned. 'What do you mean?'

'You will fade away if you don't eat more, my dear!' said Reg suddenly as he thrust a silver platter covered in delicious-looking *bruschetta* between them. 'Eat up!'

Henry took one just to keep the man happy, but wished he could have continued talking to Ditty privately. There wouldn't be many more opportunities to do so, he knew. It wouldn't be too long before she would be gone.

'Thank you, Reg,' Ditty said enthusiastically, taking two and popping one immediately into her mouth. 'I didn't have breakfast or luncheon,' she said apologetically, in way of explanation. 'I was just too nervous!'

'Now, that's no way to look after yourself,' Reg said sternly. He glanced at Henry. 'You're the doctor, tell her!'

Henry tried to smile naturally as Reg drifted away.

'He's right, you've got to look after yourself, Ditty.'

'Oh, Calliope will get a stew inside me as soon as I get back home,' she said in a bracing voice. 'She's always cooking and baking, trying to feed me up. But they need me—they've always needed me.'

As soon as I get back home.

There it was. Henry had hoped the phrase wouldn't come up somehow. Perhaps if it wasn't mentioned between the two of them, he could go on pretending it wasn't going to happen.

But he couldn't. She would be going, and Brexley would be bereft.

He would be bereft.

Henry swallowed, wishing he had the right words to say but nothing came to him. How he longed for that template of hers, that proposal speech outline to help him explain just how he felt.

Georgiana had left. Now Ditty would leave. What on earth had made him think she would stay?

And Ditty had said herself, she didn't believe in romance. It was all biological to her; this was like a play, a stage with musicians and actors who had been given their lines and performed accordingly.

'You look very serious.'

He tried to grin. 'Just thinking about all the preparations I'm about to be dragged into, that's all. The wedding,' he added, seeing her confused face.

Her confusion disappeared. 'Oh, goodness, yes. I can imagine, as the brother of the groom, you may be called upon for a great deal of help.'

He groaned. That was all he needed, more responsibility, more things to do. 'Goodness knows how I'm going to fit it all in, what with supervising the building work up at the Lodge.'

'I'm glad it's going ahead,' said Ditty with a small smile.

His heart twisted. 'It's all thanks to you.'

She pretended not to know what he was talking about, but it was true. Henry had never seen anyone do so much for people she had only met weeks ago, yet she had transformed so many people's lives.

They'd be able to live there, all his residents, in warmth and comfort. In a building that wasn't falling apart, eating food that wasn't scraped together from the butcher's scraps. They'd be able to hire two more nurses, a clerk for that disaster of a study of his.

Yet Ditty wouldn't be there to see all the fruit of her labour. She was going.

'Roses,' Henry blurted out.

Ditty frowned, sipping her champagne before saying, 'I—I beg your pardon?'

'Roses,' he repeated, embarrassment curling inside his chest. 'I mean, you got all the roses you wanted, then? Miss Vivienne was able to come through.'

'It was the fireworks I was really worried about, but in the end I cancelled the order,' Ditty said with a dry laugh. 'You just can't rely on some people.'

I want you to rely on me, Henry wanted to say. His throat constricted with the unsaid words, but he couldn't bring himself to do it. He'd fallen in love with Ditty, but she clearly hadn't fallen in love with him. Oh, she desired him, and that was flattering in itself, but she had said nothing of love, of affection, of a desire to stay here and make a life with him.

He didn't want to make her life more complicated than it already was.

'The roses are nice,' he said again, hating his inability to think of something else to say.

Come on, man! This might be your last chance!

Ditty's gaze flickered about the place, taking in the hundreds of red and white roses. 'Yes, they are pretty. But as I said before, I always preferred daisies.'

Henry smiled painfully. Here was a woman who didn't buy into the trappings of romance, or Valentine's Day. Her preferences, her likes and dislikes were genuine. Who she was.

And it was that person he had fallen in love with.

'Well, I'm glad I got to celebrate Charles's proposal with you,' he said aloud, knowing the inevitable could not be put off any longer. 'You know. With you going home after this, and everything.'

He was usually an eloquent, calm, measured man. But being this close to Ditty, standing just a foot from her, was making his brain turn to mush.

'Yes,' she said, not quite catching his gaze. 'My place on the stagecoach back to London is booked for tomorrow.'

'It's a shame. You'll…you'll miss the Valentine's Day Festival.'

Silence fell between them as happy chatter surrounded them. Henry desperately wanted to ask her to stay, but how could he?

There wasn't anything for her here in Brexley—nothing except himself.

She had no family here, no friends. No one, even someone as outstanding as Ditty, could make a living by matchmaking in a town this small.

And they had met only nineteen days ago. Nineteen days! Henry could hardly believe it himself, but the time had both rushed by and been one of the most intense, incredible times he had ever experienced.

He knew Ditty so well, loved everything he discovered about her—and wanted the chance to learn more.

But that chance was passing him by.

'Unless…'

Henry's ears perked up. 'Unless?'

Ditty was looking at him with a nervous smile, the candlelight shimmering in her eyes. Her champagne flute was gone, he noticed suddenly. Someone must have taken it from her.

He'd never had one. That meant both her hands and his were empty.

Why couldn't he reach out and take one of them?

'Unless,' Ditty said gently, under the hubbub of the celebration. 'Unless there's a reason… I should stay?'

Henry swallowed. This was it. His moment. His opening. A chance to ask her to stay, to beg her—to tell her if she got on that stagecoach tomorrow, then all his chance of happiness would be gone with her.

Brexley needs you, Henry tried out in his mind, as Ditty stared up, waiting for him to respond. *The Lodge needs you.*

But he knew none of those things were the real reason he wanted to get on bended knee, right here and right now, and ask her to stay. To be his wife.

He loved her. He loved Ditty Oliver, and if he didn't do something about it, he was going to lose her.

Henry opened his mouth. Then he shut it again. 'I…'

Excruciating embarrassment flooded through him as

he tried to speak, but he couldn't do it. Not here. Not in the same place he had once asked Georgiana to marry him, and heard those painful words still echoing through his mind…

How can you even think to ask me that? After everything I've been saying to you for months…and you ask me to marry you? You're a joke!

Ditty smiled sadly. 'Thank you for everything, Henry.'

'Ditty—'

'Yes?' she whispered.

Henry's mouth dried. He couldn't do it.

Ditty nodded slowly. 'There's no need to drive me to the staging post tomorrow, Henry, Reg has already said he'll do it. Good luck. With the Lodge. With planning the wedding. With everything.'

And with that, before Henry could say anything, before he could call out, before his boots would unstick from the ground or his heart slow down enough that he could think…

Ditty Oliver walked away, turned a corner onto the forest path and walked out of his life.

Chapter Eighteen

February 13, 1812

Ditty's key scraped in the lock, as though it had become unformed through lack of use. It took three goes to gradually turn the key, and when she pushed the door open, a wash of memories soared over her.

The umbrella by the door they never put away. The pair of boots she recognised immediately as Thalia's. A pelisse, Calliope's or one of her own, Ditty couldn't tell, just visible on a hook.

I'm home.

And yet, as Ditty stepped in, pulled her trunk in and shoved the door shut, it didn't feel like home. There was a strange emptiness to the place, as though no one was living there.

Which was foolish, Ditty tried to tell herself as she hung up her pelisse and pulled off her winter boots. She'd lived here for years, with both of her sisters and their mama. It was silly to think the place was empty.

'Hello?' she called out.

No answering voice replied, no happy squeals that she was, after almost a month, home. No rushing footsteps to welcome her.

No hint of hot chocolate on the air, or stew in the kitchen.

Ditty's shoulders slumped. Then she started to drag her trunk toward her bedchamber.

It was foolish of her to just assume they would be home. Calliope would be out somewhere on one of her painting commissions, and Thalia was surely on a walk seeking more inspiration for her poetry. It was only now, as she heaved her trunk onto her bed and looked at her books, all lined up in colour order at the moment, that Ditty realised just how cold it was.

Not their lodgings. London.

At Brexley, she could not help but think, there would be someone here to welcome her. Mrs Fletcher, or Miss Vivienne. Certainly Mavis and Avril would want to see her.

And even if they were not there at… Ditty pushed aside all thoughts of Brexley. Home was not with Henry. It was here.

But even on the streets of Brexley, she had felt the camaraderie and connection of the people around her. Reg would smile, the baker and butcher would wave, Vicar Melview would greet her warmly and offer her a cup of tea. Kids would play in the street, giggling all the while, with no fear of rushing carriages.

Here, in London, she'd had to shove her way along the pavement or else she would have still been at the coaching inn. Someone had glared and Ditty had smiled back, but her smile had swiftly faded.

'Well, I'm not in Brexley,' Ditty said to herself, falling backward onto her bed and looking up at the ceiling. 'I'm in London.'

And she was needed here, wasn't she? Her sisters could not do without her, and she needed that in turn—needed that purpose. Purpose she could not get from a duke.

Not that he had *said* anything. Henry. No promises had been made. He hadn't misled her, not really, she thought wretchedly. It was only...

Unless there's a reason... I should stay?

Ditty had really thought, for a moment, he would say something. Something like what he had been about to say, maybe, when they had danced the first dance at the Lodge's Valentine's Day Ball. They had made love and yet the vulnerability that truly mattered, that of the heart, had never occurred.

It was just a fancy of her imagination, she told herself sternly. If Henry had felt anything more than mutual respect, he would have said something. He was supposed to be the big romantic of the two of them, after all! Wouldn't he have said something?

Her smile faded.

If he had asked her to stay she would have thought about it. Definitely considered it. Maybe even—

'Goodness, whose pelisse is— Ditty! Ditty, are you here?'

The front door to their lodgings slammed, and Ditty

could not help but smile at the sound of Calliope's voice. The scatty artist had immediately noticed her pelisse on the rack.

'I'm in here,' she called out, then added hastily, 'I'll be out in a minute.'

For some reason, she didn't want Calliope in her bed-chamber. Not just yet. She needed a moment to collect herself, to remind herself she was back in her old life. Her life in London. Her matchmaking reputation was saved, she reminded herself severely, and that was the whole purpose of going to Brexley in the first place.

Not to fall in love with emotionally distant doctors who happened to be penniless dukes...

'Oh, my goodness, a small town suits you!' Calliope exclaimed as, a few seconds later, Ditty stepped out into the drawing room. 'Thalia's out, busy being inspired by nature. You look wonderful!'

Ditty looked down at herself. She couldn't see any-thing different. Well, except...

'Oh,' she said helplessly, pulling at the fabric of her scarf. 'Mavis knitted it for me. To keep me warm in the big city, she said.'

Ditty had been painfully touched when the two older ladies had taken her aside after Charles's proposal. It had been nice, of course, to say goodbye, but it was the fact they had made her parting gifts that had brought a lump to her throat.

'And those ear-bobs, are they new?' asked Calliope from the sofa, where she was curled up with a blanket before jumping up for an embrace. 'You went on a spending spree without me?'

Ditty grinned as she slipped onto the other half of the sofa, drawing up her feet and tucking them under her skirts. 'Not quite. A gift, from Avril. She made them, you know.'

Calliope beamed. 'You met some creative people, then? People you think you'll write to?'

And Ditty had to hesitate.

Mavis and Avril had promised to write. She'd promised Reg she'd keep in touch, too. And Mrs Fletcher. Both of their businesses were going to surge after this, she told them. Ditty told her she'd recommend all her friends to her inn. Even Miss Vivienne had asked to be kept up to date with her news. Charles had promised her references and a guest bedchamber anytime she was passing through.

Everyone had wanted to stay in touch...except Henry.

'Ditty?'

She blinked. 'Yes?'

'You sort of drifted off there for a second,' said Calliope with a frown. 'Like you were thinking about something unpleasant. Nothing happened there, did it? What happened in Brexley?'

Ditty swallowed. What had happened in Brexley?

In a way, nothing. She had gone there to do a job, and she had done it. Memories of Charles and Miss Yorke's proposal drifted through her mind, and a swell of warmth overcame her. She'd done an excellent job—the perfect proposal.

And she'd done more, hadn't she? Reg's restaurant was being buoyed by a market stall now which was apparently taking the town by storm, and if she was any judge, he would keep it up even when the restaurant roof was fixed.

The Brexley Lodge for Gentlemen and Ladies of a Certain Age was saved. Ditty's heart fluttered as she thought of the celebration she'd put on with only two days' notice: the laughter of the children playing the games, the craft room selling out within the hour…the frantic kisses by the gardener's shed and the dance she'd shared with Henry.

Even Miss Vivienne had mentioned she'd be stocking more daisies in future, now she knew they were Ditty's favourite.

Yes, plenty had happened in Brexley, Ditty had to admit. She had changed the town, irrevocably, and it had changed her.

But one thing had not happened in Brexley, and that was why she could not bring herself to speak.

Calliope was waiting, patiently at first, and then not so patiently. 'You know, the way you talked about that town in your letters, I honestly thought you were going to pack up and move there. I thought you'd want to stay there forever.'

Ditty bit her lip, and apparently that was all the hint her sister needed.

Calliope's mouth fell open. 'You thought about it! You actually considered not coming back to London?'

'Only for a moment,' Ditty said hastily, as though that

changed anything. 'But in the end he—I mean, I thought it was best to come home. How about a hot chocolate? I might tidy my books while you make it…'

But her sister was not to be so easily distracted. Ditty winced as Calliope fixed her with a firm glare, one that told her in no uncertain terms she was not going to be let off the hook that easily.

'Aphrodite Oliver—'

'I can't believe you're full-naming me,' said Ditty with a gasp. 'You—'

'You fell in love while you were in Brexley, didn't you?' Calliope said, her finger pointed at her sister.

Ditty could not help but laugh. 'Well, it's not like I planned—'

'Aha!' Calliope sounded triumphant, and Ditty winced at the second clue she had let slip. 'So you did meet someone! It's this Henry gentleman, isn't it? The one you very carefully made sure to mention in your letter, but gave no additional details about when I asked?'

'No,' Ditty said defensively.

Her sister raised an eyebrow. 'Come on. Tell me all about him.'

With a heavy sigh, Ditty shook her head. 'There really isn't much to tell.'

Which was odd, because it took the best part of an hour to tell. Ditty tried to explain, as best she could, how she and Henry had started off on entirely the wrong foot. How he had criticised her matchmaking, argued with her in front of her client—

'The audacity!'

But how eventually, after seeing just how much this proposal mattered, he had promised not to get in her way.

'Well, I should think so!'

And then, over time, how their friendship, for want of a better word, had grown. The kisses, Ditty decided not to share. Nor the bedding. Some things had to remain private, even from sisters. But she shared how he had helped her find the perfect place for a proposal, had opened up about his own conundrum, and how eventually she had helped him just as much as he had helped her.

'If not more!' interjected Calliope, a third time. 'But I don't understand, Ditty. You and Thomas—you two seemed well-suited. You wanted the same things out of courting, you wanted to keep it all businesslike and easy. But this Henry, he sounds a proper romantic.'

Ditty sighed. 'That's what he said, but—'

'He danced a waltz with you in front of all those people,' pointed out Calliope, with the confidence of someone who had been there. 'A waltz! It sounds like he likes you.'

Ditty's stomach twisted. 'I'm sure he does like me.'

A cushion whacked her arm. 'You know what I mean!'

'Well, you know what I mean,' Ditty said defensively, trying not to think of whispered words that could not be heard just beyond the realms of her memory. 'I mean, he didn't ask me to stay! There was this perfect opportunity, at his brother's proposal, when he could have just asked…and I didn't offer, I'm not about to make myself look a fool.'

For some inexplicable reason, Calliope had a very knowing look on her face.

'What?' Ditty asked warily.

But just at that moment, before Calliope could answer, the front door slammed.

'Only me,' called Thalia, her voice echoing down the corridor. 'Goodness, that walk was exhausting. I was thinking, when Ditty gets back we should— Ditty!'

'Don't hug her now, we're fixing her life,' said Calliope sternly.

Ditty lowered her arms which had been ready to welcome Thalia into a hug. 'Fixing my— There's nothing to fix!'

'It's this Henry gentleman, isn't it?' said Thalia knowledgeably, dropping her reticule, pelisse, bonnet, gloves and scarf all over the floor and sinking into a chair.

'No—'

'Yes,' interrupted Calliope with a grin. 'There was a moment—'

'I'm sure I was just fooling myself,' said Ditty, heat flushing through her body.

Couldn't they see? Henry had the perfect opportunity to ask her to stay, and he hadn't. That was it. The end.

'Perhaps you were,' said Thalia lightly.

Calliope threw a cushion at her. 'Thalia!'

'Well, I'm just saying it's easy to get wistful!' Thalia protested with a laugh. 'The question is, did you want to stay? Did you want to see what happened between the two of you?'

Ditty swallowed. *Of course.* Being courted by Henry,

where she was vulnerable and they shared romance and everything she and Thomas hadn't had...

It was frightening and ridiculous and foolish and wonderful.

'It just wasn't meant to be,' she said eventually.

Both Thalia and Calliope groaned.

'You love him!' said Thalia.

'What were you doing, waiting for romance?' Calliope persisted. 'You, the person who has said for years you can just manufacture it whenever you need it.'

Ditty's heart skipped a beat. She *had* always said that.

'You told me once you could always make your own romance,' said Calliope, pointing at her once again. 'So why didn't you? In that moment, when you were saying goodbye to Henry and you wanted him to ask you to stay, and he didn't, why didn't you make your own romance?'

It was a good question, and not one Ditty had considered. But as she did so now, something deep within her rebelled.

Romance, it cried from the rooftops, *could not always be made with a formula.*

'Because it wouldn't be enough,' she said quietly, looking sadly at both of her sisters. 'Coming from me, the queen of manufactured romance? I would know it was false. It...it wouldn't be enough.'

Henry heaved the wad of paperwork over to the other side of his desk, and attempted to look at it critically.

Well, it was organised. Sort of.

He had definitely made a space on his desk where,

he knew with a groan, he would merely make another mess with another stack of paperwork he was trying to go through.

He really needed to write out that job advertisement for a clerk. He was still drowning with paperwork and more seemed to arrive every day. Quotes from roofers, invoices from plumbers, builders from town…

Henry tried to smile. He should be grateful really, he knew. It was only because the Lodge was going to survive another winter, financially, that he was being inundated.

All thanks to Ditty.

He swallowed, stomach swooping and chest tightening, as he thought the name he had managed to push from his mind for…oh, what?

He glanced at his watch. *All of two minutes?*

'She's gone,' he said heavily, sinking onto his desk chair and looking out at the paperwork. 'She's gone, and she's not coming back.'

That was the truth. Why, only that morning he'd risen early and driven his dog cart over to Mrs Fletcher's, determined to see her. Ditty, that was. He had to see her, had to tell her he'd made a terrible mistake by not saying anything the day before.

He'd had it all planned out.

Henry snorted dryly, leaning back in his chair as a heavy weight settled in his heart.

That had been the plan, anyway. He hadn't counted on his dog cart almost falling apart just off King's Street.

He'd been delayed as himself and a few other men

from the town moved it out of the road, and only then had Henry started off for Mrs Fletcher's inn.

He'd ran. Heart pounding, chest heaving, Henry knew every step was worth it to see Ditty, to tell her he wanted her to stay…that he loved her.

'Goodness, you look hot,' Mrs Fletcher had said just hours ago, looking at him in astonishment as Henry bent double. 'You didn't run all the way from town?'

'Ditty,' Henry panted. 'Ditty, I have to speak to—'

'Oh, you missed her, not ten minutes ago,' Mrs Fletcher said blithely. 'Reg took her to the staging post. I'm going to miss that woman, you know. She had some excellent ideas about how to make my inn— Henry? Henry, are you quite well?'

In the here and now, Henry shifted in his desk chair. He hadn't been quite well from the moment he'd heard Ditty had already gone. He'd missed her. She'd probably driven right by him, he thought bitterly, as he was running to where he'd thought she was.

But it wasn't to be. And he just had to accept that.

'—down here?'

Henry's head jerked up. He knew that voice, and was rather surprised to hear it here, in the Lodge.

Charles's head peeked round the door. 'Henry! I didn't think you'd be here, I thought you'd be at home, or out in the town. It's the beginning of the Valentine's Day Festival tomorrow, all the last finishing touches are being put together.'

Henry tried to smile. 'Oh, yes. Maybe I'll go down later.'

He couldn't let his brother see just how miserable he was, Henry told himself sternly. This was his own problem, and he'd work it out of his system soon. He was sure.

After all, how long did it take to get over a woman?

He almost laughed bitterly at that. Well, it had taken almost a year and a half to get over Georgiana, and he hadn't really loved her. Not like Ditty, he could see that now.

But this wasn't about him. This was about Charles— he'd only just got engaged, still full of that joy which came with fresh love. Besides, wasn't he supposed to be in a carriage on the road by now?

'I thought you and Miss Yorke were going to visit her family?' Henry said aloud, hoping to move the focus of the conversation away. 'You didn't change your minds, did you?'

'What? Oh, no. We did not plan to leave for a few hours yet,' said Charles easily, stepping into the study and helping himself to the smallest available space left on the sofa. 'I came about Miss Oliver.'

Henry stiffened. Ditty? What on earth could his brother be wanting her for?

She'd done her job, hadn't she? Done it admirably, from what he could tell. The whole town was still talking about his brother's proposal and if he knew Brexley, they would be for many weeks to come. Months, even. Years, perhaps.

It was the most romantic thing that had ever happened here, Henry thought dryly.

'Ditty?' he repeated warily.

'Yes, Ditty,' said his brother brightly. 'Well, it was such a rush yesterday, after the proposal. I didn't really get a chance to thank her, so I wanted to see her, thank her for all her hard work. Where is she, with Mavis and Avril?'

Henry swallowed. *Ah. So his brother hadn't heard, then.*

Well, he should have expected that. He evidently wasn't the only resident of Brexley who had assumed Ditty was going to stay here, make a life here…a life with him.

'Why would she be here?' he said guardedly.

It was a silly thing to say, and Henry knew it the moment the words were out of his mouth.

His brother frowned. 'Well, where else would she be? Everyone knows the two of you—'

'Nothing happened,' Henry interrupted with a warning glare at his brother.

He wouldn't allow her reputation to be mixed up with his when she had only just managed to restore her good name.

And besides, nothing had happened.

Nothing except a friendship, deeper than he could ever have expected. Nothing but laughter, a sense of belonging whenever he was with her. Nothing but a few hugs that had seemed to both ground him to the earth and make his heart soar. Nothing but frantic kisses, a desperate lovemaking that had felt closer to ecstasy than he had ever—

Perhaps something of his thoughts showed on his face, for Charles grinned. 'I knew you liked her!'

'I don't like her,' said Henry instinctively.

But he couldn't lie to himself, and he certainly couldn't lie to his brother. He didn't need a looking glass to see he was flushing furiously, and there was no point in attempting to continue the pretence.

'Fine,' he said heavily. 'I like her.'

'I think you like her more than you expected,' said Charles.

Henry blinked. That was almost insightful from his brother, who, though a clever man when it came to the law, was often rather oblivious to the people around him.

'But I don't understand. If she's not here, where is she?'

'Back in London, I suppose.' Henry had tried to put as much nonchalance into his words as possible, but he did not fool his brother.

With a sudden movement that caused an avalanche of paperwork, Charles turned around. 'What do you mean, London?'

'I mean she finished her job here, getting you engaged, and now she's gone back to London,' said Henry defensively. 'Back home.'

'But—but Brexley is her home now. You don't mean to say— I thought she was going to stay here, in the town? What happened?'

Henry's stomach lurched, and he tried to tell himself it was the avalanche of paperwork that made his chest feel as though it was tied in knots.

Nothing happened. That was the trouble, wasn't it?

'Now, that does surprise me,' said Charles with wide eyes. 'I really thought— And she left, just like that, even after you told her you wanted her to stay?' With just one look at his face, his brother sighed. 'Oh, Henry. Why didn't you tell her?'

'I couldn't—'

'Do you mean she's left us, left Brexley, without knowing how you truly feel?'

'I—' Henry swallowed. 'I… I had nothing to offer her.'

'Except your love!'

He could not help but snort at that. Love. Yes, that was what he could offer her; naught but love. Love, and a crumbling down manor with debts up to his eyeballs, and an affection that was entirely hers but…

But how could that ever be enough?

'Sometimes love is enough,' said Charles, far more gently than Henry would have expected.

Hadn't he tried, struggling alone, to keep going without hardly any money? Without her ability to matchmake, Ditty wouldn't be able to live here. She'd grow stagnant, bored, tired of him. And then she would leave. Henry knew that. He'd lose her all over again, and it would be his fault. All his fault.

Explaining that seemed impossible, so Henry merely said, 'She's gone.'

'But she knew you loved her, didn't she?' said Charles, his voice softening now. 'You did tell her, before she left, that you loved her?'

Henry hesitated. His gaze flickered between the occupant in his study and the sofa where just a few days before, the woman he loved had sat there, concocting a plan to save his Lodge. 'No. Not in so many words.'

Chapter Nineteen

February 14, 1812

Ditty's heart was beating so quickly, she could hardly hear herself think. She certainly couldn't hear the rush of people around her. That was probably why she had become so confused after stepping out of the stagecoach. For a moment, she truly thought she had got on the wrong coach and ended up in the wrong town.

Brexley seemed entirely different. Oh, the road outside looked similar, but other than that, Ditty was astonished at the difference. When she had arrived in the middle of January, she had been one of three people on that coach. And today…

The staging post was packed. Couples were everywhere, arm in arm, some of them wearing red, all of them bundled up against the cold. Carriages and barouches and chaise-and-fours were everywhere, horses and coachmen milling about. There was laughter and giggling, happy chatter all around her. Some women held flowers, some men clasped gifts and excitement was rushing through the air.

Only then did realisation sink into Ditty's mind. Of course, the St Valentine's Day Festival. The place was packed!

That would explain why it had been so difficult to get a ticket for the stagecoach.

In a small way, she was glad. The people here needed this. Faces flashed through her mind as Ditty pushed her way to a part of the path not entirely taken up with carriages.

Miss Vivienne. She was going to be popular, though Ditty hoped she hadn't bought too many daises. She knew well enough that most people here would want roses.

Mrs Fletcher. If she'd taken half of Ditty's suggestions, she thought with a wry smile, then she was not only going to be booked up, but booked out—couples would want to return here for their anniversaries, weekend adventures…

She could only hope Reg would be able to expand his market stall, with this many people coming to Brexley.

Ditty almost stumbled over someone's trunk and was forced to stop as a horde of people strode past her, following someone holding up an umbrella.

'Follow me! Carriages to Brexley are this way, everyone who has tickets follow me…'

Ditty smiled, though her heart twisted. It was odd, seeing the place come alive.

But no, that wasn't quite right, was it? Because it

wasn't as though the place had been dead before. Brexley had been alive in a different way, and now she was seeing it not only at its best, but at its most welcoming.

Her heart skipped a beat. The question was, would her sudden arrival be as welcome?

Ditty smiled, despite herself. To think, she had left Brexley, the town that had welcomed her with open arms! She could hardly understand it. The moment she had realised she couldn't live without him, she had booked a seat on the next stagecoach.

It was a strange coincidence it was on Valentine's Day…

'If everyone could just be patient, we're getting you out of here as quickly as we can,' one of the staging post coachmen called over the hubbub.

Standing here, so close to Henry's location, she felt as though she could sense his presence, and excitement welled up within her. She was going to see him soon. Henry, the man she had completely fallen in love with.

You've…you've changed something here, Ditty, you have to know that.

Brexley is eternal.

But you've brought something new to it. Here, right now in this room… I can feel more love than I ever have before.

Ditty shivered. Now she was here, she was going to have to think carefully about what to say to him. She hadn't given it much thought, to tell the truth. Everything in her had been focused on getting here, and now she was…well, what could she say?

'Here for a visit, my dear?' said a voice beside her.

She turned. An elderly gentleman was beaming, just the sort of person who would make conversation with a stranger.

She tried to smile. 'Well, yes. Kind of. A visit.'

The man nodded cheerfully. 'I always think it's a good idea to visit new places, you know. And Brexley is a wonderful place. Have you been here before? Do you know it?'

Ditty's stomach lurched. *Did she know it?*

Better than she knew parts of London, which didn't make any sense. She had lived in Town for years now, had worked there a while, and yet she didn't really know anyone, except Thalia and Calliope and their outrageous mother.

But here?

Here she knew Mrs Fletcher, and Miss Vivienne, and the butcher and baker. She'd exchanged daily pleasantries with the coiffurist at the end of King's Street, and helped Reg turn his business around just when it was going to fall apart. She knew half the Lodge's residents by name and all the rest by face…and she knew Charles and Miss Yorke, and Henry…

She swallowed. *Henry.* Henry felt affection for her, she was certain. Perhaps even loved her. True, he hadn't said as much, but he'd had his heart broken before, hadn't he? What they had shared, that night, that wonderful night. Oh, how could she have left him after that?

Her heart skipped a beat. No wonder he was afraid to take that leap, to make himself vulnerable once again, just as…just as she was telling him she was about to leave precisely as Georgiana had done.

Leave him.

Ditty turned to smile at the old man. 'Yes, I do know— Hello?'

No one was behind her. Turning around, she couldn't see where the man had gone—but there was now a gap between her and the queue for carriages to Brexley. In just a couple of moments most of the new visitors would be gone and she could hopefully hail a hansom cab to get her to King's Street. Why, even if she couldn't find one, she'd walk!

Ditty stepped forward. She had no plan. No plan at all! The thought would have given her a heart attack only a few weeks ago, but it gave her a strange sense of exhilaration now, which she had not expected. Here she was, in Brexley, with no plan other than desperation to see—

'Oh! I'm so sorry,' Ditty said hastily as she knocked into someone.

'Not at all,' said the man she had knocked into, then, 'Ditty?'

She stared.

It was Henry.

Henry stared. He had to be dreaming. This couldn't be real—this was the sort of thing that happened to other people.

But when he blinked, the picture before him remained unchanged. A picture of Ditty, looking a little worse for wear for the travel, her hair pulled back under a bonnet, her pelisse half buttoned and the scarf Mavis had knitted for her wrapped around her neck.

It was her. Ditty.

Affection soared in his heart, the crowd around them starting to thin.

Ditty. The woman who always had a plan, always had the right things to say. Always knew what to do. He could never live up to her, never, but he would spend the rest of his life trying if she would let him.

Though now he came to think of it, Ditty looked less calm and organised than she normally did. And where was—

'Where's your trunk?' he blurted out.

She coloured, and he wished he had managed to say something romantic, rather than a statement about her luggage.

No wonder she was looking at him as though he was spouting nonsense!

Someone jostled into them. Henry suddenly realised, heat sparking across his chest, that they were standing right in the middle of a queue.

'Come on, over here,' he said.

Before he knew it, Ditty had slipped her hand into his as they quickly moved away to where it was quieter. Her hand felt so right there, her fingers intertwined in his. His breath caught in his throat and it felt like a real bereavement as their fingers parted.

To be separate from her even just for a moment felt terrible.

'You're here,' Ditty said, breathlessly.

Henry swallowed. 'So are you.'

He could hardly believe it. Even in his dreams, which had given him no rest all last night, he had imagined he would have to make his way to London and then…well, after then he hadn't much idea of how to find someone in a city as large as that.

But she was here.

'Wh-what are you doing here?' Henry could not help but ask.

His gaze raked over her face, her brilliant eyes, the rosy colour tinging her cheeks now they were standing out in the cold. But at least here, twenty yards away from the disappearing crowd, they would not be overheard.

'I—I just—when I got back to…and the moment I arrived, I realised,' Ditty said, her gaze fixed on him. Finally, she muttered, 'I—I don't know.'

Henry could see the vulnerability in her expression, hear the fear in her voice, and wanted to draw her up into his arms and tell her just how much he cared.

But he couldn't. Not without knowing, for definite, that his declaration would be welcome. He wasn't about to make another woman push him away.

He wasn't sure his heart could take that.

'You didn't leave something here?' he hazarded, heart thumping heavily in his chest. 'Something at Mrs Fletcher's, or perhaps something with my brother? He left yesterday actually, but I've got a spare key to his home, if you left something in his dining room I can—'

'I think I did leave something here,' cut in Ditty across

him, her cheeks reddening. 'But I don't think it's in Charles's house.'

Henry swallowed. There seemed to be so much suggestion in the air, but it was ephemeral, slipping from his fingers whenever he thought he could catch hold of it.

What was he supposed to say? How did one navigate a situation like this?

He smiled weakly. 'Mavis and Avril were sorry to see you go.'

Only then did he catch sight of a pair of ear-bobs which absolutely had to be made by Avril. He knew the design.

And a rush of longing swept through him. Even Avril had known Ditty deserved to be given something precious after her time with them at Brexley. It had only been him who had been so foolish as to let her go without anything.

'I was sorry to leave them,' said Ditty quietly. 'I found it harder to leave Brexley than I thought.'

Henry nodded. 'And…and are you here for long?'

It was impossible to say he wished she would stay here forever, but it was a start, Henry told himself. He was getting there.

He looked for her trunk. 'Oh, you've left your trunk by the stagecoach—I'll go look—'

'No, I didn't bring one,' said Ditty hastily, grabbing hold of his arm as he moved away from her.

To Henry's disappointment, she released him the moment he halted. 'You didn't bring one?'

She shook her head. 'Just this bag.'

She held out a carpet-bag and his heart sank. It was a short visit, then. She'd be gone tomorrow, perhaps even the day after. She must have forgotten to do something, or left something here, wasn't that what she'd said?

Ditty Oliver wasn't here for him. He was just fooling himself, hoping she had come all this way for him.

He should have known. Well, he'd just have to harden his heart, that was all.

'Right. Well, I'm sure you've got someone meeting you, so—'

'Henry,' she said urgently.

His heart softened at once. There was such tenderness in her voice, tenderness he could only have dreamed of, and she was looking at him like she never wanted to look at anyone else ever again.

Or was that just his imagination?

'Ditty,' Henry said quietly.

He reached out and took her hand in his and the movement felt so natural, so obvious, he wondered why he had never done it before.

This hand, her hand, it belonged in his own. It was his responsibility to hold it, keep it safe and warm.

Ditty looked at his hand, then back to him, and when she spoke, it was in a whisper. 'I... I don't know what I'm doing here.'

His heart skipped a beat. 'I think I know.'

A gentle breeze rustled past them, but he didn't notice. He wasn't even aware of who else was around them. What did it matter? In this moment, in this place, there was only himself and Ditty.

'You do?' Her eyes were wide, her lips parted.

Henry nodded. 'I do.'

And the magnitude of the moment suddenly hit him. Perhaps it was the particular words they had just spoken, the echo of marriage vows spoken between them.

You do?

I do.

Perhaps it was the fact he was still holding her hand in his. Perhaps it was the way she looked at him, open and trusting. Perhaps it was her beauty, beauty Henry was sure he would never tire of. Perhaps it was a reminder of when they had given themselves to each other, unrestrained and unexpectant of any promises.

Perhaps it was just a special moment, created by the town of Brexley on this Valentine's Day Festival.

Whatever it was, he wasn't going to question it. He was just going to embrace it.

'Ditty,' he said, and he was surprised to find that a lump in his throat was making his voice thick. He cleared his throat. 'Ditty, I— This is hard for me to…'

He hesitated as tension crept along his shoulders.

Why was this so difficult? Why was it so hard to speak his feelings, to say what he felt to this beautiful, kind, bold, contradictory woman before him?

And then Ditty squeezed his hand.

That was it. Just a squeeze. But it was enough.

'Ditty, I don't want to do life without you,' said Henry simply.

He heard her breath catch in her throat, felt the

change of her pulse in her hand, and knew he could keep going—he had to.

'Life without you—Brexley without you, it just isn't something that's even worth thinking about,' he said quietly. 'I was foolish not to say it before, but I wanted to, many times. But whenever I thought about it… I'm not a brave man, Ditty—'

'I think you're one of the bravest men I have ever met.' She did not take her eyes from his. 'You carried that burden of the Lodge for months without asking anyone for help.'

'And I shouldn't have done,' Henry said firmly. 'You've taught me that. Asking for help isn't weak. Look how many people you've helped, and you were only here a month!'

She smiled. 'I suppose I did.'

'This town needs you, but more than that, I want you,' he said softly. 'I never thought I was enough for anyone to choose to stay in Brexley—'

'Enough?' Ditty looked astonished. 'Henry, you— you are everything.'

Joy soared in his chest but he could not lose himself to it now. 'And I know you have a responsibility to your sisters—'

He was interrupted by her laughter. 'Oh, don't you worry about that. I have already engaged Thalia and Calliope to assist with the Lodge. Painting and poetry for your residents. What do you think?'

Henry grinned. 'I knew I would like them.'

He needed to keep going, needed to find the courage to say what was truly in his heart.

If he could.

'I have thought this through,' he said firmly. 'No, really, I have thought it through far more than you would imagine, Ditty, and I'm set on it. I have a plan for us both to be here, and be happy.'

The words had almost tumbled from his mouth and he wasn't surprised when Ditty just stared in wonder.

He was a little surprised when she then started to laugh.

Embarrassment, hot and scalding, roared through his veins. 'What are you laughing at?'

He hadn't intended to sound so defensive, but it was difficult not to be. Here he was, unburdening his heart to her—

'You have a plan?' she said with a giggle.

Heat scalded his cheeks. 'Yes, why?'

'Because,' she said with a beaming grin, 'I don't!'

Henry's jaw dropped. 'You don't? *You* don't?'

Ditty shook her head, a curl descending from its pins and bouncing off her shoulders as she continued to laugh. 'I have absolutely no plan. I just knew I had to be with you. I grabbed my reticule and stuffed a few essentials into a carpet-bag, and jumped on the first stagecoach to Brexley with nothing in my mind except... except being with you.'

And that was just what Henry needed to hear. Relief, joy, giddiness roared through his body, his mind hardly able to take in what was happening.

But his heart knew. All the cracks, all the pain that had been caused before, they were gone now. In a way, he thought they'd never really been there.

Georgiana had been lovely, but she wasn't Ditty. He hadn't known real love until this wedding planner had stepped into his life, and now he could not imagine life without her.

'I love you, Ditty,' he said, the words coming so naturally, it was a wonder he hadn't said them before. 'I want you to be my wife—my duchess.'

She beamed. 'And I love you, Henry. I love you. I came back for you.'

'You never will have to again.'

He pulled her into his arms and she came willingly. As he placed a loving, passionate kiss on her lips, lips that parted to welcome him in, Henry knew it wasn't just Ditty who had finally come home.

Epilogue

May 1, 1812

There was nothing quite like a May Day party.

At least, Ditty thought so. As she put the finishing touches onto the bunting she, Mavis and Avril had worked on together, she couldn't help but feel proud of her work.

Even if her stitches were only half as good and twice as wide as those of her friends.

'You'll get the hang of it one day,' said Avril with a smile.

Mavis snorted. 'Perhaps. She still can't bake to save her life!'

The three of them giggled, Ditty hardly able to believe this was her life now.

Of course, it wasn't the plan. There had been no plan. Just love, love of Henry and his love of her. Love for Brexley. Love for the Brexley Lodge for Gentlemen and Ladies of a Certain Age, for everyone who lived in this wonderful town.

Making the decision to move here and start building a life, a real life, had seemed so obvious. And even now, months later, she knew she had made the right decision. There was no better place for her than Brexley.

'And you like it? The bunting, that is?' asked Mavis carefully.

Precisely why it mattered so much what she thought of the bunting, Ditty did not know, but she smiled. 'It's beautiful.'

'Well, I'll ask Jim to help me hoist it up,' said Avril, carefully folding up the bunting. 'Mavis, aren't you needed in the kitchen?'

Mavis sniffed. 'I'm always needed in the kitchen—you leave those people alone in there for five minutes...'

The two older women bustled away, leaving Ditty alone for a moment in the study.

Not Henry's study. *Her* study.

Ditty smiled as sunshine poured through the windows—now mended and watertight—onto the carefully organised study.

A new filing cabinet in one corner was expertly labelled with all the different categories a housekeeper of the Lodge would need. Medical records, lists of birthdays and anniversaries, schedules for pottery classes and waltzing classes and baking classes...

Ditty had made sure they ordered three filing cabinets. There was no point in being organised, as she had told Henry countless times, if you then couldn't find the things you'd carefully put away.

She had been able to justify that decision just two

weeks after she had made her permanent move to the town which had so captured her heart and Charles made an exciting discovery.

'Henry, what is this?' Charles had interrupted them.

'How should I know?' Henry muttered, his temper so obviously flaring that Ditty had been forced to hide her smile.

The three of them had been clearing out the study, and her future brother-in-law was holding out a piece of paper with a serious expression.

'I think you should read this,' said Charles quietly.

It was only when Henry took the paper that she realised just how pale Charles's face was. 'Oh, you know I never trained in the law, man, how am I supposed to—'

'It says that you are rich,' Charles said bluntly.

Ditty stared between the two men. Rich? No. No, surely the man she adored could not have been so foolish as to be accidentally sitting on a fortune—

'No it doesn't,' Henry said, wide-eyed.

'Yes, it does,' his brother said quietly. 'A mine the duchy owns, that the Duke of Glanyrafon owns, it's found gold! Look here. That number?'

She moved to stand behind Henry, and was forced to grab his arm as her head swam. 'Th-that is a lot of zeroes.'

'How could you not have known this was here?' Charles demanded. 'You're the Duke of Glanyrafon, you'd think you'd read your own letters! You have been sitting on a fortune!'

And so he had. Ditty had investigated, with Henry's

assistance, and discovered that the great-uncle who had driven the duchy into the ground had also made some fairly wise investments, which Henry had immediately shared with his brother, before the repairs to the Lodge began.

And such repairs. There was a large calendar behind the desk, a week by week look at the activities hosted at the Lodge. Avril would be giving another talk on the history of the town, Ditty could see just by glancing at it, and waltzing would be stopping for the summer. It was too hot, she had told Henry more than once, and they needed to take care of their residents.

That's why the new bathing pool would be opening today, as part of the May Day celebrations.

Ditty sighed happily. Laid out on the console table before the sofa where she was sitting were her plans for the next three months. The roof had been sorted and there was now no concern of damp—but she would like to extend the plans for the kitchen gardens. There was already a waiting list in the Lodge for plots. Brian had told her in no uncertain terms that if he didn't get one soon, then he wouldn't be able to plant spinach in time, which to Ditty had sounded rather serious. In fact, if she just spent an extra five minutes—

A knock on the door made Ditty look up, and the person who had entered made her smile.

'You are working too hard,' said the Duke of Glanyrafon with a grin.

She returned his smile. 'Occupational hazard of the job, I suppose.'

'I don't know, the last housekeeper was never this organised, never had this many plans,' teased Henry as he stepped into what had been, until a few months ago, his study.

She could not help but laugh. 'I know. That's why I took over.'

Their laughter mingled in the air as he sat beside her, but she was right.

It just made sense. Within weeks of her settling into one of the spare bedchambers at the Lodge—though they were engaged to be married, it would be scandalous for her to take a bedchamber in the manor itself—Ditty had already reorganised the meal plan to make better use of the space in the kitchen, started a treat night on Fridays when the residents could gorge themselves on Reg's best Italian dishes, and started clearing through Henry's paperwork.

Their wedding? Well, it would have to wait. They hadn't exactly ceased their nighttime adventures, and there was just so much else to do, wasn't there?

You don't have to keep going through my paperwork! Henry had protested, more than once. *It's not like you work here!*

But that hadn't remained true for long.

'Do you ever miss it?' Ditty asked, placing her head on his shoulder.

'What?'

'Being the one in charge here. This place being yours to run,' she said quietly, looping her arm into his.

She'd never asked him before, but it had been weighing on her mind for a while. The closer they got to the May Day party, Ditty had realised just how much she was doing now at the Lodge.

It made sense, on paper. She was the organised one, he was the one who could finally concentrate on being a doctor. Being a duke. Understanding his responsibilities as a landowner with tenants and an income—thanks to the discovered goldmine—that would make most of the peerage's eyes water.

But still. Ditty's stomach twisted painfully. Since they had become engaged to be married, she didn't want to change him. Or Brexley.

Henry sighed, squeezing her arm. 'You are a far better person in charge than I ever was.'

'But—'

'Will you just take the compliment, Ditty?' he said with a laugh. 'You were an excellent proposal planner, yes. I won't deny it. But you are a truly inspirational leader.'

Joy curled around her heart.

She was. Oh, she knew it was not appropriate to think that, let alone say it. But when you looked at it, Henry had never been suited to that sort of thing. He was still learning what it was to be a duke, Ditty had learned with a roll of her eyes.

Now there was a man who never read his own letters. All those months, with a small fortune hidden in the paperwork of his own study!

'Well, I have to admit, I do love it,' said Ditty with a smile. 'And I've been looking forward to today for—'

'There she is!'

Ditty sat up hastily and squealed with delight as she saw Calliope, blond hair and crisp white gown as she always wore in the spring, standing in the doorway. 'You're here! I thought you were coming tomorrow, I was set to collect you from the staging—'

'I decided to come a day early!' Calliope said with a grin.

Ditty stepped forward and pulled her sister into a tight hug. Oh, it was wonderful to have her here. She never regretted her decision to leave London and make a life here in Brexley—all except leaving her sisters. Their mother, on the other hand, well, she could be Calliope's problem.

She looked behind Calliope, but could see no one else. 'No Thalia?'

'She's busy planning a poetry tour with her friend Alexandra—you know how she gets,' said her sister, rolling her eyes.

'But you're here! Oh, I must show you around,' said Ditty excitedly. Then she turned back to Henry, who was laughing. 'If that's quite all right with—'

'Go and spend time with your sister,' said Henry with a laugh. 'It's good to see you again, Calliope.'

'Come on, I want to be shown around!' said Calliope, slipping her arm into Ditty's. 'Where shall we start?'

There was so much to look at, Ditty hardly knew where to begin. The May Day party had started in earnest as she and Calliope left her study, and it took almost an hour to do the whole tour.

They started in the drawing room, now with a mended fireplace; then the kitchen, packed with culinary contraptions of the height of fashion all down one wall; next her bedchamber upstairs which looked over Brexley Forest; and ended with the celebration outside by the bathing pool, Reg's food going down a treat and Miss Vivienne acting as watchdog.

'Oi! Careful there, we'll have none of that!' she yelled across the pool as Avril came up spluttering, gown plastered to her skin, but with a huge grin. 'Who told you jumping into the bathing pool was allowed?'

Ditty giggled as Calliope stood agog in the sunshine.

'Did that woman just—'

'That's Avril. We haven't been able to keep control of her,' said Ditty with a laugh. 'Come on, let's see what's over here.'

Mavis, that was what. She was managing a table where delicious sandwiches, cakes and a huge vat of lemonade was being shared out.

'And that's one each, I said,' she snapped at Jim, tapping his fingers as he tried to pick up not one, not two, but four macaroons. 'There's got to be enough to go around!'

'You can always make more,' wheedled Jim with what he evidently thought was a begging smile.

It was Calliope this time who giggled as the two of them walked farther along the garden, the shouts of laughter from the bathing pool echoing around them.

'I just can't believe you've created all this,' she said

wistfully, as the sounds of music starting to drift on the air. 'Are those musicians?'

Ditty nodded, face beaming. 'Turns out, half the residents play instruments and all I had to do was—'

'You know, this life suits you,' interrupted Calliope, that wistful look still on her face. 'I mean it. I think you made the right decision, coming here. Building a life here. Falling in love. Preparing to become a duchess.'

Ditty flushed. It sounded strange when her sister put it like that, but she couldn't deny the truth. She had never expected to come to Brexley and fall in love. She had come to work: to create the best proposal anyone had ever seen. To be the best proposal planner.

And she had. But it hadn't only been Charles's and Miss Yorke's hearts which had been affected that day.

Ditty saw Mavis approach them and hissed hurriedly under her breath, 'Now, whatever you do—'

'Here, you're the artist, aren't you?'

'Yes, that's me,' said Calliope brightly. 'Why, do you need an artist?'

Mavis grinned and winked at Ditty before grabbing Calliope's arm. 'Come on, I need someone else who can decorate a cake.'

'But I—'

'Be careful with her, Mavis,' Ditty said cheerfully.

Her sister looked horrified. 'But, Ditty, I've never baked a cake in my—'

'I keep telling you, you need a rest,' Ditty said sternly,

trying not to laugh at the panic rising in her sister's expression. 'Consider this your long weekend rest—of a kind!'

Ditty was giggling at her sister's predicament when Henry came upon her, just past the kitchen garden.

His heart soared. She was just wonderful. It was hard to imagine the Lodge without her now, and he hoped he never would have to.

Of course, that question was about to be finally put to bed.

'There you are,' Henry said impulsively, grabbing at her from behind and lowering her into a romantic dip.

Ditty shrieked with the surprise and grabbed at his neck, her fingers curling behind it as she held on. 'Henry!'

He laughed with her, unable to believe he had this wonderful woman in his life. What were the chances? Here she was, a Londoner—or at least, someone who had lived in London—coming out here to the little town of Brexley, all to help his brother of all people get engaged. And now...

'Your romance lessons are coming on apace, then,' Ditty teased, as he righted her and slipped an arm about her waist. 'I told you, there's always a formula.'

Henry rolled his eyes. 'So you keep telling me. Come on, I want to show you something.'

Excitement started building in his chest as he led her away from his residents, the shouts of laughter by the bathing pool, the contented munching of Reg's and Mavis's food, the delight of those just starting to enter the sunshine.

This was it. He had promised himself it would be today, and—

'Don't tell me there's going to be a proposal,' said Ditty with a laugh.

Henry halted just outside the craft room, its door shut, as his heart skipped a beat.

'Well, actually,' he said quietly, turning to look at Ditty. 'Yes.'

Her eyes widened. She had evidently been joking, and had not expected him to agree. 'I beg your pardon?'

'Well, maybe not exactly a proposal. There's a fresh notebook in the craft room,' Henry said wisely, knowing precisely what she would want. 'Why don't you go grab it?'

She grinned. 'You always think of everything.'

She stepped away, threw open the door to the craft room and— 'Oh, Henry!'

'Not quite everything,' he murmured, his heart skipping a beat.

Ditty stepped into the craft room. It was filled to the rafters…with daisies.

He followed her and closed the door behind them. There were a great many things he would share with his residents, but this precise moment wasn't one of them.

'Ditty Oliver,' he said quietly, lowering himself onto bended knee.

Ditty turned to face him, shock and delight on her face. 'Henry!'

'No, you're going to have to let me say this without interruption,' he warned her with a grin. 'I've practiced and everything, but you know what I'm like.'

She breathed a laugh, her eyes filling with tears. He hoped that was a good sign.

'My life entirely changed when you arrived at Brexley,' Henry said simply. It wasn't a complicated speech, after all. Just a heartfelt one. 'And I never thought I would find someone who understood me, who cared for me as you do. As you have. As…as I hope you will for a very long time.'

Ditty did not look away as Henry slowly pulled out a notebook.

'Is that—'

'What did I say about interrupting?' Henry said with a mock severe tone.

Ditty laughed, a tear finally falling down her cheek, but she nodded.

He took a deep breath. 'Ditty, you are my everything. I wish I could have given you the perfect proposal, but I didn't need to. Because you are perfect. And though our lives may not always be so, I can't wait to finally start organising them together. So…so will you marry me?'

'I've already said I will marry you,' Ditty breathed.

And he grinned. 'Yes, I know, but I actually meant now. Today.'

Before he could quite get the last word out, Ditty had

pulled him to his feet and thrown her hands around his neck.

'Yes,' she said, her voice muffled by his hair. 'Yes, Henry. I will marry you.'

He kissed her passionately, desperately, knowing that this was the last kiss they would share before they became man and wife.

That was when the doors burst open and everyone entered the room.

'I knew it!'

'Who would have thought the man could prepare anything?'

'Excuse me, please, coming through. I'm the reverend!'

There was suddenly a stricken look on his beloved's face. 'But my mother, Thalia—'

'Thalia could not be persuaded to get on a coach, and your mother, I am almost terrified to say, has gone to Weymouth,' Henry said, trying not to grin. 'Apparently she would not wait.'

Ditty smiled as she groaned. 'My family! What on earth are we going to do with them?'

'Nothing. They'll sort out their own troubles, I am sure, in time,' said Henry firmly. 'And in the meantime, we have a wedding to attend.'

The woman he loved was laughing, pulling his notebook from his hands. 'You truly have planned everything!'

'I don't want to go another day without you being my wife,' he said simply. 'Dr and Mrs Paisley. The Duke and Duchess of Glanyrafon. I don't care what you call us, I just want you to be mine. Forever.'

'Oh, Henry.'

Their kiss was gentle, warm, loving, and Henry wished it could never end.

'Ahem,' said Vicar Melview, with a slightly dour frown that was undermined by the twinkle in his eye. 'Is everyone ready?'

Henry smiled and took Ditty's hand in his.

'I've avoided your displeasure long enough,' she whispered as the crowd behind them quietened for the wedding ceremony to begin. 'Time to enjoy ourselves for the rest of our lives.'

And his stomach lurching, knowing that their pleasure had only just begun, Henry grinned. 'Forever.'

* * * * *

Whilst you wait for the next instalment of
The Unconventional Oliver Sisters miniseries,
why not check out Emily E K Murdoch's
The Wallflower Academy miniseries

Least Likely to Win a Duke
More Than a Match for the Earl
The Duchess Charade
The Prince's Wallflower Wife

MILLS & BOON®

Coming next month

THE DANGERS OF DECEIVING A DUKE
Louise Allen

Celebrating Louise's 75th Book!

The kiss was not gentle, but hungry, as though both were famished.

She was not an innocent. She had been married. But this was not right. Not there, not now. Not ever.

That was his conscience, shouting at him against the thrum of his blood, the aching need and desire for her, the answering desire Cat's body was signalling. Her mouth was open under his, the heat, the dart of her tongue and the nip of her teeth acting like a shot of brandy in his blood.

They were as one in passion and, it seemed, in tune in more ways than that, because, in a split second it was over. She drew back, even as he lowered her carefully to the floor and straightened, stepped away.

'That was a very bad idea,' Quinn said, controlling his voice with an effort. 'I apologise.'

'That realisation appeared to strike us both at the same time. No apology is needed.' Cat sounded equally breathless.

She moved away a little, but not, he thought with relief, out of wariness, but to brush the dust from her skirts.

'We agreed that a cat may be friends with a duke, did we not? But friendship is as far as it can go.' Her clothes apparently ordered to her satisfaction, she looked up and met his gaze squarely. 'I am not in the market for a *carte blanche*, Quinn. And no other offer is conceivable, is it?'

Continue reading

THE DANGERS OF DECEIVING A DUKE
Louise Allen

Available next month
millsandboon.co.uk

COMING SOON!

We really hope you enjoyed reading this book.
If you're looking for more romance
be sure to head to the shops when
new books are available on

Thursday 26th February

To see which titles are coming soon, please visit

millsandboon.co.uk/nextmonth

MILLS & BOON

LET'S TALK

Romance

For exclusive extracts, competitions and special offers, find us online:

f MillsandBoon

X @MillsandBoon

⊙ @MillsandBoonUK

♪ @MillsandBoonUK

Get in touch on 01413 063 232